Story Girl

storygirlnovel@gmail.com

ISBN: 0-9866-7092-8
ISBN-13: 9780986670923

Story Girl

A Novel

Katherine Carlson

Dedication

For Anne, Bo, and Bradley...

Acknowledgements

Much love and gratitude to Anne, Bo, Brad, and Jasmin Carlson.

Many thanks to Kathy, Dale, and Kerri Hauer – as well as Mike, Steph, and Garrett Lidin.

I am thankful for Nicole M. Weatherly and wish to extend thanks to Bea and Edward as well.

Thank you also to Val Yegorov, Rylie T. Lowry, David Alley, Amy LeJeune, Luisa Marshall, Nicholas Snow, Lucy Pereira, Marie Prasad, Anja Offermann, Rowan Tully, and Jasmine Whenham.

I also want to thank Yiota Maldovanos for her unwavering support and friendship.

And kudos to all the Story Girls and Boys out there who brought their imaginings to fruition and delivered us countless epics, spectacles, and flights of fancy.

And finally…

Thank you, Lin Elder, for being so consistently amazing… and for showing me that real life is the most wonderful adventure of them all.

~

Part 1

Hives,

Uneaten Scripts,

and Happy Accidents

chapter 1

HOLY CRAP.

My hand mirror revealed a face I'd never seen before.

It was the morning after my thirtieth birthday, and I was swollen silly with blood red hives that were merging together like some strangely hideous second skin. And my torso was cramped as though I'd spent the last three nights traveling by Greyhound.

I hobbled to the bathroom, took two Benadryl, and sat in an empty tub. My naked and bloated body had somehow turned against itself. I turned on the tap and tried to squish my entire bulk, limbs and all, under the faucet. Hot water burned through the itch, and my tormented hide turned a rather violent shade of purple.

My God. I held my breath to better endure the scalding and squinted at myself in the shiny tub fixtures. I had no reference point for an event such as this, and wondered if I might be suffering from some sort of raging food allergy; considering I hadn't eaten anything in twenty hours, I was left to conclude that I was having a really bad reaction to my own life.

I squeezed my eyes tight and tried to remember yesterday – *the turning point*. I'd eaten breakfast with my cat, Lucy, and stared blankly at the news. An hour later, Ray called – he was the latest in a string of apartment managers, informing me that I had two birthday packages sitting in the lobby.

My little sister had sent a stationary set with a butterfly pattern, and my high-school friend Molly had sent me a bottle of Cabernet and a box of last year's Christmas chocolate. For fun, I set a lighter to some of the chocolate squares and watched as the stale candy melted into a sticky puddle.

At noon, I received a dozen lavender roses from my parents. And fifteen minutes later, they called.

"Hello," I asked, already skeptical.

"Happy Birthday, sweetheart." My mother sounded like she was on the verge of tears. I could hear my father's heavy breathing on the other line.

"Thirty years ago today, I was holding you in my arms," she said.

"Yes you were, Mother."

"Twenty-five years ago today, you were celebrating your first half decade on Earth. Twenty years ago today, you were about to enter grade five," she paused to take a breath, and I broke in.

"I feel good, Mom – I feel fine." I wanted to add that only one hour ago I'd been plucking dark hairs from around my nipple.

"Well honey, your father and I are so proud of you. Not many people just up and leave their family for Hollywood."

She waited for a response from me, but there was nothing. We'd been having this exact discussion for almost six years.

"Have you written anything lately?" she asked.

"This and that."

"No big money offers yet?"

I couldn't admit that the only thing I'd been offered was a twenty-dollar bill to write a phony doctor's note for a co-worker – which I regretfully turned down, "Not unless my secretary's keeping secrets."

"You have a secretary?"

"I'm kidding, Mom."

My father laughed but I could almost feel my mother stiffen.

"I'm glad you can be so light-hearted, dear."

My father sneezed and wished me a happy birthday.

"Thanks," I said.

"You were always such an adventurous type, Tracy."

I was squeezing my pillow like someone possessed, bracing myself for the other shoe to drop, but I knew from the tone of her voice that it might well be a kick from a steel-toed boot.

"Thirty's different, sweetheart. Thirty changes everything. Time to be thinking about direction and security. When you're our age, there will be no such thing as a pension."

"Not if they privatize social security," my father hollered.

I had to put the phone down and rub feeling back into my ear. The phone looked better on the floor but I eventually picked it up and placed it against my other ear.

"Just stop it, Herb," my mother was scolding. "All I'm asking is that you don't interrupt me."

"She's my daughter too, right Pebbles?"

"Right, Dad."

"As I was saying, dear. Security and retirement are important concerns."

I was expecting a Suze Orman style lecture on 401(k)s and Roth IRAs; instead, my mother delivered the dreaded strike to my most vulnerable region.

"Maybe it's time you thought about marriage."

I suddenly remembered that the cupboard was bare of vodka.

"You know, Tracy, there is absolutely nothing more rewarding, or fulfilling, or meaningful – "

"Or expensive," my dad interrupted.

"Stop it, Herbert. You don't want to give her the wrong idea."

"But they are."

"As I was saying..."

But don't say it.

"There is nothing more substantial in life, nothing that makes a woman feel more whole than finding love and having children."

But I barely even know what a child is.

My throat tightened for the grand finale.

"Trust me, sweetheart. Trust me on this one thing. It's fun to tinker around in your teens and maybe even your twenties, but thirty is a turning point in every person's life. Thirty means it's time to grow up. We're not meant to be alone, my dear. And it's just that – well – you've tinkered enough."

"Okay."

"Tracy?"

The entirety of my existence had been reduced to tinkering.

"Okay, Mom – great!"

"I mean it, Tracy. We really aren't meant to be alone – it's unnatural."

"Someone's at the door."

"Have you really taken in what I've said?"

"Yes, I've taken it in," I mumbled. "Like a mallet blow to the gut."

"What was that, dear?"

"Someone's at the *door.*"

"Well, for God's sakes, do not answer it."

"Why not?"

"Is it someone you know – it could be someone with bad intentions."

Or maybe even worse, Mother – it could be someone with unnatural intentions! Maybe it's me at the door, carrying a spine, ready to tell you off and reassure myself that my lack of desire for kids is as natural as the nose on my face – possibly even supernatural.

"Is the person still there – you have to call the police."

"They're gone."

"They could be lingering."

"I don't think so."

"Then let's get back to basics. I really want you to consider your age now. Alone won't be fun."

I already knew that.

"Old won't be fun either, Tracy. And anyway, isn't it time to be responsible for someone else?"

I summoned the most frenzied voice I possibly could, "Oh my gosh – I really *really* gotta go!"

"Why, for heaven's sake?"

"I'd rather not say."

"Now you're really worrying me."

"I just got my period."

I slammed the phone down in horror – the phone that was shaped like Mickey Mouse. Sure, of course I was ready to be responsible for someone else.

Some other voice had now seized control of my head, and it had started chanting:

Old and alone.

Immediately after the birthday phone call, I remembered running to the bathroom and staring at my reflection. All I could see were crows-feet and sun damage. I would soon end up an old woman, living in a cardboard box, and without the love of sweet children or a brawny prince. Yes indeed, I had forfeited the fairy tale. I was a shrew in the making, and all because I'd been stubborn and unbending.

I'd spent the rest of that treacherous day in bed. My dreams had been filled only with crows, carrying away my youthful green eyes with their big ugly feet.

And now, almost a full day later, I was sprawled in a tub covered in ghastly anxiety. The memories of the phone call had ignited more tingling. Luckily, I had a large supply of flour in the kitchen – a holdover from an ancient goal of baking muffins. Muffins had never materialized but I was happy to have a reason to finally slit the bag open. God knew I needed to slit something.

I doused my entire body in the baking staple, face included, and wandered around my studio apartment – wet, pasty, and inflamed.

My cat seemed nervous, as though she'd encountered a stranger or a lunatic, but ultimately, all she could do was lick the sticky powder from my aching body.

This was clearly my punishment for floating through my youth with such arrogance – so oblivious to the perilous path I'd been traveling, the one that ended up right in the center of Spinsterdom. I had been so damned determined to transcend my biology, but now shuddered to finally understand what so many before me had always known – no woman could ever transcend her biology. It would be forever impossible, similar to setting up ice colonies on the sun. I had played such a cruel trick on myself, and pilfered away non-renewable years.

My mother had successfully unleashed the monster within, and it was now playing nasty with my immune system. I could always kill myself, but I really was afraid of guns and knives and usually gagged when trying to swallow any more than two pills at a time. To make matters worse, the studio 'room' I lived in was located only on the second floor; a jump may not even guarantee a broken bone, let alone the finality of my misery.

So if I were going to jump at all, it would be onto that popular bandwagon. It was a terrifying thought but I could not allow myself to wander any deeper into the ghastly forests of barren despair. I now knew what had to be done. The mission was as clear as my aversion to it.

It was time to smarten up and find myself a man.

Pronto.

chapter 2

THE DATE WAS going super well; dates driven by desperation usually don't.

But this was something close to a miracle. Jason – the guy sitting across from me – was utterly, painfully gorgeous. He was the kind of gorgeous that inspires double takes and jaw drops. I had to pinch myself under the table to make sure it was really happening. And I still wasn't quite sure how this breakfast meeting had come to be – especially considering the online ad I'd posted:

DESPERATE GAL SEEKS HUSBAND.

And this rare Adonis actually responded with EQUALLY DESPERATE FOR WIFE.

So perhaps it was time to rethink my avoidance of all things traditional. As I watched him smile at me with snow-white teeth and healthy-pink gums, I had to wonder if the universe was paying me a royal bonus for finally coming around and reclaiming my senses. After all, it was plausible that I could see myself shacking up with this guy – in a formal sense – and maybe even having a kid. As long as he took care of it – as I'd be way too busy writing or something.

I certainly didn't have to tell him all that just yet.

"So what do you do for a living?" I asked.

"I'm a trainer."

"Where?"

"Just down the street – Guy's Gym."

"Cool."

Maybe he could also help me get in shape. I'd certainly have to be in some kind of shape if I was going to be appearing regularly on his well-toned arm.

My cell phone was vibrating frantically in my battered purse, the one covered with small rips and fraying threads. God willing, it would be good news from my last job interview. I was one of three people short-listed for a receptionist job at the William Morris Agency. It really was the last hope I had for getting a script developed in this town.

"So – Tracy – your ad really intrigued me."

"Thank you, Jason – your reply intrigued me more."

"Why are you desperate for a husband?"

I looked down at my cold, shriveled eggs, "I'm afraid that – well – I think it's time to try something new."

He studied me with his shiny brown eyes, "That doesn't exactly scream of desperation."

"No – I guess not."

Even his eyebrows were sexy.

"So – should we treat this breakfast as some kind of weird interview?" he asked.

"Sure – why not."

He cleared his throat and smiled at me, "So – Ms. Johnston – do you have any dreams, goals?"

I looked out the window and thought about the William Morris Agency again. I would be hired as a receptionist and would quickly befriend one of the top agents. We'd casually go for lunch and I'd bring up my latest script. He or she would become increasingly excited as I pitched the story. They would interrupt me with an excited yelp, and demand that I have a copy of the script on their desk without delay. The project would be fought over by all the major studios. It would eventually go on to dominate the national box-office for a full season, and triple its numbers in the international market. I would be catapulted into the dizzying stratosphere of fame and glory where only fellow A-listers were ever welcomed.

But no, I couldn't alienate this guy so soon.

"I don't know, Jason. Dreams? I've never really thought about it."

"Really? You look like a woman with dreams."

"I do?"

"I can almost see them swirling around in your eyes. You should think about it – I'm sure you have a lot to offer the world."

I'd also have to reconsider my disdain for the concept of perfection.

"Wow – thank you."

"I'd like to own my own gym one day. Maybe even a spa."

He took a bite of his egg white spinach omelette and I poured more syrup on the large pancake that came with my jumbo breakfast.

"Actually, Jason – I lied just now. I'm a writer... I want to be a writer. Make some sort of a living at it."

"That's more like it. I was gonna say that you're the only person in L.A. without a dream."

"Well, exactly."

"But I bet you'll achieve yours."

"You do?"

"In the five minutes I've known you, I can tell you've got heart. And just for the record, I'd certainly support you in all you do."

"You would?"

"Yes. And I can cook."

"Well, that's good... because I don't."

"Italian is my specialty."

"And I don't eat meat."

"I make the best vegetarian lasagna this side of the Valley."

My God, I was ready to get on both my knees and start begging.

"Do you want kids?" he asked.

"I'm not sure."

"That's okay. I'm not either."

"The truth is, I don't really know what I want. My mother thinks it's time for me to settle down or end up alone forever. And she may be right. I feel like my life needs a jump-start."

"I totally understand. You're treading water in the rough seas of expectation."

"Yes."

Wow – this guy was a cinch to talk to.

"And I just had my thirtieth birthday and broke out in hives – big horrible splotches all over my body. Red itchy bloated little bastards. I was gonna take pictures of myself and take them to the clinic, but I've actually put on a couple extra pounds and felt I looked too disgusting – like the pictures might cause trauma."

I stared down at my pancake. Oh my God – what was I doing – where was my OFF button? I was going to frighten this guy away before I finished my first dose of caffeine.

But when I looked up, he was laughing – and not in a mean or mocking kind of way, "Oh, Tracy – I can totally relate. I used to get stress headaches and my left eye would twitch at the worst moments – and so, I'd devour macaroni and cheese by the barrel full – to make myself feel better. That's what I love about the gym. It's a better way to deal with my fear and insecurities."

"You have insecurities?"

Jason sighed, looked around the diner, "I often feel inadequate. Like I'm not worthy of my existence unless I'm perfect. Unless I have everything figured out – and I really don't have anything figured out."

"Uh – yeah. I get it."

"So what do you do for money?" he asked.

"I'm a garden-variety production assistant. But I'm really trying for a receptionist job at William Morris. It's a way to make connections and try to get my scripts read. Although, if I do get the position I'll need to upgrade my wardrobe – doubt they'll let me wear flannel shirts or boxer shorts."

Jason threw his head back and laughed, and I had little doubt that he also possessed exceptional tonsils.

"I am kidding about the boxer shorts."

"Oh, Tracy – you're refreshing. And if you do get the job, I think I can help in the wardrobe department."

"How's that?"

"A friend of a friend is a designer. He specializes in upscale women's business attire – not the size zero glam stuff."

"That's a relief – 'cause I don't do zero."

"More like a ten?"

"On my good days."

"And you're tall?"

"Yes."

"Anyway, he often has extra showpieces. He usually has one or two extra blazers hanging around."

"That would be fantastic – especially on my budget."

"And let me guess – you hate shopping for clothes?"

"Loathe."

We smiled and giggled and let the waitress fill up our coffee mugs.

"You're a very special girl. And I can see why you'd have some trepidation about trudging down the *path*."

I solemnly nodded my head and we sipped our coffee like we were founding members of some sort of resistance movement.

"So you wouldn't care if I wore slacks on our wedding day?" I asked.

"Not at all."

Finding this guy was like winning two jackpots in one day.

"Which brings me to an important question, Jason."

"Yes?"

"Why are you desperate for a wife? Seems you could have them lined up around your block."

"Well," he sighed. "That's the rub."

For the first time all morning, Jason seemed to deflate – just a little.

"My parents are major players in the Christian church. And I mean *major* – and I'm not talking about the Unitarian church. I'm talking about the conservative values, hyper-traditional variety."

I suddenly felt queasy.

"Anyway, I just turned thirty-five and they're extremely suspicious of everything. Why don't I have a wife and children, why don't I volunteer at the church – on and on. The thing is, I love my parents dearly and I don't want to hurt them. They've literally built their life around a very specific idea of who I should be. And part of me would really love to fit into that idea for them – at least make them think that I do."

"Okay?"

"And you and I could solve both our problems in an instant – with one quick trip to city hall. You could have your own life, of course – sleep with whomever you wanted to… or not."

He paused and I had to stifle an urge to reveal that it was him I wanted to sleep with.

"I could cook your meals, lay out your clothes, pay the bills. All I'd ask is that you accompany me to a function now and again – maybe come with me to church once a month."

"I don't get it."

"I'm talking about an arrangement that works for both of us."

"But…?"

"Tracy – I'm gay."

Well, somebody order me a crap soufflé. I should have known – the guy could write a manual on how to be super-fabulous. I imagined the cosmos laughing at me – for daring to think I could do a quick fix on my life by having one measly breakfast with a gorgeous guy in a grimy booth.

"The thing is, Jason, I'm trying to – well – I'm going for my truth."

"Then why let your mother dictate it?"

"Good question."

I left perfect gay Jason with some reluctance and the absolute certainty that the William Morris job had gone to someone else.

chapter 3

NOT EVEN TEN minutes after I'd pulled out of the diner, Jason called me. He wanted to sweeten the deal with gourmet cooking lessons and free karate.

I needed a rain check on my reality.

Looming billboards seemed to mock me as I drove east on Sunset Boulevard. Hot sexy women with impossibly flawless skin whispered "old" through full, luscious, lightly glossed lips. Hot studs flaunting perfect abs and all manner of Bling turned their heads with cruel indifference as I drove past. Even the well-dressed pedestrians seemed to sneer, "So did you get the job at William Morris?"

This could not be my life, and yet... it was.

I was already thirty years old, heading back to my tiny studio apartment *room* and my frozen dinners that I would eat while sitting on my bed – since there wasn't enough square-footage to allow for a table and chairs. And even sleeping wasn't easy since the mattress was too large for the box spring – so every time I moved, the entire situation would wobble – not unlike a small boat adrift on a cruel sea.

How could the dream that lured me here curdle so completely? I had moved to Los Angeles six years ago, hoping to write blockbusters and meet my match – something like Harrison Ford and that lady who wrote E.T. the Extra-Terrestrial. They were a smart, handsome couple and they struck me as equals.

But my writing hopes were crippled somewhat when Harrison traded in said writer for Ally McBeal. And so it was his fault completely that in the last year, I'd only managed fifty-one pages of an odd inner excavation piece entitled, *Space Boy*. And now I was officially stuck – firmly embedded in that treacherous state known as Writer's Block, although it felt more like a block of concrete.

Nine out of ten agents totally ignored my previous script, *The Chains of Matrimony*. The tenth agent sent me an email that was probably meant as encouragement but came across as a near threat: NEXT TIME, CONSULT A SCRIPT DOCTOR!

And when I wasn't blaming Mr. Ford for my woes, I resorted back to my standard position: blame my parents for everything. They'd been the ones who'd praised my haikus throughout childhood. They'd encouraged me to read voraciously and take English classes at the local community college. In a weird way, they were the ones who had pushed me here, and now they were selling me out to what I'd had the courage to flee in the first place.

My father had worked as a truck driver and my mother as a homemaker. The only person who'd had any ambition was my father's younger brother, Derek; after what seemed like an eternity of school, he finally ended up as a dentist. Despite nearly naming his practice Jaw Breaker Dental Works and situating it in an isolated and crumbling strip mall, I was still quite pleased with his accomplishment. My younger sister seemed tailor-made for her roles as wife and mother, and I simply assumed she'd been born *after* her time. She didn't seem to question anything that had already been taken for granted as unalterable reality, but on the rare occasion she would, it was with the same intellectual vigor one might expect from Elisabeth Hasselbeck.

But I did relate to Mary – my father's mother. My grandmother seemed to be going through a never-ending metamorphosis, from Betty Crocker to Jane Fonda to Jedi Knight.

I pulled over at a Wells Fargo bank machine and studied myself in the rearview mirror: green eyes, nice mouth, messy brown hair hidden neatly under a ball cap — standard issue Tracy. I was now cutting my own hair to save money but could no longer tell what length it was. Maybe I really did need gourmet cooking lessons.

Shit.

I withdrew twenty bucks to pump into my Corolla. My remaining balance read $56.80, which would have to hold me for the next eight days. No more buffet lunches at Whole Foods, unless karma willing, I could somehow score the job or make something happen with one of my scripts. I had an older one in circulation at a couple of small production houses. In a last ditch attempt to make absolutely *anything* happen in this town, I wrote a cheesy horror flick entitled, *Morbid City.*

In the meantime, I just bounced around town working as a production assistant on various independent film projects. A few production coordinator opportunities had come my way, but the job looked way too scary and involved far too many details. So I was stuck with an unstable underling job and huge rent in refurbished Hollywood.

I had dared to roll the dice on total freedom in the search for my truest self; but the moments I had spent *looking* for ME were those I could never regain, and I was still lost — and without a thing to show for it.

And now my mother wanted me to just up and produce a family, of all things. But after that health depleting phone call from my parents, it was hard to even look at a kid; every time I saw one, I'd do the math and it wasn't pretty. I'd probably be over half a century before the little bugger even left home.

When I finally pulled into my apartment garage, someone was already parked in my spot. Normally — like everyone else in L.A. — I'd freak out over such a thing, as a parking spot of one's own is such a psychological asset that it almost makes up for the overpriced squalor that must often pass as an actual home. Still, I could no longer afford to go spastic over such trivialities – not after the skin fireworks I'd just suffered through.

I was now very aware of the mind-body-spirit connection and had to be careful to keep my thoughts somewhat calm, although I wasn't sure that I could trick myself in such a complicated way. It was more likely that my subconscious anxiety was already sending dangerous mail to my physiology – much like some sort of sadistic Unabomber. So I wasn't really sure what to do – bring my misery to the surface and dwell on it or try to focus on soothing things like flutes and sunsets and soap bubbles.

My cat was curled up on the hood of the culprit's car. I wasn't quite sure how to take that, so I just assumed she'd been waiting for me – ready to assuage any of my one million possible fits. She jumped through my open window and sat in my lap as I circled the block looking for street parking. It seemed half the cars were immobilized by a big yellow wheel lock, thanks to unpaid tickets and frighteningly efficient parking attendants.

I walked into my room wondering if I could end my gloom-fest with an overdose of frozen veggie dinners or just knock myself out with one of the mystery blocks of foil-wrapped freezer burn. I fired some broccoli hot-pockets into the microwave, and fell face first on my swaying bed.

The fork in the road had finally appeared and I wanted neither path, but the one that whispered *ogress* was by far the most intimidating – like walking straight into the nightmare of old age without an emergency kit. And I could see myself a little farther up the road – the long shabby grey hair, blowing wild in the fierce wind. As the old woman came closer, I could see that I was wearing every single rag I had ever owned. I suppose the layers kept me warm, and I probably had no other place to store them.

It was a horrible possibility, but I could clearly see her as myself – and man, was she pissed off at my choices.

Mickey Mouse rang me out of my nightmare.

"Hello?"

"What's wrong?"

It was my sister, Jenny.

"What do you mean?" I asked.

"You sound like you're in a major funk."

"I sure the hell am not."

"Anyway, I tried calling you on your birthday but you must have been sleeping."

"I wasn't sleeping on my birthday."

"Funk," she said.

"Give me a break," I said, yawning. "I had a lot of things going on."

My sister was the perfect weight and height for her twenty-five years. She was the type of woman people referred to as "petite doll". She lived in Denver with her dapper husband "Luke the orthodontist" and their three-year-old daughter, Clarice. The name always reminded me of the Hannibal Lecter movie, but I never told her so. She had a staunch rule of never seeing violent films. Oh well – it was best to leave it alone – one small glitch in her picture perfect life.

"How's the writing career coming along?"

"Just peachy keen."

"I'm forever telling Luke that I can hardly wait for the day you're nominated for an original screenplay Oscar."

"Don't be so insincere."

"I am not! Oh my God, is that really what you think?"

"Yes."

"I'm trying to encourage you."

"Right."

"I really am."

"Listen, Jenny, I gotta go – dinner's burning."

"Is the microwave on fire?"

I hung up the phone, sick to my stomach. Claustrophobia was setting in – everything was too close together. The bed, television, microwave, closet, and toilet all crammed into one large square for

55

only $1,025 a month. Oh, and a laundry facility in the basement and a parking spot I couldn't use. What a bargain.

Tracy Johnston now starring in, *Lonely Adventures in The Room*.

I wanted to knock on every door in the building until I found the despicable thief who'd made me park half a mile away, but then I noticed the baking flour all over everywhere and was once again forced to let it go.

But then the phone rang again. It was the William Morris Agency, informing me that my position had gone to someone else a little more qualified.

No kidding.

chapter 4

THE NEXT MORNING brought more hives.

This time they were of the more subdued pinkish variety. I almost called in sick but didn't want to hasten the onset of my home-less and decrepit state.

Today would consist of me driving around the smoggy mega-lopolis in my own car with my own gas picking up random things for so-called important people on a movie set. It usually meant pick-ing up donuts for craft services, props that the art department had forgotten, and extra film or tape. The job wasn't hard, but it was starting to feel beneath me and I was always spending more money on fuel than I was reimbursed for.

The only thing that got me moving was the rumor that some hunky movie star would be putting in a cameo appearance on our little low budget fiasco. Hunky movie stars are good for igniting fantasies that can sometimes last a week or two, a special place far removed from the daily toil.

Patrick Dempsey lasted me a whopping thirty-three days, still a record in my fantasy department – where I had played the triple roles of nurse, patient, and mistress to Dr. McDreamy. Prior to that, George Clooney had got me through a ten-day stretch of a more bru-tal than usual menstrual cycle. But so far, none of my fantasies had ever included children or cooking or forced monogamy.

I washed down my Benadryl with strong coffee, and wandered around the neighborhood trying to remember where I'd parked my car the day before. My phone rang just as I walked up to a street that I'd swear I never heard of before – so I assumed that's probably where I'd find my car.

"Hello?"

"Is Tracy Johnston there?"

"This is she."

"Hi. This is Eric from Cold Blooded Productions. You sent us a copy of Morbid City."

"Oh yes!"

"I'm Mr. Riley's assistant. Anyway, when we turn down a script... we don't normally call. I just wanted you to know that your premise is sort of cool, and you should continue writing."

"My premise is sort of cool?"

"Yes."

"Does that mean you're sort of interested?" I had one eye closed and my fingers crossed when I asked this.

"No."

"Okay!" I could've slapped myself for sounding so eager over a rejection.

"We're passing on it."

"Really?"

"Absolutely."

"Okay, thanks."

"You're welcome."

I hung up the phone feeling more dazed than usual. Another desperate hope dashed on an unfamiliar street in Hollywood – so far my day was shaping up to be just like any other.

We're absolutely not interested, but keep writing.

What the hell kind of encouragement was that? Well, fine. I'd keep on writing. And while I was at it, I'd just keep on counting particles of sand for the fun of it. Fuck it, I wasn't going to think about scripts, or ambition, or annihilated dreams one second longer.

Well – maybe just one more second because I couldn't help but think that *Morbid City* still had a shot over at the Bloodhound Group – an eager little company known for producing a large percentage of the B movies and cheap horrors that came across its desk.

Even finding my car felt like a let-down.

Traffic on the 101 South was barely moving, and my radio had decided that this would be the day that it died. That was fine – I could deal. There were many ways of dealing with traffic grid-lock. Even though my imagination hadn't brought me any sort of an income, I could always count on it for more lascivious purposes. I was already in McDreamy-ville when my cell phone started to vibrate.

It was my best friend Sheila, a woman I secretly loathed but could not cut loose for fear of not having a best friend. And like a few others in Hollywood, I had no real idea what she did, but she seemed to have connections everywhere.

"Hi, Sheila – yes?" I said, hoping to get back to my tawdry scene before the imminent fade-out.

"Whuzzup, girlfriend?" she asked. I hated it when she tried to sound cool or hip, being that she was a tall lanky white girl like myself. Although – truth be told – her boobs were extravagant.

"Worming to work on the 101."

"Anyway, listen, I met a man for you. His name is Fly-Dawg and he manages some upstart hip hop band."

"Fly-Dawg?"

"More emphasis on the 'w'."

"Sheila, please."

"So what do you say?" she asked.

"No."

"Why not? He's cute, sexy, *not* broke."

"I'm still recovering from Jason."

"Who's Jason?"

"The perfect guy who got away."

"Okay, whatever. Anyway, listen – Fly-Dawg leaves for Atlanta in two days. So get over yourself – he's really cute."

"Is he African American?"

"How did you know?"

"I had a feeling."

"Don't tell me you're still not over last time," she said.

I put the phone in my lap and stared down at it. After a count of twenty, I brought it back to my ear.

"Did you hear me?" she asked.

"I was changing lanes."

"Just because a couple of black girls accuse you of ruining their chances of ever finding a husband."

"It was a big deal, Sheila. I didn't even know the guy, and all of a sudden I'm guilty of depriving unborn African American children of a father."

"Don't be such a wimp. All of my couple friends are either interracial or gay. Cool *cool* people. And that reminds me, I have this friend – Anita – who says she'll go out with you – as long as you pick up the tab."

I was stunned.

"Well?" she asked.

"Sheila!"

"Don't yell in my ear, Tracy!"

"Now you're hooking me up with lesbians?"

"I'm more concerned that she's cheap."

"Are you for real?"

"What?"

"I'm straight! And am I really so pathetic to you? You sound just like Jenny. Maybe you guys could hook up and take notes on the best ways to rub my nose in the dung that has become my life."

"What are you talking about? Excuse me for thinking you were progressive, adventurous, cutting-edge – willing to try something new or different at least once."

"But I'm not gay."

"How do you know?"

"Because I like guys."

"In what way?" she asked.

There was really nothing more I could say.

"She will be calling you in one hour," she said, and hung up.

chapter 5

THE LESBIAN AND I were facing each other in *Tacos Tacos*.

It was a bit of a dump, but it was the best I could do on my dung-life budget. Anita was a rather calm seeming girl with large blue eyes. Not so bad for my first ever Sapphic date. Except that this really wasn't a date at all. Women had never really entered into my fantasy realm, except as peripheral characters or to function as reminders of just how truly fabulous I was. But maybe Sheila sensed something in me that I didn't. Maybe I *was* gay. It would definitely explain a lot – like why I didn't seem to want much of what other straight women did.

Unfortunately, I didn't believe it.

What I really wanted was to feel better about shirking my feminine responsibilities. For one night only, Anita and I could be united in our man barren, childless life. Maybe she could even make me feel empowered by my wayward choices.

"Sheila tells me you're straight. That true?" she asked.

"Uh yes," I said, feeling my cheeks flush. "Very true."

"I was straight too, until last year."

"What happened last year?"

"I met Gwyneth," she said, matter-of-factly.

"Paltrow?" I asked. It wasn't an unreasonable question in Hollywood.

"Of course not, although I did meet Ethan Hawke once – at a rummage sale in the Valley."

She shifted her cleavage with a middle finger, and I took a gargantuan suck of Corona.

"Anyhow, this other Gwyneth – well, she knocked my socks off. Literally."

"Wow – that's great."

"And now, Tracy, I've ditched the dogs for a little pussy."

She looked at me tentatively until we both giggled. I was relieved that she had a sense of humor, but when she used her tongue to get at the dribble of enchilada sauce working its way down her chin, I squirmed in my seat hoping the tongue aerobics weren't meant for my benefit.

"Don't get me wrong, I still love men. It's just nice to know a girl's got options."

I raised my beer, "Here's to the possibility known as full-fledged lesbian."

I was trying to be funny, but she didn't laugh.

"I despise that word."

"What word?"

"Lesbian. It sounds icky and slimy, like something that just crawled out of a slough."

A small rush of satisfaction pulsed through me as I realized this woman could use the word *slough* in a sentence.

"Why not just call me a sticky swamp thing?" she asked.

"Exactly," I nodded.

"I think lesbian is a sexist word. Gay is better, easier on the ears – more sophisticated."

"I think the word comes from that island – you know, Lesbos or something." I had read it one day when I had nothing better to do than look up controversial words on Wikipedia.

"Lesbians are usually sloppy and broke," she said. "At least that's the stereotype, and I think it all stems from that damn icky word. Words define how we think about ourselves. I mean, when you think of the word God, don't you automatically think of a man, Tracy?"

I reached for my old dusty constructs, and was incensed to discover that my image of 'God' was something like Dick Cheney with a long flowing beard. Something had gone terribly *terribly* wrong. I guzzled back the last of my Mexican beer and tried to focus on Anita.

"Listen, Anita – I'm definitely not gay."

"But maybe you're bisexual."

I shook my head, "I would have had an inkling by now. So I really don't want you to think of this as a date, because I'm not thinking of it that way. I'm actually sort of thinking of myself as a covert agent."

"A covert agent?"

"Yeah. I'm trying to get an insider's perspective on what it means to completely buck the system. And I'm thinking you and I could be friends. You could offer insights into what it's like to navigate through life without the need for a man. And when I'm really low, I can turn to you and feel better – knowing that you forged ahead in your own way – as an individual first, woman second. I really admire you – just to know that there are women out there who can live a man-less, childless life and not suffer one iota of guilt over it. Not have a nervous breakdown over it. And you know what, I'm starting to feel better already. I really am. So good, in fact, that I could actually go home and write a page or two. So thank you, Anita. Thank you."

"Uh – Tracy?"

"Thank you."

"I should tell you something."

"Oh – okay. Anything. Lay it on me."

"I'm pregnant."

I could feel the hard shell of my vegetable taco slicing through the tender supple stuff lining my throat. Anita saw my distress and passed me her apple juice. I immediately gulped it all down to keep from choking to death.

"Yeah, my last encounter with a male was a potent one."

"Oh. My. God."

"Are you okay?"

"Not exactly."

Anita would actually be a mother before I would. Now I really felt on the verge of some sort of major collapse.

"What's wrong?" she asked.

"You're *pregnant*? For real?"

She nodded her head apologetically.

"I just had breakfast with the perfect guy who turned out to be gay, and now I'm having dinner with the perfect lesbian who happens to be pregnant? I mean, somebody – anybody – cut me a break. You were supposed to make me feel better."

"Excuse me?"

"About my choices. My man-free, childless life."

"Oops."

"Don't you want to be with the father of your baby?"

"Turns out I'd rather be with Gwyneth. But she's moved on and I'm trying to do the same. I'm sorry if I've upset you."

"Forget it."

"I really am, Tracy."

"I'm okay – just give me a minute."

As she began chatting about environmentally friendly baby clothes and new age toddler camps, I came face to face with a new version of myself. I'd won some bizarre contest that was happening only in my head, and I was indeed the last woman standing. But I was forever standing on the outside, perpetually looking in. And my prize was a nice big bag of empty.

"So I'm excited about all the organic stuff – especially the apples and pears."

Suddenly estrogen was the last thing I wanted to deal with. I wanted my fantasies back.

"Can you just, like, morph into Johnny Depp?"

"Pardon?"

"Nothing."

"Are you sure you're alright?"

I put my head in my hands, "No, I'm not alright. Even *you're* not reneging on your biology."

"It's not like I was planning on getting pregnant."

"Just forget it."

"I think you need a stronger drink."

"I think it's time for me to go home."

"Because I'm pregnant?"

I shook my head like a spoiled child.

"I'm sorry, Tracy. I'm clearly not turning out to be the person you wanted me to be."

"It's just that I thought you might make me feel better about being an outsider. You know, someone who is comfortable not following the rules?"

She tried to speak but I shushed her, "And now I discover that you're *with child!*"

"Have you maybe thought about therapy?" she asked.

"No, but I think my throat is bleeding."

Anita watched as I put five fives on the table, picked up my paper plate of food, and walked out of the restaurant. I drove back to my room with less cash, but at least I'd reaffirmed my never-in-doubt heterosexuality.

chapter 6

AFTER AN ENTIRE night of bizarre visions, I awoke in a very odd mood.

My dreams had been filled with bisexual horses galloping through unknown galaxies, and pregnant lesbians were busy re-writing the English language – the word for God was now Utera.

It was six o'clock, and I had seven minutes to get out the door – but Lucy was splayed across my chest. She was purring at me in the most comforting and unconditional loving sort of way. This was just exactly the kind of acceptance I needed right now. I could easily call in sick, but I knew there were countless others who'd be willing to take my place – those dreamers who'd practically beg to work for nothing if it gave them a chance to climb the Hollywood ladder.

I scarfed down leftover mushy tacos at the sink, and put a Dodgers cap on my unwashed hair – nothing in me felt even remotely guilty as it seemed the appropriate attire for the character description known as *typical, unsuccessful 'artist'*.

Traffic wasn't moving and the radio was still dead. The commute would give me time to wrap things up with McDreamy. I rewound the production and started at the beginning with Anita now co-starring as the woman rejected by the doctor, in favor of myself.

My phone started vibrating just as he was leaning across the table with a tiny suede mahogany box (if I had to bite the bullet, this is how it would have to go down). I almost didn't answer but assumed it was Sheila calling – since she usually calls when I'm jammed and helpless on the freeway.

"So what's the deal, Sheila? That girl you set me up with is pregnant."

Silence.

"Sheila?" I asked.

"It's your younger sister – the one who's supposed to look up to you."

I turned my mute button on.

"Sheila set you up with a *girl?*"

Mute.

"Is there something you're not telling me, Tracy? Do I need to prepare Mom and Dad? No wonder you don't have a boyfriend. It's all starting to add up."

"What do you want, Jenny? I'm really busy."

"Don't change the subject."

Many seconds passed in absolute silence.

"God, you're stubborn. I was just wondering if you were gonna come home for the anniversary?"

"You know they don't want a big fuss."

"Of course they want a big fuss, especially after thirty-five years."

"They really probably don't."

"They do so."

"I can't afford it."

"Luke and I can offer you a low interest loan."

I wanted to gouge her eyes out with a corroded spoon.

"I'll think about it," I said.

"Call me later then."

I hung up without saying goodbye.

Damn it to hell.

I tried to conjure Patrick and the box and the ambience, but it was too late; the mood had been completely tasered. I comforted myself with the thought that tonight I could be alone with frozen vegetables and my own friggin' fantasies, the last enjoyable thing in my dung life that I was truly in control of.

And then, as if a gift from a pitying universe, traffic started moving. Slow at first, but soon I was moving along at a bearable clip.

The phone started vibrating again and I did not hesitate to scream into it, "I said I'd think about it, Jenny!"

"It's Jason."

"Oh."

Mr. Perfect.

"I was just wondering if you got the job at William Morris because I'm at the showroom and I have some slacks here for you. They're a size twelve but we could easily take them in. And there's a dark blue Escada blazer here with your name on it. You'll be an absolute smash on your first day."

"I didn't get the job."

"What?"

"A wham-bam – no thank you, Ma-am."

"Oh – I'm sorry. They don't know what they're missing."

"Tell me about it."

"Why don't you let my boyfriend and I make you a meal. Something with lots of vegetables – good wine."

"I think I need to just fantasize my way through a box of Ding-Dongs."

"Really?"

"Yup – preferably in a pair of stretch underpants."

"You're really sure?"

"Yes."

"Take care then – sweet Tracy."

"You too."

You too... perfect gay Jason.

I was sick with a new kind of grotesque despair. But then I started thinking that such a gay man may well be perfect, but he surely wasn't perfect for me. And did I really want a boyfriend anyway? Was I really letting stress and a few nasty hives dictate my future?

I was so deeply engaged in matters of such profound importance that I didn't notice the car stopped dead in front of me.

chapter 7

THE EMERGENCY ROOM reminded me of a teleplay I'd once written.

Dr. Stetson McQuaid was the only script I'd ever burned, but this place had the exact look of what I'd been trying for on paper. The place was packed with all manner of injury, mine being by far the least gory.

The ambulance had insisted on taking me in because of the severity of my expression. The officer on the scene said he'd never seen anyone look so utterly dopey – not at least without some form of brain injury. They were afraid I might be suffering from intense whiplash or a blow to the head. I withheld the impulse to reveal that my expression had more to do with the gathering stench of my life than any trauma I might have sustained.

The driver of the crappy car I hit would apparently be arriving any moment. I was already preparing my defenses, although I wasn't too worried, as I'd heard emergency workers talking about the need to take such junk heaps off the freeways.

As I was figuring ways to retrieve my own car from the towing company, a younger cousin version of McDreamy limped into the waiting room. He sat across from me between an elderly woman and a small child who had a mouth stuffed with gauze.

He nodded at me with recognition, "I'm really sorry about that."

Even his head slanted in the exact same way as McDreamy,
"Pardon?"

"Weren't you the one that smacked into me?" he asked.

"Oh yes, sorry. I wasn't paying attention." God was I a buf-
foon, blowing my entire defense just because a cute guy asks me a
question.

"Oh no, it was my fault. You had no reaction time. My engine
just died on the spot. It was dead. That car has over 200,000 miles
on it."

"200,000 miles? Okay, it was *your* fault."

"Told you so."

"But still. I should have been paying more attention. I could
have stopped a couple of seconds sooner."

"Not really possible. My car just up and died. I always wondered what that might feel like on an L.A. freeway. Anyway – don't
worry about it. I have insurance. Or I can pay you out of pocket."

Cute *and* nice.

"Well, I'm hoping the damage to my car isn't too bad."

"But the front didn't look good, and it's totally my fault."

"Maybe."

He shrugged and we both sort of laughed in a goofy way; then
he extended his hand. I immediately scanned the powerful forearms –
steel cord pulsing. My hand in his hand felt strangely intense; the
textured flesh was not of my imagination this time.

"And my name is James, by the way."

"Are you straight?"

Fool – why not just pounce on the poor guy?

"Uh – yeah – although sometimes my shoulders droop."

So maybe we were both a little asinine.

"Anyway – it's sometimes hard to make ends meet, but I really
shouldn't have been driving that thing. And all the stop and start
stuff is hard on a good car, never-mind a bad one. My parents warned
me a million times. It's a '78."

"My God, I was still in diapers. How does it pass the smog test?"

He started to tell me and I really wanted to listen but I was far more interested in analyzing his sexiness — it was low-key in a lanky sort of way. He had a huge head of wavy brown hair that was so healthy it gleamed purple at certain angles.

"So I'm thirty-one and sometimes I think I should just hightail it to Hawaii and make pucca shell necklaces on the beach."

"Where are you from?"

"The east coast. Washington... my parents are political people."

"What type of political people?" I asked.

He shrugged like he didn't want to talk about it.

"Involved in the daily running of government?" I pressed.

"More like lobbyists, both right-wing. Sixties backlash stereotypes. Every time I take money from them I feel like a sell-out."

I stared at his purple clean hair, "Why don't you stop taking their money then?"

He winced at the obviousness of the question, and I was amazed at how quickly this beautiful man could be hurt by a stranger — even one who ate dinner on her bed every night, alone but for her cat.

"I've tried and tried and then things get so tough."

There was the unmistakable trace of a whine in his voice. I wondered if Mr. Clooney would accept parental charity, but then I remembered his aunt Rosemary and thought about family dynasties. Nothing was going to dampen James for me, even if he was a spoiled brat.

"What do you do?" I asked.

"Screenwriter," he said, without a trace of embarrassment.

"Yeah, I can see why you need help."

"Last three months they've paid the entire rent plus utilities plus car insurance, gas and groceries."

He was looking a little less dashing. I quickly conjured a vision of Rosemary helping little Georgie, sending him out the door with a Superman lunch box.

"Makes it hard for me to argue with their neo-con ideology," he said.

"Are they really neo-cons?" I asked, amazed.

"War is peace, right?"

"Neo-cons indeed," I said incredulous, as if he'd just presented some rare species of dinosaur. I also loved anyone who could quote Orwell in the proper context.

He nodded but not without a touch of sadness.

"Makes my parents seem progressive," I chuckled.

"Makes me feel like I'm taking blood money and it depresses me something fierce."

"Couldn't you get a job?" I asked.

He shrugged and sighed as though such a thing was out of the question, as though I was being unreasonable.

"You look like a strong, healthy guy."

"Can't give up my dream."

"Lots of people have dreams and zero money, and so they have to work at jobs in the meantime. You know, *jobs.*"

"I know. But it's like there's a money tree in the front yard. It makes any sort of struggling seem pointless and unbearable."

"If taking the easy way out makes you sick, then what's the point?"

I could barely believe I was being so argumentative – maybe it was because he just ruined my car and probably lost me my crummy job.

"I just want to be respected, you know. I want to really move people, like a visionary. Can you dig that?"

"Isn't a visionary more concerned with something *other* than being considered a visionary?" I asked.

"Not necessarily."

"Oh, okay."

"All I've ever wanted to do is move people," he repeated.

"Do you move *you?*"

"What's your name?"

"I'm Tracy – guess we missed that in the intro."

"No, Tracy – I don't move me at all. Some days I can barely look myself in the eyeballs."

I absolutely loved the way he said my name. *Tracy*. It made invisible hairs quiver, "Well then, how do you expect to move me or anyone else, James?"

"You're quite blunt, Tracy."

There it was again.

"Maybe it's time to uproot the money tree."

"Yeah," he said. "Maybe it is."

chapter 8

WE WERE EVENTUALLY released back into our separate streams.

But we wanted to stay together – so Sheila picked us up outside the emergency entrance. We were only waiting at the curb fifteen minutes, but standing together while ambulances passed made him feel like my boyfriend. There was an easy energy between us, and I didn't once feel like I had to 'people please' him. Perhaps I was just running out of energy, but I'd never felt more real.

James and I had neck x-rays taken, but the doctor could immediately tell that we'd both suffered military neck – which I assumed meant bad whiplash. I'd already started nagging that I'd never be able to handle the medical bills. I don't know what it was about him, but I was having no problem being fearlessly authentic.

We carefully contorted ourselves into the backseat of Sheila's Paseo, and everyone agreed on Thai Town for noodles. I checked my messages: my sister wanted an answer regarding the anniversary, and work informed me that I'd been officially replaced.

All I could do was look on the bright side – maybe now I'd have the time to feed my long starving characters. The panic would probably come later, when I was no longer in the dizzying state of my newfound orbit.

After a quick drive, James and I bent our way out of the back-seat to find Sheila standing before us in a miniskirt and heels. Her make-up looked like it had been professionally applied, and in one sexy move, she pulled her long hair out of its scrunchy. I wanted to charge her like an enraged bull, and ram her into the next car until she was nothing but a heap of crushed bone and flesh.

Instead I said, "You look nice."

Earlier in the waiting room I had text messaged her that I had just met a gorgeous heterosexual man and that he'd be accompanying us for lunch – apparently, a big mistake on my part.

She led us into the restaurant, and I watched James stare at her toned calf muscles, made all the more pleasing by the four-inch pumps she was struggling in. In the five years I had hung out with her, she had never once worn any footwear other than fancy sandals or Asian slippers.

James and I sat beside each other in a booth across from her, and I couldn't even try to hide my scowl. I should have expected that she'd betray me like this. Women could be cutthroat when it came to snatching up the dwindling resource known as cute and single straight guys. Small wonder she set me up with a lesbian.

"So, how was your date last night, Tracy? Anita's her name, right?" Sheila looked right at me when she asked the question.

I was so shocked that I couldn't speak.

James turned to me, "You're gay?"

"It wasn't a date," I coughed. My military neck was throbbing.

He squinted at me and then at Sheila.

"I keep telling her to just come out already, but whatever. It's her decision, not mine. I mean, I was also against outing Jodie Foster."

Sheila smiled across at us in the most enticing way possible, and it required all of my will power not to stick a fork in her eye.

"I must admit I like the boys, the men, the stronger sex," she said. "Love their hands and feet, love the sexy line of their neck – the bobbing apple, the contour of the muscles, the way they walk, their masculine musty scent, and the casual charisma."

"Is that all?" I asked.

She ignored me without once taking her eyes off of James. It was obvious that she was trying for Marilyn Monroe but came much closer to Rue McClanahan.

"Now, if you'll both excuse me, I'm off to the ladies room where I'll powder my nose," she said, and choked a little. The throaty whisper must have got stuck in her throat.

James turned to me, "Is she out on a day pass?"

"Probably."

"Really kinda wacky."

I relaxed instantly, almost grateful for Sheila's antics. She was making me seem relatively sane.

"But did you really go out with a woman? Because if you are gay, I'll be really bummed out."

"You will?"

"Yes."

"I went out last night, with a woman – who just happens to be pregnant. It wasn't a date, though."

"What was it?"

"Research."

"You're not reassuring me, Tracy."

"I'm not gay – trust me."

I also wanted to admit that my stomach was now a frantic dance of the willies, thanks to the big sexy veins that were almost bulging free of his hands.

"But I do have to tell you something, James."

"Okay – you're seeing her again because men suck?"

"No, although they do suck – sometimes."

I wasn't sure how to continue.

"Continue."

"I've just been feeling a little stressed lately and a little gross."

"And?"

"And that's enough."

He was quiet – just looked at me as though I might be as mad as a hatter.

"What do you think of that?" I asked. I figured the only way to deal with my insecurities was simply to present them, air them out in the open.

"I was just admiring your green eyes, alabaster skin, perfect nose, and sweet little mouth."

Alabaster skin?

"Othello?" I asked.

He nodded and downed a packet of artificial sweetener.

I was thrilled. Not only had I never thought of myself in those terms, but how many hotties – plucked from the freeway – can quote Orwell *and* Shakespeare, "Thanks, but I don't have a shred of lip and my nose is crooked."

He studied me to see if I was kidding, "You're a little delusional."

We said nothing further on the topic – just studied our menus. And it was all okay because I could literally feel his attraction for me, and it felt rather overwhelming – especially since it matched my own for him.

"Just how many hours were we in that hospital?" I asked.

He looked at me the way Rob Lowe looked at Demi Moore in *About Last Night*, "I don't know – I've lost track of *almost* everything."

Oh yes, indeed.

Sheila came back and positioned herself into the booth so that her breasts literally surged forth, threatening to overspill her fuscia tank top. Now that James and I had firmly re-established ourselves, we began to giggle. The laughter started off mild but quickly strengthened in intensity until we were both roaring and crying and struggling for air.

"What's so damned funny?" Sheila asked.

"I was just telling James how much I love beaver."

"And it kinda grossed me out," he said. "Being, of course, that I'm also gay."

Though my eyes were spurting tears, I could still see the black rage cloud that had engulfed her face. She was on to us, and our rock-solid alliance.

"You two queers can find your own way home," she cried, and fled the restaurant in a major huff.

We watched as she broke a heel and nearly flew into the back-seat of a restored convertible bug. A parking attendant grabbed her and steadied her and folded her into her own car. She sat there at least five minutes before driving away.

I stared at my phone until the angry text arrived: YOU ARE A FIRST CLASS FUCKING COW!

chapter 9

THE HEAVENS WERE full of winking stars.

Not that I could see them in the L.A. sky – but I knew just the same.

James and I were walking west on Franklin, all the way to my room. We didn't hold hands, but I could tell that we both wanted to. I also noticed that his limp was gone.

I invited him up, and he smiled a big happy yes. It was at this point that I regretted not washing my hair for three days – not even when I'd been stuck in the tub with hives. Not even before my desperate date with Jason. I was also aware of the two small nests of underarm hair that had been left untouched for the past three weeks. Perhaps I had been in a funk – as Jenny had so generously suggested.

I placed the key in the lock with near palpitations; the place was small and cat-smelly and Lucy had probably added a few droppings to the shambles. She was never consistent when it came to using her proper potty. I opened the door and turned on my new eco-friendly bulb, which set the entire mess ablaze in a Wal*Mart glow.

"It's one big litter box," I said, trying hard to sound as cool and indifferent as Janeane Garofalo. As if this wasn't really my life, and I didn't really care.

"At least you earn the rent," he said. I could tell he really meant it, and I was again at ease with my bare self. No bells, no whistles.

I heated tea in the microwave. James looked around at my books and pictures and the tiny toothpick people I handcrafted when bored or depressed.

"I have never seen so many toothpick people," he said. "You literally have a forest worth of wood in here."

"Yep."

We sat on the floor near the big window – overlooking a square of the adjacent building – and sipped chai from large beige pottery mugs.

I didn't want him to feel guilty but I had to be honest, "I don't know what I'm gonna do for money now. I was fired for not showing up today."

"Oh fuck."

"Yeah, exactly."

"Maybe this whole accident thing is a sign from the universe."

"A bad sign," I said, slurping mightily at my chai.

"Maybe we were both on the wrong track, heading in the wrong direction. And the accident derailed us."

"But you were headed for Hawaii," I said.

"Not really."

"Are you saying we saved each other from something?" I asked.

"Well, were you happy with the status quo?" He smiled big and wide, and his eyes sparkled accordingly. I could see his nipples under his baby blue cotton shirt.

"You did save me from a crappy day on the set. Although I guess some hotshot was set up for a cameo."

"Do you like hotshots?" he asked.

"Sometimes."

He shook his head and sipped his tea. He didn't slurp.

"What?" I asked.

"You don't strike me as that type."

He was mostly right. And now was not the time to reveal my marathon fantasy life, not when I had the real thing alive and breathing in my room. I absolutely had to see this guy's nipples.

"Are your nipples pierced?" I asked.

"Of course not."

"I don't believe you."

He lifted up his shirt and showed me his pectoral muscles, just exactly as I'd predicted he would. They were hard and soft and hairless and masculine all at the same time. I had to look away for fear of lurching across the carpet and chewing at a handful of his chest.

"See," he said. "No piercings."

"I stand corrected."

To my absolute and secret delight, he took off his shirt and tossed it across the floor.

"The walk made me sweaty, and now I feel gross," he said.

"You're not gross."

I was sitting on my hands much like a guy in a strip club awaiting a lap dance. It had been quite some time since I'd been with a man – unless I count John. John and I had great chemistry until I found out that he was one of those sorry souls who have to stand on the corner dressed like a sandwich. He explained to me that he really enjoyed waving to people, and that the 'gig' was only two days a week. I felt bad for being such a snob, but I could no longer allow the pastrami king access to my privates.

"I hope you don't mind," he said.

"Pardon?"

"That I'm topless."

"Not at all. Topless is good."

"Okay."

"I mean, feel free. Whatever."

James began to stretch his upper body, giving me an eye-full of his torso. I had more body hair than he did.

"Do you shave your arm pits?" I asked.

"Yeah, just an old habit. I used to swim."

"And so that makes you faster?"

"Something like that."

Now I felt beastly – once again aware of all my overgrown areas.

"Hey – there's half a script over there," he said, as if talking about one of John's uneaten sandwiches.

"Want some?" I asked blandly.

"You never told me you're a writer."

"I'm not."

"You are so, unless your cat wrote it."

"Lucy deserves more credit."

"What's it called?"

The damned script was the last thing I wanted to talk about.

"Space Boy. I've completed fifty-one pages in one hundred and fifty three days. That does not make me a writer."

"You keep track."

"I do not."

"So is that like one page every three days?"

I watched him calculate the math in his head, and I made a hurried scan of his features: thick black eyelashes, ice blue eyes, and a small vertical scar running the length of his cheek.

He looked right at me, caught me in the act, "What?"

"Would it be rude of me to ask how you got the scar?"

"Oh, that." He ran his finger along it. "I was a little kid – tried to shave with a knife."

"How little?"

"I think it was the day before kindergarten," he said, looking instantly sad.

"Did you get much sympathy?" I asked.

"My parents were pretty worried."

Despite his primo ability to feel sorry for himself, I immediately wanted to lick the scar, give it the good ol' Popsicle treatment – up and down, circle, and again. I imagined it would taste like thick skin – smooth, hard, and salty.

"Are you okay, Tracy?"

"Now?"

Story Girl

"Of course now."

"Yeah, yeah I'm fine. Why?"

"You look a little dazed."

I couldn't admit that I wanted to Popsicle his scar.

"Well gee, I was just in a car accident," I said – amazed at my ability to transform my goofy moment into his.

"Of course. I'm sorry."

"Plus – I'm just not a writer."

"Why not?"

"Because I fooled myself into thinking I had a passion for it, when it was really just a mad dash scramble to get out of Bumble Fuck."

"Otherwise known as?"

"Small-town Minnesota."

"Tell me more."

"I really don't want to talk about it."

"Why not? I've told you my stuff."

"No."

"Please."

"Fine. My father drove a rig. He hauled grain and sugar beets across the plains. Blah blah blah, he's retired now. And my mother was Betty Crocker homemaker. There. Nothing too exciting."

Now he was running the side of his thumb down his scar – I could almost feel it on my own cheek.

"Oh, and they think I'm insane for not copying the life they have. They think I'm just wasting my time here."

"Are you?" he asked.

The light was changing angles, casting enticing shadows across his chest. "I don't know. Maybe."

"So what do you like about being here?" he asked.

I wanted to throw myself at him, and declare that the only thing I liked about being here was the fact that he was right here with me – but I chickened out at the last second.

- 55 -

"I like the energy here, all the ambition and drive. I like to be around it, but I can't really say that I have it myself."

An image of me scaling the wall of the William Morris Agency flashed through my head.

"I don't really believe that," he said.

Thoughts regarding my complete lack of success threatened to drown the sex hormones that were wildly raging.

"But I do get it, Tracy. Sometimes I know that I don't have the stamina for this place, but yet it's the only place that feels like home. It's the only place that makes me feel alive."

I pulled my knees up to my chin and hid my face from him.

"What's wrong?" he asked.

"I don't know."

"Tell me."

"Do you ever feel like you're just trying to stay afloat in a pool of self-absorption?"

"What?"

"What if we're just splashing around in our own narcissism?"

"Is that really how you feel?"

"Not really."

"You sure?"

"Yeah – I was just wondering."

"It's not a crime to want to create stuff and express yourself."

"Have you written many scripts?" I asked.

"A few. I made one short – it festival hopped for a couple of months. My dad ended up changing everything. Can you imagine? It was humiliating."

"So why did you let him?"

"Because he funded the damn thing. So not only did it not really count in the first place, but my own words and ideas didn't even make the final cut. It started out praising the values of the sixties and ended up warning against them."

"It counts, James – a lot of people here are launched by their families. Look at the Fondas and the Coppolas and the Bridges and the Douglas people and the Hiltons." I wanted to bring up the Cloo-neys but couldn't bring myself to do it, "The list is endless."

"The Hiltons? Great, now I feel much better about myself."

"Sorry."

"It still doesn't count, Tracy. Not in a real sense – no matter how you try to justify it."

"Couldn't have been that bad."

"Evil Terror Plot was the final title, about a misguided bleed-ing heart who thinks love is the answer – but later comes to his senses and learns the value of fear. Totally demoralizing."

"That really is a horrendous title – worse than some of my own. So what was the original title?"

"Blaine Walker – about a bleeding heart who finally comes to his senses and discovers that love is the answer after years of drown-ing in bullshit muck."

"Yes, I'd say that's an overhaul. Is your name attached as writer?"

"No, thank God. My dad and his business partner took the credit. I got a DP nod just because most of the footage of Blaine Walker was already shot. A few voice-overs and inserts changed the whole thing. It's only six minutes, Tracy."

"I'd love to see it."

"Never."

"Then don't harass me about Space Boy."

"Fine."

"And don't call me a writer – at least not yet. It's bullshit."

Lucy snuggled herself into my lap, sensing that I was strug-gling to ward off a bout of depression. She was steadfast that way, always around when I felt most like a loser.

"What's in those boxes?" he asked.

Damn. I'd almost forgotten about the four cardboard mon-strosities that were stacked in the corner of the room.

"Just nothing," I said.

"Can I take a peek?"

"It's just old junk."

"Then you won't mind me looking." He tossed a box lid across the room before I could stop him, and Lucy practically leapt through the air to get inside what had once been forbidden.

"Is she okay in here?"

"Yes – just leave her," I sighed.

James maneuvered around her and carefully lifted out a pile of journals, diaries, loose pages, and old scripts.

"Not a writer, huh?"

"Oh please – that stuff's from high-school. Old crushes and crappy poetry."

"I'm not buying it."

He un-stacked the boxes, and Lucy quickly disappeared inside another one. He rifled through everything – all of my various notes, scribbled commentaries, and crummy screenplays.

"Why do you pretend it doesn't matter?" he asked.

"Oh God, James – please. It's a bunch of childhood doodles."

"Is that why you haul it around?"

Shit.

"It's just a lot of very light, very silly stuff."

James read the titles of a couple of the bulkier scripts, "The Meaning of Everything Before I Died and The Existential Trench."

Even Lucy peered out of a box to cock her head at me.

"Really light and really silly," he said.

"Can we just not talk about it right now. Please."

"Why not?"

"Just because."

"Why not, Tracy?"

"Because I don't want to."

"Okay, I'm sorry."

We both sort of went slack against the floor as if we were inflatable dolls who'd had our plugs pulled. I wasn't sure how long we stayed crumpled up like that, but finally James spoke.

"I wanted to be a self-made man. My father was a self-made man – he had businesses in everything. He's a true entrepreneur. I figured if I came out here, at least I'd be charting my own course."

"Okay."

He turned over to face me, "I just want to chart my own course."

"But you're not really charting your own course," I said, unable to stifle myself. "Not if your parents pay for *everything*, and not if you've let your father change the entire theme of your film."

I thought of my own parents, and was happy they hadn't funded my life or taken over my tepid ambition. As frustrating as it was, it was still mine alone to make, break, or transform into something a little more plausible.

"So am I a parasite or a sell-out?"

I couldn't tell if he wanted to kiss me or punch my lights out.

"You're a kid with rich parents and it's all been a breeze, and now it's time to grow up."

"Anything else?"

"Trust me, James. You'll feel a lot better about yourself."

He shook his head like he wasn't convinced.

"Otherwise, you'd rather be depressed than not, and all because you're lazy."

"So are you saying you're not attracted to me?" he asked.

The question put me on vibrate mode. It took me half a minute to recover my voice, but I willed myself to forge ahead – for the sake of any possible future we might share.

"I am very attracted to you, but I can't respect you if you don't respect yourself."

"Stung."

"What?"

"You're being a little harsh."

"No, I'm not – just honest."

But I really couldn't remember ever being so harsh or honest before, not with a guy – especially one I wanted to devour whole hog.

"Let me demonstrate what I'm up against."

I wasn't quite sure what he was talking about. He pulled out his cell phone and pushed a button.

"Mom? Yeah hi. Fine, fine. Well, actually, not so fine. My car died on the freeway today, and this sweet girl ploughed right into the back of me. Yes, yes, I'm fine. We're both fine. Nothing is broken. Yes, I know you warned me this would happen. I'm over at her place now. Her name is Tracy. I don't know – I'll ask."

James covered the mouthpiece with his hand, "What's your last name?"

"Johnston."

"Tracy *Johnston*. She made me tea. No – she's not gonna sue me."

As I watched his lips move, I couldn't help but wonder what his tongue would feel like inside of my mouth.

"She was really understanding about the whole thing, especially since she lost her job today for not showing up – a production assistant for film. Okay. Yeah. Really? Thanks so much, Mom. I'll ask her. Hold on."

He looked at me with questioning eyes, "My mother wants to know how much you'll need?"

"Come again?" I asked.

"How much, you know, money? For the car, towing, medical, lost wages, and the unavoidable emotional scarring?"

"Are you serious?"

"Yes."

Now the room was expanding. Visions of knights and castles and unicorns filled my head, and I again found myself mute. Lucy scrambled out of my lap and I was sure I was going to pass out. James was watching me as if I were some predictable little equation – as if he knew the drill by heart.

chapter 10

I SWIFTLY CAME to realize that a money tree isn't so bad after all.

In fact, it's quite a joy. How foolish my earlier assessments had been – based on pure ignorance. The morning after the car wreck, James' mother – sweet Paulette – deposited twenty-five thousand dollars into my bank account with a promise of additional compensation if needed. She also bought her son a Prius. I had never seen so much money in an account belonging to me. I had no job, no kids, and a pile of money in the bank – plus, a simple phone number could grant me quick access to more. As a matter of fact, my whiplash was really starting to hurt. Real, real bad.

It was amazing how rapidly the universe could wipe the slate clean. The poles could switch places and the pendulum could swing with such force that perhaps it was even time to register as a Republican.

James called later in the afternoon and invited me to dinner. I thought of Jenny and Luke and their perfect Colorado life and asked him to make a reservation at Spago Beverly Hills. I had never eaten there before; it would be the perfect spot for our first date and the beginning of my new life.

I found an old copper dress that was now three sizes too small – thanks to countless boring hours hovering around the craft services table. All that underling production assistant crap had finally come to an end, forever. So black dress pants and a baggy yellow blouse would have to do, and only because they were still hanging fresh in dry cleaning plastic. Every other article of clothing I owned was now a crumpled rag dropped onto various piles around the room. I smiled with the realization that I even had the cash to hire a clean-up crew. Someone else could haul the laundry around for a change.

My amazing fortune was almost too much to contemplate. I had a bath, groomed all overgrown and un-kept areas, and crawled into bed to cuddle with Lucy. The sound of her purr seemed a little lighter, as though a heavy burden had been lifted from her own kitty shoulders.

"You'll be eating tuna tartar from now on, little lady."

I could have sworn she winked at me.

"Tonight I have a date with a prince."

She touched her paw to my nose, and soon we were asleep.

Three hours later, James and I were sipping lemon drops in the outdoor courtyard of Spago Beverly Hills. We were giggling under the open night as he nibbled house smoked salmon and hog island oysters. I was happy with my platter of beet cakes. There was a gentle breeze playing with my blouse and teasing the little trees around us.

James was wearing a white silk shirt and an expensive yellow tie from Pink's London. He'd called me so that we could match our outfits, just like other moneyed couples in L.A. I had been forced to admit that I only had one available choice. But now I realized that opulence was rather cozy, and it was hard to imagine that I'd ever thought otherwise.

"How ironic that a man driving an ancient heap of shit could afford whatever he wanted," I said.

His smile faded, "My parents could afford whatever I wanted."

"What's the diff?" I asked, finally feeling like part of the worthwhile crowd.

"See how quickly integrity wears away in the face of ease and luxury?" he asked.

He asked this lightly, but it felt like a calculated stab, "I think your mother was very gracious in light of your carelessness. I mean – you could have killed us both driving that rust can."

"I thought you said it was your fault."

"And I thought we split the difference."

"One little lump sum and you turn yourself inside out – immediately abandon your lefty ideals?"

"What lefty ideals?" I asked.

I wasn't sure what he'd said under his breath, but I heard the snicker.

"No, I would just accept my good fortune and be thrilled for it, instead of accepting my good fortune and sulking for it."

James ignored me and ate a piece of salmon.

"Why not just appreciate your roots, and make your movies?" I asked.

"Because there are always strings attached, no matter how subtle."

"Well then – grow up and get a job."

He looked in every direction but mine.

"Do you ever want to be married, James? I mean – like with a wife and kids?"

I wasn't quite sure where the hell *that* had just come from.

"It's not a big desire of mine."

"Why not?" I asked.

"It's someone else's idea of happiness."

"Is that what your parents want for you?"

"Of course it is."

"Really?"

He wiped his mouth with the perfect cloth napkin and tossed it across the table, "I can't tell you how many dinners I've suffered through with well-meaning Republican girls."

"Suffered through? So are they all like Ann Coulter?"

"No, they're not. Some are very beautiful, and well... poised."

I nearly choked on my beet cake, "Poised? Okay. So I bet you grew up in a gated community?"

"What's with the sarcasm?"

I gulped back my lemon drop, and signaled to the waiter that I needed another one – fast. I wasn't exactly sure what was up with the sarcasm, or the surging resentment I was now starting to feel for my knight in matching colors.

"I grew up in a couple of places – one of our summer condos *was* gated. So what?"

"So quit pretending you could ever understand what it means to struggle."

"I never said I could."

The lemon drops were surely to blame for my sudden and acidic turn. Or maybe it was something else. Maybe the possibility of a real-life man had me in way over my head. Maybe I just didn't want any of it. Maybe my mother could go take an extended hike.

"What does it mean to be a man in the twenty-first century, James?"

"I haven't really got a clue. What does it mean to be a woman?"

"I think it's more complex."

"Why is that?"

"Because of roles and biology and choices. I don't know. It's hard. It's like that Chaka Khan song. But I can't be every woman."

The damned alcohol went straight to my eyes, but I wouldn't let him see me cry.

"Tracy, it's okay. I'm not expecting you to be every woman."

His gentleness unnerved me somehow, as if he were meddling with the core that even I'd been denied access to.

"What are you gonna do with the rest of your life, James?"

"What are you gonna do with the rest of yours, Tracy?"

"Well, tomorrow I'm going to the spa."

The waiter placed another citrus delight in front of me, and I instantly gulped it down. The tears could come if they wanted to – I didn't care anymore.

"After that, maybe I'll sleep for a month and then deal with that space thing again."

"Is that really the level of passion you have for your writing?" he asked.

"Yes."

"I still don't believe you. Not at all."

"Don't then."

"Maybe you're just scared. Maybe you don't feel worthy of your own voice."

"Don't lecture me on issues of worth. You're an adult man who acts like a ten-year-old. Do you really think that's attractive to women? When Mommy and Daddy Warbucks swoop in to take care of your doodie poos? And rather than appreciate your fabulous karma, you find a way to hate them for it."

I couldn't believe I had uttered *doodie poos* nor could I believe my dream date was now swirling down the shitter. All thanks to me and my runaway mouth. It was like my damn opinions had a mind of their own.

James was silent, wounded to the core by the big bad scary woman. I had just unloaded nearly six feet of Amazonian terror on him, and now felt like the most unattractive thing ever to be tolerated in Beverly Hills.

"I didn't realize you were so angry," he said.

"Neither did I."

We sat in silence as he was served plates of meat and I was served plates of greens.

"James, I'm really sorry about that. Sometimes I just go off like a wing-nut. Maybe I do want a husband and kids. Maybe I thought I was too cool for it before, maybe I thought it would be some sort of boring trap. I mean, maybe I was thinking marriage isn't even necessary anymore."

"Maybe it is, maybe not. Maybe you don't have a clue what you want. Maybe you're just as wishy-washy as I am."

"Maybe," I said, as sweetly as possible.

I was trying hard to salvage the evening and heal the puncture wound I'd delivered, but he looked as though he'd lost his essential spark. It bothered me to know I could snatch it from him so completely.

"You know, I already feel bad enough about myself. And you make me feel worse, Tracy."

My tongue licked at the sides of my empty glass.

"I have my struggles too, you know," he said.

"Like what?"

"Stuff."

Despite my better, lust-driven self, my smart-mouth was not going to let him sit and whine about his life predicament, "Where to go on vacation? What stocks to invest in?"

"It's a struggle for meaning," he said.

"Well, it's a luxurious struggle then."

"But it is a struggle."

"I just really don't care."

"You don't like me then," he said. "Why the hell are you here when you don't even like me?"

"Yes, I do like you," I said, unsure of myself. "It's just that your self-pity is boring and your so-called struggle has about as much depth as an ingrown hair."

"You're an asshole," he said.

"Probably so, James. But no one is ever gonna feel sorry for you – not ever. And maybe it's that fact – more than any other – that makes you feel so sorry for yourself."

He nodded at me and drained his cocktail.

I'd been looking forward to the most extraordinary evening of my life, but my romantic interest in James was disappearing like a magic act. He was a lost little boy, and I guess I'd been hoping for a man.

"Do you want me to give the money back?" I asked.

"It's not my money, Tracy. Besides, didn't I ruin what was left of your life?"

His scar was beaconing, inviting me to touch it, "You wish."

We had the Spago feast wrapped to go, and left all of our hopes for each other on the luminous patio beneath the cold black sky – as if the stars had all abandoned the heavens to sit and be seen in this eatery.

Oh well. Another crushed possibility left to die in a La La Land landmark.

James dropped me off outside my lonely room, and I spent the rest of the night crying into my dirty pillowcase. Maybe I was only content if my chances for happiness were on life support. Lucy licked my tears with her rough little tongue, and I thanked God for not pulling the plug completely.

chapter 11

THE NEXT DAY I bit the bullet, and decided to drown myself in clichés.

I bought a ticket home for my parents' surprise anniversary celebration. With the newfound money, this was simply the way the ball had to bounce – but I was hopeful I'd find a silver lining in even the darkest cloud of whatever it was I was in for.

I called to let them know I'd be dropping in for a long overdue visit. They were both ecstatic that I'd be coming home, and I was careful not to drop any hints, although the timing of my trip would surely make them suspicious. I was happy that I didn't have to rely on Jenny's faux charity, and decided I would no longer answer her calls. Nor would I answer any calls from Sheila or James.

Oh, God. James.

I sat on the floor next to the window, exactly where we had sat the other night. The view was the same, but everything looked different. I still couldn't believe how sarcastic I had been to such a sweet guy, but he disappointed me in a profound way. And that's probably because I disappointed myself in the same way. I was really no different than he was, and would endure precisely the same struggles if I'd been lucky enough to be born into his life.

Maybe he was right about me – perhaps I didn't feel worthy enough to succeed. I stood up and skulked over to my floundering screenplay – the way one might move towards a killer spider. It felt light and meaningless in my hands.

Lucy and I sat on the bed, and I closed my eyes until all I could perceive was black. My perfected ability to fantasize now took me deep into the heart of a movie theater. With extra buttery popcorn in one hand and an iced cold Coke in the other, I found a seat as far back as I could. I sat through preview trailers until a serious score finally took over, signaling that *Space Boy*, a film written by Tracy Johnston, had indeed begun.

I opened my eyes to the first scene, just as I had written it months ago. We, the audience, are seeing Earth through the eyes of *The Space Station*. This station isn't really a place as much as it is a force. It beacons only to those who long for freedom – a freedom so vast that it can only be compared to space. It is neither a good force nor a bad force – but it is there, and it exerts itself on all those who would seek expansion. Like a mirror, the space station ultimately serves to reflect.

And then we CUT TO a young blonde boy who is standing alone on the balcony of a large house. He is staring up at the heavens through a large telescope – and when he pulls his face away, we can see that he is longing for something. We can also see the traces of sadness that he carries. Who knows who this child might be or who he will become, but it quickly becomes clear that his insatiable curiosity for the unknown will take him wherever he needs to be.

The phone rang just as I was about to advance my protagonist. Shit. I ignored the phone but the mood was lost. So far, the blueprint I had layed out with words was translating well to the screen in my head. I would have to use my powers of fantasy to guide me through the first fifty-one minutes so that I could find the visual track to write the rest. And when it was done, there was no guarantee that it wouldn't just languish in a drawer or on a shelf – for the rest of its life.

Such would be a tragedy, similar in scope to the Taj Mahal or Eiffel Tower never having been built – only existing as stacks of blueprints disintegrating into dust. Except it was almost a sure thing that my spectacle would never be built or seen, and the architect would never be admired or remembered forever throughout history. It was simply the way of Hollywood, a giant graveyard for lost and forgotten blueprints.

Maybe my ideas of self-importance were too grandiose – instead I should be humble, and just write without any regard for outcomes. That's what all the wise people seemed to suggest. It was best to be without expectation and watch the magical moments unfold. But it was in these waters that I always capsized.

It was hard to do anything at all without an expectation of some kind, unless you were kidding yourself. I loved writing but it was so damn hard, and I needed incentives to continue. Fame and fortune were huge bonuses, but then I'd be writing for all of the 'wrong' reasons.

Now, with money in the bank, there was no reason not to write – unless of course, I lacked the sufficient passion for such a monumental endeavor. Or maybe I was just drained from the effort of piling up so much pain.

My head throbbed, so I took a taxi to Coffee Bean and Tea Leaf and had a large fix of caramel flavored caffeine. I slurped and pouted – exactly like James might – until it was time to take another cab to the spa.

The waiting room at Spa-tastic felt very Zen-like. Birds chirped and a pan flute floated across scented air. Water gurgled gently from various fountains and white flowers soothed the eye.

A small elderly Asian woman appeared out of nowhere and gently guided me into a tiny room with bare walls and a massage table. She informed me that her name was Miss Tan and that she'd come here from Korea thirty years ago. Her countenance was sweet, but she was also no-nonsense – something like a cute but maturing tiger.

But nothing could dampen my anticipation. It had been a long time since I'd treated myself to such an indulgence and I could hardly wait to feel her capable hands gently massaging away my broken heart.

Miss Tan removed her buckled slippers with great ceremony and then lit a stick of musky incense. I stood as still as possible out of respect for her ritual until she barked at me to hurry up, disrobe, and slip under the sheet – face up.

It was a mighty good thing that I'd shaved everything so pristine. I was expecting her to leave the room as is proper etiquette but she remained where she was, with hands on hips. I tried to undress as quickly as possible without giving her much visual access to my ample thighs and hips. Soon I was safely concealed under the cool sheet. But she promptly positioned herself over me – studying me with a very concerned, almost puzzled expression.

"You don't need massage," she said.

"I don't?"

"You need reike."

"What's that?"

"I spin your circles – they clogged up."

"Circles?"

"The chakras are stuck, the chi is backed up – like a clogged pipe," she said, rather annoyed.

"Oh."

"What wrong with you?" she asked.

"I don't know."

"We find out."

"Okay."

Before I could inquire further, she was pulling invisible bands of energy out of my chest.

"Spin spin spin," she cried. "Spin the sex, spin the dust, spin the crown."

I had no clue what was happening but my tummy felt the way it does when a roller coaster plummets.

"You squirmy inside," she said. "A big ball of mix-up."

"Yes – that seems about right."

Tan closed her eyes and motioned her hands in slow ovals over my body – she looked like a human metal detector.

"Ahhhhhhhhh," she said. "A-ha."

"What?"

"You shut yourself off like a light."

"I do?"

"You in off mode."

"I am?"

"Yes."

"How do I turn myself back on?"

"Only you know," she said.

"Know what?"

She shrugged her shoulders.

"How?" I asked.

She shrugged again.

"Miss Tan?"

"Call me Tan."

"Tan."

"Stop whining, child – this is half your problem."

"Yeah, but – "

"But nothing. The answers in your chest."

"They are?"

"You not foolish – you know already."

"But I'm confused."

"No, you not confused. You stuck."

"Isn't that the same thing?"

"No, stuck is to know and not act."

"So then what is confused?"

"To not know and not act."

I scratched at the palm of my hand.

"Empowerment is to not know but act anyway."

"Or maybe that's the definition of reckless," I said.

She ignored me and concentrated on wiggling each of her strong but tiny fingers.

"Do you have any juice?" I asked.

"Stop distracting," she snapped.

"But I'm thirsty."

"Distracted."

"But even you said I was a big ball of mix-up."

"Until I examined your chest."

"What about it?"

"You in love. Simple."

I was shocked. How could she possibly know such a thing? And how could it possibly be simple? But even more importantly, how could I be in love with someone after only a few hours together – a guy too spoiled to ever even hold a job.

"I am not."

"Stop judging."

"I'm not," I said.

"Don't lie to me."

"So now you can see my thoughts?" I asked.

"Your energy. Your heart."

"Am I that transparent?"

"Yes."

"Well, could I at least get a massage now?"

"You also spoiled."

"I'll have you know I was just in a car accident."

"Not surprised," she said.

"What does that mean?"

"It means you daydream."

"I am a writer."

"Then write something."

"How can you know all this?"

"Easy," she said.

"I'm easy to read?"

"Your generation is restless – too much stuff, too many choices of stuff. You become bored and selfish – listless, even. Listless – that my new word. Even I lazy sometimes now."

"It all sounds terrible, Tan."

"Am I wrong?" she asked.

"No."

She started to massage oil into her hands and I was hopeful I'd finally get my massage. I wondered if I should tell her about the hives – maybe she could cure them somehow.

"You should be massaging *me*," she said. "That could be your life lesson."

"What?"

"To be of service. Make you happy."

"I broke out in hives the other day – I thought I was going to die."

She busted out a big grin, "Of course you do."

"How do I fix it?" I asked.

"In your chest."

"What?"

"All answers there," she said, poking a sharp finger between my breasts.

"But?"

"All answers in your chest."

I wanted to press for more information until I felt her oily hands begin their work – her skin was soft but the pressure she exerted made me cringe. We never spoke another word but I left her a triple digit tip and by the time I walked out of Spa-tastic, I was sure the car accident had been rubbed right out of my neck.

chapter 12

ANOTHER CAB DROPPED me off at my room.

My muscles felt brand new, but I'd been thoroughly laid bare. I'd always thought I carried myself with a touch more subtlety – even a dash of mystery. But Tan was right – I was as obvious as garlic breath in a phone booth.

James was waiting for me at the front entrance. He was messy in wrinkled clothes and I reluctantly invited him up with a cranky sigh, even though I was secretly elated that he had come. It felt good beyond measure to know that I mattered to him.

We sat on the floor in front of the window and ate through a bulk package of mini raisin boxes.

"You're glowing," he said. "And you smell like mint."

"I've just been debunked."

"Pardon?"

"At the spa."

"Of course, the mint."

"Forget the mint. Tan told me I was selfish. And stuck. She said I knew things but didn't act on them."

I didn't dare mention the fact that she also accused me of being in love.

"Tan?"

"The old lady at the spa."

"Oh."

We sat quite comfortably in silence, watching a gorgeous couple move furniture into a nearby building.

"I still think I'm confused, no matter what she says."

"She doesn't think you're confused?" he asked.

"She thinks I'm stuck."

"What's the difference?"

I ignored him.

"How would she know? She doesn't even know me. The audacity – telling me I know more than I think I do."

"I would say that's a compliment," he said.

"It's not."

"Okay."

"If I do know more than I think I do – I don't know that I know it."

"Was it expensive?"

"What?"

"The spa?"

"What's that supposed to mean?"

"I'm just making conversation – maybe I'd like a debunking or whatever the hell it was you had."

"The money gives me some squirm room, James."

"I didn't say anything."

"I'm just telling you. It helps me breathe."

"Just make sure you don't choke on it."

"I'm not you," I said.

"You're just like me."

"How's that?"

"You don't know what you want *only* when what you know to be true involves any smidgeon of struggle."

"You're giving me a migraine."

"So let's change the subject."

"Good idea."

"What's your space script about?"

I shrugged, "It's a metaphor."

"For?"

"Escape."

"From what?" he asked.

"I'm still trying to figure that out. I thought it was escape from the known. Escape from conditioning, escape from the well-laid path – but now I'm really not so sure. Maybe it's really about an escape from any sort of ambition."

He looked at me with his usual sad intensity. His blue eyes were dancing with all the light they'd caught from the window.

"Actually, that's not true," I reconsidered. "I do know what I mean. Escape from anything that would deny *freedom* – even the freedom to be stuck. Even the freedom to be an absolute nothing."

He smiled at me like I might be a genius, and I was amazed that we hadn't kissed yet.

"Yes," he said. "You should continue with it."

"It's too hard," I said, surprised that I could so readily admit the truth about such a painful subject. "I let the gap get too big. And besides, what does the freedom to be a nothing have to do with space?"

"Everything."

"But I can't stay focused."

"Why not?"

"I don't know."

"I bet you do."

"Maybe because I'm running. I've been running away for a very long time. So it's too hard to go back. And I haven't even escaped yet – I still care what everybody thinks. I can't write about something I haven't yet experienced."

He nodded intently as if I made some really profound sense rather than just rambling on in my nut-hound sort of way.

"So write about the process of trying to escape," he said.

"What?"

"The process."

"Right."

"Maybe you're a blocked creative – Julia Cameron writes about them."

"Maybe it's just not meant to be."

"I think you're blocked."

"I don't know."

James pulled up his socks and then rolled them back down.

"And I break out in hives. My parents called the other day, on my thirtieth birthday. They're worried that I have no family, no direction, no nothing."

"Is that how you feel?"

"I don't know. I think maybe I do agree with them and then I feel like maybe I'm just supposed to *think* I feel that way. And I'm going home for their anniversary."

"For how long?"

"I don't know."

"Take the script with you."

"No."

"Hash it out for fun, turn it into something else."

"That's like saying, stick a poker up your nose – for laughs."

He shook his head at me like I was a bad puppy, and I could feel the squiggles in my solar plexus.

"Just let me be lost, James. Will you?"

He didn't answer.

"Will you just let me be lost?"

"Get lost, Tracy. If that's what you really want."

"It is."

"Okay then, but you'll be wandering for a while."

"That's fine – that's what I want. Just let me wander. Please don't project your shit onto me. If you wanna write, go and write."

"That's all we do, Tracy – project shit onto each other. So why stop now?"

I didn't answer.

"I just don't want to see you give up."

I wanted to grab him by the shoulders and shake him and admit that I hadn't given up – that despite dredging up my soul time and again to a chorus of boos, giving up was the one thing I just couldn't get right. I wanted to tell him all this, but I couldn't. It was easier to let him think that my failure was something I still had some control over.

I let out a huge sigh, "I'm gonna go make us some tea – take an intermission from the intellectual jacking off. Is vanilla herbal okay?"

"Yes."

I stood up and walked across the room to the kitchen.

"Are you still mad about Spago?" he asked.

"No."

"Good. Because my parents are coming into town tomorrow and I want you to have dinner with us."

"Why are they coming into town?" I asked. "Is it about the money?"

"Of course not – forget about the money."

"Thank God."

"I think they just miss me."

"This is all very last minute."

"There's no need to be nervous, Tracy."

"I'm not nervous."

"Or defensive."

"I am not defensive."

"You don't have to come – it was just an idea."

I studied him to see if he was practicing reverse psychology on me.

"I want to come."

"Good."

I made us our tea and we sat in silence.

"I have to pee all of a sudden."

Lucy and I went to the bathroom. She scratched around in her litter box, and I peed a gallon only to discover that I was out of toilet paper.

"James!"

"What?"

"Could you bring me some coffee filters? They're right beside the pot."

He obliged me, no questions asked. I was aware that a big part of what attracted me to him was how comfortable I still felt in my own skin. He didn't activate my walls, and even better, I didn't have to turn myself into any sort of feminine caricature.

"Are you hungry?" I hollered.

"Famished."

We ordered Thai food, and filled the kitchen corner of the room with pineapple-fried rice, red curry chicken, garlic prawns, and pad thai noodles. We also sipped the wine that my friend had sent for my birthday.

"So why do you think you get hives?" he asked.

"I don't know. Maybe I'm allergic to the choices I've made."

"Your choices aren't so bad."

"Look around, James. I live in a big litter box and I'm unemployed. I have no clue what I should do or where I want to be."

"And that's bad *why*?"

"I don't know. Maybe I'm allergic to the choices I'm supposed to make."

"That might be more like it."

I twirled a huge heap of noodles around my fork.

"But I mean, what do I have?" I asked. "What have I done?"

"You're also free, a blank canvas. You are free to wander, remember? You're not anchored to anything but this moment."

Yes, that ever-reliable moment had now become excruciating. It was time to touch him. I placed my hand over his and gently rubbed his knuckles with my thumb. His hands were exquisite, and for a long time I just stared down at them – at the thick veins and bits of hangnail that he'd chewed.

Finally, I felt his other hand on my chin, lifting my eyes to meet his own. He gently pulled my face into his, where our mouths and teeth and tongues met, searching and exploring, but mostly eager to consume. Even the bits of pineapple rice in our teeth couldn't hold us back.

chapter 13

JAMES TOLD A big fat fib.

He'd assured me that the dinner with his parents would be casual, but I showed up at the restaurant completely underdressed. I'd insisted on taking a cab and meeting them – just in case things got awkward and I needed to bolt. And now I found myself sitting in bell-bottom jeans in a well-known Beverly Hills eatery famous for their salads.

"What's wrong?" James whispered – even though his parents had excused themselves to go admire a painting on a far wall... although I'm sure it was just an excuse to go compare notes on the hopeless new gal in their son's life.

"Your parents look like they're ready for the Golden Globes."

"They always dress like that."

"I have a patch in the shape of a raspberry stitched into my ass."

"They're just happy you're here."

"And what cologne are you wearing?"

"Some expensive thing my mother handed me at the airport."

"I feel like a bit of a hobo – you could have prepared me."

"Huh?"

"I'm wearing a thrift-store blouse. I thought we were going for pizza or something."

"My parents don't do pizza. Just be yourself."

"A neurotic pile of nerves?"

He tilted his head at me as though I were still the cutest, most aggravating thing he'd ever had to put up with.

"You're beautiful, Tracy. Now just be yourself."

"Okay – I'll try."

His parents came back to the table chatting merrily about Hollywood's golden age – but once they settled back into place, the table went mysteriously and terribly silent. I wiped my sweaty palms on my decorated denim and realized that his family seemed rather accustomed to the hush – one likely born not of too little to say, but rather too much, of the repressed variety.

"You really need a cleaning lady, James," his father finally said.

"Oh, Peter – not now."

"When, Paulette? We're only here for a day."

"Just not now. Why don't we focus on the menu?"

"Our salads are on the way. Anyway, there's certainly money in the budget for a cleaning lady, son."

I was afraid to look at James, but did anyway. He looked like he was in the initial stages of some really bad stomach flu.

"Your mother and I will find you one before we leave. And you should try to keep that Prius detailed – twice a month. Otherwise, it just completely depreciates."

James tossed his menu at the table, "Is a full detail twice a month really necessary?"

"Keeping your car clean and respectable will improve your spirits."

"My spirits are great," he pouted.

"Driving around in a portable dump will get you noticed for all the wrong reasons."

I choked on a lemon seed, and Paulette slapped me on the back. I felt it was only a matter of time before they asked to inspect my apartment. And then I would most surely have to give the money back.

"I'm not that hopeless, Dad. Tracy will get the wrong impression."

"Tracy's first impression was slamming into your car because it was stopped dead on the freeway. It was totally broken down, James. And that makes me wonder if you were maintaining it at all. I shudder to think when the last oil change was. And the money we gave Tracy could have been spent on a decent import in the first place."

Oh shit.

"The past is done," Paulette said. "But there is certainly money in the account for a house-keeper, detailing, and oil changes. Not to worry. And driving around on these freeways is scary at the best of times. So make extra sure that your little Toyota is well-conditioned."

I thought of the Prius at the beauty salon.

"It's called upkeep, and it's something responsible adults are expected to do," Peter said.

My face felt as red as the wine in my glass.

Peter turned to me, "James tells us you work in film?"

"Tracy's a writer," James said, irritated to the hilt.

"Oh," Peter said. "Anything I would know?"

"Well, I'm not exactly at that stage yet," I said.

"Not to worry – neither is James."

I tried to stop my eyes from widening, but fell short.

The table soon felt like a funeral again.

"I'd love to see the short film you put together," I offered.

Peter and Paulette shared a *look* – something akin to a silent groan.

"We usually don't bring that up at meal-time," Peter said.

"Oh – I'm sorry."

Peter chuckled and assured me he was just kidding, but I felt the first trickle of sweat glide down my side.

"That was a fine exercise in bad planning," Peter started. "We barely got into the short festival circuit let alone any sort of realistic distribution."

I wanted to yell "CUT!" at the top of my lungs, scoop James into my arms, and lick away all of the wounds that were surely getting worse by the millisecond, but instead I simply smiled like someone who'd just been slapped silly.

"But I guess that's what happens when the idea isn't really there."

"It was there, Dad."

"It wasn't there, James."

"That's because you came in and screwed with it until it was unrecognizable. The opposite of what I'd intended."

"We were just trying to help, son. Get this dream of yours off the damn ground."

"I didn't need help."

"Well, we thought you did. Stories about John Lennon hippies weren't exactly hot-ticket items at that time."

James sighed at his father like he was the hangman, and I realized I was casing the joint for the nearest emergency exit.

"I suppose it was an experience in terms of a learning curve, but certainly not a lesson in how profits are made."

"Not everything is about profits," James said.

"It is when you have dependents to support."

I looked around the restaurant like a wild animal, wondering where on God's green globe our waiter was hiding.

Peter turned to me, "But James is stubborn. There's an amazing real estate opportunity for him back east but he refuses to even hear about it. It's far beneath an artist, I suppose."

"Well, uhm, uh," I stammered, and then fell silent.

Our waiter finally emerged from the shadows with four chopped salads; I studied mine like it was a bar exam. I could only hope the gods of mercy would soon vaporize me on the spot.

"What is it that you enjoy most about writing?" Paulette suddenly asked.

It took me a couple of seconds to realize that the question was directed at me.

"Um, well. It's like I…"

My bra was soaked on either side.

"Yes?" she said.

"I get to create something out of nothing."

"Nothing, alright," Peter said.

"Peter, behave," Paulette said.

"It just sounds like they both have a God complex – that's all."

"Well, good for them. Now let the poor child speak."

I sort of liked the fact that she referred to me as a child – a poor one. It made her questions far less threatening.

"Go on, Tracy – something out of nothing."

"When I'm writing, life suddenly has great meaning. And I'm less empty inside."

I tried to block Peter out of my peripheral vision.

"Well, that's quite something," she said. "I certainly hope you'll allow me to read something you've written."

"Tracy's working on a script about space," James said.

"Really? Is it science fiction?" she asked.

"Not Scientology, I hope?" Peter asked.

"No. It's more about the depths within us," I said.

"Oh dear," Peter groaned.

Paulette ignored her husband and focused on me, "You've got the loveliest green eyes I've ever seen."

"Thank you."

"And I'd really love to read your script sometime."

"Actually," James said, looking at his watch, "Tracy's got to get back to it soon – very soon. Don't you, Tracy?"

"Well…"

I looked over at James whose eyes were pleading with me to put an end to whatever it was this evening had become.

"Uh, yes, I certainly do. I have to get back to it as soon as possible."

"We haven't even ordered entrees," Peter said.

Paulette studied James and me, and then she smiled, "These salads are more than I can handle anyway."

"I'm ordering something substantial," Peter said.

"Go ahead, dear. But perhaps these two have other places they need to be. Am I right, Tracy?"

"Well, Mrs. Howard, I would never want to kick a hovering muse in the teeth."

James laughed and Paulette quickly concurred with me, although I wasn't entirely convinced she knew what I was talking about.

chapter 14

WE WERE NEARLY stoned with relief.

James and I had raced down the street, hopped in a cab, and ordered the driver to take us to Griffith Park. We sat in silence in the back seat and I thought about how awesome Paulette was – helping us escape like that.

As we moved east, the streets grew noisy with traffic and angry shouting, but the dominant voice in my head belonged to Peter. He was carefully enunciating all of my failures in the order in which they occurred. I shuddered and looked to James for comfort, but his jaw was set in stone.

When we finally arrived at the park, he gave the cabbie a hundred dollar bill. I didn't say a word – just took his hand in mine and walked him around in a large circle.

"That was brutal," he said.

"I was sweating bullets the whole time. My bra's a little sticky."

"I'm really sorry about that."

"Does that happen a lot?"

"It's pretty standard."

"Well – your mother's really something – totally clued in."

James bent down to pick up a twig.

"I'm embarrassed, Tracy."

"It's okay."

"No, it's not. It's so bad that I almost want to call it off with you."

I stopped cold and stared at him with a mixture of horror and hopefulness – to call us *off* meant that we were actually on – and I so wanted to be on.

"My father emasculated me in front of you."

"No, he didn't. He just proved himself to be completely overbearing."

"You're trying to be nice."

"I am not."

James turned from me and started walking away.

"Wait!"

He kept walking.

"I think maybe your father wanted to be the artist!"

"Whatever!"

"Where are you going?" I called after him. "If you want to dump me, don't blame it on your parents."

He stopped at a picnic table and sat down. I quickly found myself sitting next to him.

"Are we even together, Tracy?"

"I thought so."

"We've only known each other a few days."

I had to grit my teeth to keep from scratching his face, "Fine – just fuck it then."

"I'm a child, Tracy."

I tried not to notice the dried clump of toothpaste on his collar, "You are not a child."

"He's so damn smug."

"He's just trying to do his duty, James."

"Just like your parents are, right?"

"I don't want to talk about any of this anymore."

"I feel like I can't really make anything work in this position."

"So why can't you change your position?"

"I don't know how. Don't you get it yet?"

"I guess not."

"And now he's even going to micro-manage how I take care of that damn car."

I looked around at the big trees, trying to stifle my irritation, "So why don't you get a bus pass?"

"Tracy – be serious."

"I am."

"This is L.A. – the city's way too fucking big."

"Other people take the bus."

"People without money?"

"Sensible people who don't want to be slaves to car payments, insurance payments, gas and repairs."

"People without money."

"It's an option, James."

"I'm not getting a bus pass."

"Well, then why complain about the Prius? So your parents want you to take care of it – so what?"

"I don't want to talk about the fucking car."

He peeled away a section of loose paint from the table.

"Look James, we're both a little screwed up and confused."

I tried to hold his hand but he made his fingers go limp.

"Why take it out on me?" I asked.

He shrugged his shoulders and looked at me with eyes that turned all of my strong intentions to mush. And he continued looking at me until my flesh was covered in something that felt like desire but probably ran much deeper. I wondered if he knew this was the effect he had on me, and I wondered if I should try harder to be less obvious.

"Why are you looking at me like that?" he asked.

"It's cold and I was thinking we should get back."

"Get back to what?"

"Someplace warm."

"You're leaving for the mid-west."

"Not tonight."

"Still."

"Don't bring up the mid-west right now."

"Why not?"

"Just don't."

He continued peeling the table until he had a small stack of old paint strips.

"I'm scared to go back, James."

"Why?"

"I don't know. I'm almost afraid of what I'll find. Some buried truth that affects me somehow – that has always affected me."

We both sat at the picnic table like a couple of rejected artists.

"This seat is cold and uncomfortable and hurts my ass," I said.

"Do you respect me, Tracy?"

"Oh God, James. Haven't we had this conversation?"

"It's a simple question."

"Of course I do," I sighed.

"But?" he asked.

"I didn't say anything."

"You sighed as if you had more to say."

I wanted to reach out and gently touch the curve of his eyelashes, the perfect frame for such intensity, "You're being paranoid."

"No – you have more to say."

Maybe I did, but now was not the right time to say it.

"You think I'm a loser?"

"I do not."

"You're full of shit."

I couldn't believe that this man who so easily turned my knees to pudding could look at me with such accusing eyes, as if I were somehow the enemy.

"Excuse me?"

"What does it mean to be a man in the twenty-first century? Didn't you ask me that?"

"Well I have no idea what it means to be a woman, James – or where I fit in. I've been struggling with these questions forever. I mean, marriage, kids – the whole thing. What does it even mean?"

He shrugged like it didn't even matter – stood up from the table.

"Where are you going?"

"Don't know."

"James, come on. I'm just trying to talk to you."

"Forget it."

I tugged at his sleeve, tried hard to pull him back down.

"Just let me go, Tracy."

"I don't want to."

I wrapped my arms around his knees and we both fell onto the hard dusty ground. For a moment, his blue eyes and purple hair were all mine – like a fissure in the prison wall, offering the light of freedom. I put my thumb on his bottom lip and gently pulled it down until I could see the pink of his gum-line.

"James?"

"I can't."

"Can't what?"

He closed his eyes, "Do this."

I should have dug my nail deep into the gentle tissue beneath his teeth, but my signals were rapidly scrambling – the circuitry burning itself to the ground, "Please don't say that."

He pushed my hand away from his mouth and quickly jumped to his feet, leaving me to stare helplessly at the points of his boots.

"Why don't you just kick me?" I asked. "It would hurt less."

He yelled over his shoulder as he walked away, "I just need some space."

"No you don't," I whispered at the small rock I was clutching in my fist.

I wanted to scream after him that he was a fucking quitter, but I threw the rock instead. It landed behind him with a pitiful thud – he didn't even bother to turn around. I sat up and watched him fade away – his eager strides ever increasing the space between us.

Part 2

A Bingo Hall,

Aunt Mertyl,

and The Used Appliance Prince

chapter 15

I'D FINALLY ESCAPED the two-faced temptress.

Ms. Holly Wood. She'd lured me here with her dazzling smile and empty promises, but all she'd ever done was snap my dreams in half. I waved down at her big, white-lettered grin. She was such a tease, after all. But she'd continue on her merry chaotic way long after I was gone – as if I'd been nothing but a non-existent blip on her radar screen.

The flight was long and uncomfortable and I'd decided that I wouldn't think of James – but it was like trying not to breathe, so I gave in at thirty thousand feet. If he wanted space, I'd give it to him. Loads of it. I'd give him all the space in the world – pasturelands full. He could graze all day on the endless, empty fields of a life lived alone – not a whiff of me ever to be had again.

And I needed to steer clear of the implications – how empty my life would also become – yet moving through my mind was like traversing a gloomy terrain of bottomless pits. I gobbled a bag of peanuts and dug my fingers into the armrest, trying to steel myself against the dread.

But my body shuddered with the memory of his fingers in my mouth. We had stopped short of undressing. I had insisted on it, for a thousand reasons I was no longer sure of.

Damn him.

He was like an explorer determined to discover my landscape, especially the treasures he'd sensed underground – buried deep in stacked boxes against the wall. And I'd been so close to signing over my most guarded territory – fertile soil that might miss out on any chance to bloom.

As the miles between us multiplied, I wondered if the gathering distance might somehow bring us back together – like a boomerang that finds its way back to the hand that flung it away.

I fell asleep and awoke to something strangely familiar and instantly demanding – rendering the immediate past something closer to a dream. I remembered that I was coming home.

Flying over the green of Minnesota felt like drinking water after an endurance test of concrete. The round bushy trees and thick grasses only added to my relief; I watched from the window as the light danced and sparkled and gleamed across the surface of the emerald lakes.

Jenny and Luke met me at the airport. Their outfits matched – crisp ironed beiges and blues. Clarice was wearing a little pink sundress, and she happily toddled into my arms. I buried my head in her curls and deeply inhaled their baby smell. We giggled together; it made me feel confident in my decency that tiny children and small animals had no qualms about getting close to me.

"Hey sister," Jenny said, and flung an arm around my waist. "You look... good."

I was wearing jeans with holes and construction-type work boots.

"Glad to see Lucy again," she said, and poked a finger into the carrier.

We all heard the hiss, and I was almost thankful when Jenny's finger emerged unscathed.

"Alright, listen up," Jenny said. "Aunt Mertyl and Uncle Harley are coming in tonight, and so are Derek and Trina. Meanwhile, Luke and I need to pick out a dessert. I want something different, maybe a cherry or vanilla something or even a pudding-filled sponge.

And then we need to figure out the place settings. I haven't decided on the color schemes yet but I'm leaning toward light pink and peach or a bright red apple with an understated gold."

My sister's eyes bulged as she spoke, like she wasn't breathing. Clarice started to cry in a rather mournful way; even Luke looked odd, like perhaps he should be wearing some sort of a leash.

I never wanted to see James wearing that expression.

"Is there time for a salad or something?" I asked.

Jenny let out a long sigh, as if I were an unruly pet in training, "Didn't you eat on the plane?"

"They didn't have anything," I whined.

"They have snack boxes," she snapped.

I looked at Luke, but he wasn't able to make eye contact.

"I suppose we can run through a drive-thru somewhere."

"Thanks."

"Wait until you see our latest purchase, Tracy."

I carried Clarice on one arm and my duffel bag and the cat carrier in the other as we walked to their new vehicle: an 8 cylinder giant hog of an SUV.

"Surprise! Isn't it nice?" Jenny gushed.

I was speechless.

"It's so wonderfully black – you should see it shine in the sun. And so much room for everything."

"What do you need room for?" I asked.

"We're a family now, Tracy. There's plenty of room for the car seat."

"Ten car seats," I said.

All four of us situated ourselves in the dark behemoth. Even Lucy and her little cage got a full seat.

"Must cost a lot for gas," I said.

Clarice was sitting merrily in my lap, blowing spit bubbles.

"Way too much," Luke said. He sounded grave and I was slightly startled to hear him speak.

Jenny let out another colossal sigh, as if we were all trying to rip up her pretty flowers.

"It's just practical for a family to have an SUV, Tracy. You'll see one day. Think about it."

"How is it practical?" I asked.

"When our kids get older, they're going to play sports. They will have *equipment*. You know, hockey sticks and football gear." Jenny spoke down to me as though I were a complete idiot.

I didn't really want to get into this, but her snotty attitude deemed it obligatory, "Clarice will play hockey and football?"

"Uh, sons. Duh."

"What sons?"

"Our sons!"

"So you're planning on sons in the future?"

"Uh, yeah. Is that so odd?"

"It would be even more cool to let Clarice play hockey or football," I said.

"Uh no, Tracy. My baby girl will not get busted up playing hockey or football. Thanks, but no thanks."

"So you bought this thing for your future hockey-football playing sons?"

Luke was making strange sounds, sort of like a choppy wheeze.

"First of all, that's what people do, Tracy — responsible people, that is. They make plans for the future. Fu-ture, two syllables — sound it out. Second of all, it's spacious. Luke is six feet tall. Where exactly would you have him put his legs, the glove compartment?"

"5' 10, sweetie," Luke interjected.

"You are *not* 5' 10," Jenny barked.

"Last year, remember? The tailor measured me top to bottom — when I got the custom suit you wanted me to have for Mark's wedding."

"You must have shrunk," she said, her cheeks now a hot rose.

"So I'm really taller than you, Luke?" I asked.

"You are not taller than him."

"5' 10 and one half," I said.

"Yep – you're half an inch taller," he said.

"You were definitely six feet tall when I married you," Jenny said.

"Nope."

"Yes!"

"I don't think so, precious."

"I am not precious!"

Poor Jenny – everything was coming out so wrong, "You guys are upsetting the baby!"

I looked over at Clarice who was happily engaged with an old Smurf key-chain I'd given her.

"I never noticed that I was taller than you, Luke."

"That's because I wear higher heeled boots," he said.

"Fruity boots they used to call them," I said.

Jenny reached back for Clarice like a mad woman, and I handed her over without delay. The entire scene was endlessly amusing and took my mind off the big jerk that abandoned me in Griffith Park.

"Exactly," Luke said. "Fruity boots. That's what they called them back in the seventies. My father had a pair. He's 5' 8. So he wore a three inch boost."

"I think they're cool," I said. "Especially on Prince."

"Well no," Luke said. "Prince wears a full-blown pump."

"Stop it!" Jenny screamed. "I did not marry a man who wears heels. And Luke, I do not want you comparing yourself to Prince."

"I wasn't. I was just saying he sports a pump and I wear a lift. I don't need as much extra height as he does, which is a good thing."

"Or what?" Jenny asked. "You'd wear a pump too? Well that's just great – maybe we can share shoes."

I let go a sound that sounded too much like sheer delight.

Jenny turned around again and stared me straight in the eye, "So, do you have a literary agent yet?"

"I'm working on it."

"Won any writing contests?"

"Haven't really been submitting for contests."

"Why not?"

I shrugged.

"Internships? Seminars?"

She had me in a vice-grip, so it was time to remedy the havoc I'd wreaked on her self-image. So, in a performance tailored to a network dramedy, I turned my attention to Luke and tried not to focus on his slender hands holding the wheel, "For what it's worth, I think that you are the very prototype of what it means to be masculine."

He looked at me in the rearview mirror, making a face like I'd just opened a bag full of sweaty old rugby togs, "Uh – thanks."

"I really do. And the shoes could never diminish that in any way – they only add character."

I turned back to my sister, "I'm sorry, Jenny – what were you asking me about?"

She eyed me with suspicion, but soon calmed down and allowed my absent writing career to continue to wander lost.

Luke pulled into McDonalds and headed for the drive-thru.

"What are we doing here?" I asked.

"I thought you were hungry," Jenny said.

"I don't eat meat – remember?"

"You're still on that kick?" she asked.

"It's not a kick."

"Get a salad then."

"I can't eat here on principle."

Jenny sighed with almost painful resignation, "Fine. But we don't have time to drive around forever because of your stupid principles."

"Just take me home. I'll eat there."

Luke pulled a u-turn in the parking lot just as Clarice started screaming about "boogers and fwys."

We arrived at my old house, and I was both relieved and appalled that nothing had changed. Even the row of shrubs along the driveway appeared to be the same size. The dark green brick and white windowpanes looked exactly as they had the day I left.

The yard was meticulously kept, and the white picket fence was coated with fresh paint. The three-bedroom/three-storey structure still resonated with a sense of safety, but it also whispered of something else. And I could almost feel the undertones once again – dragging me away to a life far removed.

"Not so close to the house," Jenny said. "They'll spot us for sure."

"They don't even know we own this thing," Luke said.

Jenny turned around in her seat to look at me, and I had to recoil from the scary grimace she was wearing.

"Now remember, you are not here for the anniversary. As far as our mom and dad go, we've all forgotten about it – completely. You took a taxi from the airport a little early – to save them the drive. And you're just here for a visit, or a breakdown or whatever. We'll be staying at the Comfort Inn. So just enjoy your dinner and don't screw up the surprise."

"I won't."

Although I still thought it was ridiculous that my parents wouldn't be suspicious of my timing.

"Good. Now we need to go pick up more relatives. So, we'll see you tomorrow afternoon. I will give you more details tomorrow. Wear something decent – it's not a lumberjack convention."

I nodded that I would, glad that Jenny was such a control freak. It meant that I didn't have to do any of the work – for the price of merely having to show up at this thing, I would happily wear a rhinestone-encrusted unitard.

The ice-melter honked as it drove away – probably a passive aggressive action on Luke's part. I wondered if my mother had been watching the street from her familiar perch at the kitchen window.

Whatever. At this point, I could deal with just about anything.

chapter 16

THE PANIC SPRANG at me like a coiled snake.

I swallowed hard and braced myself for the homecoming, wondering if I'd erupt into a mass of flaming hives the second I sauntered through the wreath-laden door. I stared down at the welcome mat, and noticed that the little smiley face seemed to be smirking at me, but I already knew I was entering at my own risk.

My mother began sniffling the second she saw me, "Oh sweetheart, now you're here. Not just a little voice on the phone. We've been so worried about you."

"I'm okay."

"Did you take a cab? We would have been delighted to pick you up."

"No worries."

"Things will be so much better now that you're home. And I'm so glad you packed your little cat."

Her embrace nearly knocked the life-force out of me, "Something smells delicious, Mom."

"I've made you a vegetable casserole – with the baby green onions and corn. Your father wanted a beef chunk stew but I held him off."

"Thanks."

"Where's your luggage, sweetheart?"

"Here," I said, holding up my duffel bag.

"That's all you brought?" she asked, trying to conceal her displeasure as she gave me the once over.

"Just some jeans and a couple of shirts."

There was a full-length mirror in the foyer and my mother and I both happened to catch my reflection at the exact same time. In that moment, it was apparent to both of us that I was in shambles. My jeans were splayed at both knees, my shirt was wrinkled and stained with old mustard, and I had no idea just how masculine my comfy work boots actually looked.

My hair had dried frizzy and I had grey circles under my eyes. Even the recent high of James hadn't alleviated my fundamental messiness. Maybe he was even shaping me into my truest and most authentic self. I didn't want to give the jerk so much credit, so I pushed the thought off the ledge of my awareness.

"Rough flight," I said. The apology in my voice irked me because I always resented feeling that I should be someone other than I was – rough patches and all.

"Well, you can borrow whatever's in my closet."

And much like my attitude with Jenny, I'd wear a triple-tiered tiara if it meant my mother wouldn't nag.

"Okay then, thanks."

"Yes, let's give you some proper time to freshen up. I've got all the goodies you'll need. Powder, shampoo, soap – have yourself a nice long bath, and help yourself to my closet, sweetheart. There's a real pretty blouse that I think will fit you. It's way too long for me in the arms. You'll see it on the bed." Her words sounded like thoughtful suggestions, but I knew well they added up to a direct command.

"But," I started.

"Since after all – " she burst.

"What?"

"We're having a special guest tonight."

My mother had that familiar frantic look in her eye, after years of dealing with my obstinate refusal to play girl. She was waiting for me to protest that I was, in fact, not a doll.

I just sighed, "Special guest?"

"Yes."

"Do I know this person?"

"I think so."

"I'm so tired, Mom. I've been cramped up all day."

"I know, sweetheart. A harmless little dinner and then you can go to bed."

She hugged me again, and I knew my choice in the matter was gone. This was a place where I'd always had to acquiesce, and tonight would be no different.

"Where's Dad?"

"Buying the dinner rolls."

"Right."

I walked upstairs and into my parents' room; something felt very different. It was hard to pinpoint exactly what the difference was, so I sat on the bed until it came to me. My father was missing from the room, not just his possessions but also his very essence.

The bathroom counter – once cluttered with both perfume and aftershave bottles – was almost bare, except for an old bottle of Chanel and a toothbrush holder that held only one brush. Now only my mother's things were here; even the grey shower curtain had been replaced with vertical pastel stripes.

Everything smelled completely of her.

I took a long, hot shower and conditioned some life back into my hair. I picked up the mushroom-colored blouse that had been laid out ever so neatly on the bed. My mother had passed it off as hers, but I knew instantly that she had bought it specifically for me. I clipped away the Jane's Boutique price tag, and slipped it on over my bare breasts, which were well into their downward sag. I searched my duffel bag for a bra, but only found two of the sports variety. My boobs looked like thick pancakes under a silk blanket. I tried on my mother's bras, but my C's were quickly lost inside of her giant D cups.

Then I tried on my mother's dress slacks but every pair was three inches too short. This would normally be the time when I'd end up wearing a pair of my father's pants, cinched up tight with a pretty belt and a long top left to hang loose over the way-too-big crotch area.

That left me with one final option, and it was the worst possible. I wanted to run downstairs and offer my mother a thousand dollars to let me wear one of her warm fluffy housecoats. But I couldn't.

It was time to break out the wool. I slowly stepped into one of my mother's school-marm skirts. It was too large around the waist and I was tempted to create a new hole to loop around the button, but I had nothing sharp except my angst, so I knotted a Disney-inspired sash around the whole itchy thing. Then I put my hair up in a tight bun, and applied a little of my mother's powder and rouge to my face and neck.

I studied myself in her oval ivory mirror, and was reminded of my days as an extra in a really bad period piece – around the same time I'd discovered that the screenwriter isn't exactly the most valued person on a movie set.

Humiliating as this dress-up nonsense was, it was far easier than the epic battles my mother and I had fought any time I'd resisted such maidenly garb. I could have solved this indignity if I'd possessed even a modicum of style, but unfortunately – I cared not.

I had no shoes for the outfit so I ran down the stairs with bare feet. The look of relief on my mother's face was rather comical. I smiled at her and started peeling carrots for the inevitable dinner salad.

"You look lovely, sweetheart."

I nodded with a smile, absolutely baffled as to how she could find the get-up anything other than ghastly. Even in her silky peach pantsuit and bangles, she looked far hipper than me.

"Do you want to borrow some nylons? I've also got knee-high hose." Given our long history with this conversation, her hopeful desire for a different outcome almost made me sad.

"I can't wear any of that stuff. It's all too itchy, remember?"

Everything from my waist down was already one big wooly torture, and I couldn't understand why women in the new century still had to torment themselves in such diabolical ways.

"Oh right – I forgot. You're probably the only girl I ever knew who hates nylons." My mother tried to be carefree about it, but there was no mistaking the hurt in her voice.

"The only one who admits it," I corrected.

She ignored the comment, "Your father should be home any second now with those rolls. And I really hope he picked up whole wheat – last time it was sour dough and I just can't eat white breads like I used to."

This was probably not the time to inquire about the half-empty bedroom.

As if on a cosmic timer, we heard the door of my father's Cadillac slam shut – maybe just a tad too hard. He walked through the door with a bag of brown buns and a bottle of wine. His grey hair was receding slightly and he'd put on weight, but he was still my sweet and handsome Dad. I immediately walked into his arms and held him, pressing my fingers into his meaty back. He seemed a little shocked to be receiving such attention. Something about him reminded me of Luke.

"Hi, Pop," I said.

"Hey, Pebbles."

I finally let go of him when I felt tears welling. We both chuckled and I grabbed the rolls out of his hand and put them in a bowl. My father and I never said much to each other, and in that, we were bonded – as if we still weren't sure of our place in life or how we'd ended up as who we were. We were like lost little moons held in place only by the planetary pull of my mother.

I followed her into the dining room where she had set the table for four, using her best china. Now I was a little nervous because she only used her expensive dishes at Christmas and Thanksgiving.

"So who's coming over for dinner?" I asked her.

She was adjusting a centerpiece of stargazer lilies.

"You'll see."

"But I don't like surprises, remember?"

"You'll see, Tracy. That's the end of it."

My mother had cooled to me by a couple of degrees, and I assumed she was hurt by the affection I'd lavished on my father.

"The table looks beautiful, Mom."

"Could you bring me the cloth napkins in the top cabinet drawer?"

"Sure," I said, eager to stitch up her feelings. The drawer was stuffed with neatly folded squares of cloth: white, beige, raspberry, peach, and teal.

"Bring four of the cream, on the top. Careful not to mess up the other ones." She had stopped calling me sweetheart, and I wondered what sort of emotional acrobatics she would demand from me before I'd hear it again.

I handed her the napkins.

"These are beige, Tracy. I asked for cream. There's a big difference."

"Oh."

I pulled out the ones I had thought were white and questioned whether I was color blind or just completely inept at the art of home-making.

My parents moved around our small kitchen just like they always had, but something in the familiar energy field had changed. They reminded me of magnets trying to maneuver at similar poles – the closer they got, the more they repelled.

chapter 17

Kyle Steinke turned out to be the surprise.

So screw the emotional acrobatics – my mother and I were now even. As a matter of fact, she'd pulled significantly ahead in the race to see who could hurt or aggravate the other more.

Kyle and I had attended high-school together, but I'd always found him to be on this side of unbearable. The mean kids used to call him 'Stinky' because of his last name, although he did possess a mysterious scent that I could never quite pinpoint. And he never failed to pass off his fuzz swirls as a promising beard. My parents had always liked him because he'd wanted to become a Lutheran minister, and because he encouraged the rest of the school to listen to Christian rock.

I caught myself in the china cabinet glass – a woman ready to greet gold-miners arriving in the Yukon at the turn of the twentieth century. No wonder James abandoned me in the park. He could surely do better. A lingering image of him running on the beach with Maria Bello helped edge me a little closer to a night of heavy drinking.

Kyle was now bald except for side patches of wispy hair. His face was pink and swollen as if his main diet consisted of red meat and vodka. It was hard to accept that we were anywhere near the same age, but he greeted me with the same embarrassing eagerness from years ago. We had nothing in common in high-school, and I was sure the divide had only widened all these years later.

We sat in the living room – drinks in hand – and my mother suggested we update each other on our current life situation, as she put it, and then maybe reminisce about past times. I was overwhelmed with the same sense of imprisonment that had enabled my escape in the first place, and I truly had to wonder if my mother was even remotely rational.

Kyle gave my mother and me a pin from the store he worked at. *Kendall's new and used appliance and automotive parts Center.* The tiny gold lettering sat inside a huge outline of an oven. The pin was so large that it would be more accurate to call it a broach. My mother pinned the appliance broach to her blouse and looked at me as though I should do the same. I simply stopped making eye contact with her, and ignored her many attempts to get my attention with intermittent rounds of fake coughing.

Turns out Kyle sold new and used mid-sized appliances to our territory and three others, which meant he had to travel around by car a quarter of the month. I had a vision of the two of us reading Death of a Salesman back in Ms. Dodd's class, and I was curious if he remembered too. He assured me that I could get a twenty percent discount on any new or pre-owned washer-dryer set or a whopping thirty percent off any line of used dishwasher in stock – the only catch, of course, being that I had to move back to Bumble Fuck county.

All three of them laughed and winked at that, as though they were in on some brilliant and monumental bribery. I wanted to scream that, short of the threat of death, I'd probably need a bigger incentive to move back; instead, I sat politely, trying to act like a lady and keep my legs crossed at the knee.

"You're just as pretty as ever, Tracy."

"Thanks, Kyle."

There were no shivers when he said my name, although my mother involuntarily clapped her hands. I thought of James, and stared longingly at my father's well-stocked liquor cabinet. I imagined what little helpers might be stored behind those two wooden doors. There had to be at least one more bottle of red wine, two more bottles of gin, cheap family-sized vodka, and at least a small quantity of port to wash down any variety of my mother's casserole.

My parents were taking turns with Kyle, asking him questions about wage levels in the area and how that made ownership of a home possible, if at all. I started to feel like a low budget film director watching some poor actor audition for an impossible role.

As I listened to the fantastically interesting debate over whether Kenmore or Maytag was the superior brand, I found myself grateful that I had secured the bun in my hair so very tightly; it was keeping my head on my shoulders and my eyes focused sharply ahead. I felt like a button, fastened firmly in place on the living room sofa – there was no chance whatsoever that I could flee.

As Kyle droned on about commissions, I wondered about who scored the job at William Morris. I also wondered what the bosses would think if I strolled in there and offered my services free of charge – I'd literally crop the job into an internship. They'd be impressed with my dedication and start coming to me for advice on everything until – eventually – I'd be the one calling the shots on what projects to acquire and which ones to drop-kick to the mid-west.

After another drink, my mother finally invited us to sit at the table. Kyle pulled out my chair, and commented that he liked my old-fashioned hairstyle.

"I love a woman with a bun. Not like all these uppity women you see in movies these days."

I downed my Pinot in a desperate attempt to keep myself from violently clawing at my head.

"So I'm hoping you'll wear this exact same one when we go to the movies."

I looked at my mother who now offered a silent clap – reminding me of a seal – and I had to wonder just how long this unfolding crime against my sanity had been planned.

"And we can bring our own popcorn. I know the guy that manages the snack stand, and he won't mind."

"You have impressive connections, Kyle."

All I could see was the man of my dreams ditching me in the ditch.

Well, screw you, James — and your pissy fit. Look where I am now — most definitely getting the last laugh — out here in the boondocks with Mr. Kyle Steinke.

The gulpfuls of wine were loosening my already flimsy grasp on decency, and I had to stare at Kyle in order to make him come into focus; unfortunately, he took this as a sign of interest on my part.

"That's a swell idea," my mother said. "About the movie."

Swell?

"Swell-I-Can't-Kyle."

"Pardon?"

"Swellicant. I have a dentist appointment every night this week."

"Tracy – you're being rude." It was Mrs. Joanne Johnston who'd spoken – the ultimate voice of reason.

"What about a matinee?" he asked.

"I volunteered for jury duty."

"Tracy," my mother said. "Don't be so coarse. Herb – don't pour her such big glasses of wine. Sweetheart – I'm sure you could find the time to accompany Mr. Steinke to a matinee."

It took everything I had not to lunge at her.

"I'm actually working on a script, Kyle. A screenplay."

"Oh, that's interesting – I had a movie idea once."

"Really?"

"Yeah. It was about cowboys defending the west."

"Defending it from what?"

"Indians."

"I think you have it backwards," I said.

He waved me off with a pudgy hand. At this point I was ready to hitchhike back to Los Angeles – wool wrap and all.

"So I'm very sorry that I can't accompany you."

It might have been a wine-induced hallucination, but I was certain that he scowled at me. And when I asked my mother if she had any honey mustard dressing, Kyle laughed and said I must have lost my mind in California.

"Who puts mustard on their salad?" he snickered.

"It's actually a honey mustard dressing made specifically as a lettuce topping." I could no longer look at him without wanting to put my fist through his teeth.

My snotty tone had silenced the table. Finally my father spoke, reassuring Kyle, "I guess us country boys are more used to Thousand Island and French."

"I'm not supporting French anything anymore. Not after what they did to us," Kyle said. I could tell by his voice that he wasn't kidding in any way.

I was praying for the linoleum floor to open wide under my chair. There was no way I could go near this topic without destroying Kyle, the dinner, and my parents' thirty-fifth wedding anniversary.

"What did they do to us, Kyle?" my mother asked. I wasn't sure if her tone indicated innocence or sarcasm.

"They didn't support our invasion, Mrs. Johnston."

I looked at my father with one eye closed, ready to cringe, but hopeful that he might say something that could redeem the evening and my steadily declining ability to stay at the table.

"Hasn't the invasion turned out to be a not so good idea?" my mother asked. She was ever vague and careful not to use her reasoning to offend any man in the room, no matter how dull he may or may not be. It was always better to ask a question than state an opinion. Jenny and I were often warned that politics should be left to the 'stronger' sex.

I wanted to scream at her to smarten up and get a life outside the kitchen, but instead I sucked the water out of a snap pea.

"Everyone should support the President — especially when we're fighting evil," Kyle said, definitively. He spoke with authority, as if his mature reasoning should be the final word at such a table of juveniles.

"No matter what?" I asked.

"No matter what."

"It sounds like fascism."

Crap. Why couldn't I just shut up and get through the damn dinner? The tight bun, indicative of knowing one's place, wasn't holding worth shit.

"Oh no, not that tired old line," Kyle said.

He was boldly smug, and I wanted to flatten him.

"You can't create peace with war, Kyle."

I kept my knuckles interlocked because – ironically enough – arguments over peace could easily turn violent.

"I wasn't talking about peace, Tracy," Kyle said. "I was talking about defeating our enemies."

"Let's not talk about politics at the table," my father said.

"Yes," my mother said. "Cool yourself down, Daughter."

"Just exactly who are our enemies, Kyle?" I asked.

"Don't you watch television?"

"Way too much."

"So then you're aware that there's evil out there – might even be sleeper cells in this neighborhood."

"The only evil in this neighborhood is the skirt I'm now wearing."

chapter 18

I WAS COUNTING specks of a mysterious substance in the dining room ceiling.

But Kyle, much like a dog with a bone, would not let it go.

"You're so incredibly naïve, Tracy."

"Me?"

"Yes – you. Evil is all around us – everywhere."

"Everywhere?" I asked.

"Yeah – I was watching a show about a guy who found a pair of devil horns in his shower."

That did it. It was the perfect excuse to spew Pinot Noir all over the skirt.

"Okay, Tracy – enough!" my mother said. "No more talking about ugly subjects. You've spilt purple wine all over that lovely skirt."

"Oh crap," I said. "What will I do now? I'm going to have to change into some loose fitting cotton sweatpants."

My mother rolled her eyes, "We didn't even make it to the casserole."

My father cleared his throat, "Well, I think she's right, Joanne. Our Pebbles is right. So maybe we should talk about the ugly subjects. War is usually a cockamamie idea to begin with – a cock-eyed plan from the get-go. Think of what that money could do for health-care or renewable energy investment."

Notwithstanding his reliance on silly vocabulary to deflate the impact of his intelligence, my father now felt like my last link to mental health.

"Stop calling her Pebbles," my mother snapped. "It's ridiculous. I mean, it's not Saturday morning, and you're not watching the Flintstones."

My father and I shared a longing glance for the good old days.

"She's not a baby, Herb. She's a lady now."

"And so she's entitled to her opinion, Joanne."

Salad fixings flew across the table as she practically threw a second helping onto everyone's already full bowl. I knew that she believed a woman should primarily express herself through the domestic arts, but such expression would render me powerless because I deliberately blew at all the games pertaining to the awesome challenge known as womanhood.

Kyle never took his eyes off of my mother as she banged condiments on the table. My father poured a generous helping of French dressing over his heaping bowl of lettuce, carrot, and radish. It was a true act of solidarity between us, although now that the battle lines were drawn, we didn't dare exchange a glance.

We were working like an echo because we couldn't help it.

"Now that's really insane, Mr. Johnston. The idea that we should leave our door open for the bad guys – just because the idea of war scares you."

"But the bad guy just keeps changing. Right, Kyle?" he asked.

Kyle didn't answer him.

"Shit," I said.

"Tracy, don't say shit."

I ignored her.

My mother paced herself into the kitchen, making the specific sucking sound that signaled it would take her at least a week to recover from the current meltdown.

"So let me ask you something, Kyle," I said.

"What?"

"Are you excited to see the day a woman is sworn in as head honcho of the land?"

"That won't be happening for a while."

"And why is that?"

"Because women are soft."

"Is that so?"

"Yes."

"Do you think a woman's place is in the home – surrounded by pots and pans?"

My mother threw a pot in the sink, and I immediately felt like a beast.

"I just don't think a woman sees evil in the same way. She'd probably want to rehabilitate everybody."

"Yes – she might even use brains instead of battering rams."

My lame attempt at something Stepford-esque was officially over.

"But we still need to destroy our enemies, Tracy – so that you can sit around in comfort and safety while you defend them so poetically."

"The world needs more poetry, Kyle."

I ran upstairs to change into sweatpants just as my mother began firing dinner rolls at our place settings like they were targets. Her old facial twitch had returned already, and I'd been home less than three hours. I knew it rattled her to the core that I could be so raw and challenging and thoroughly un-pretty like this, especially after she'd made special veggie dishes and bought me such a feminine blouse.

When I came downstairs, Kyle started in again, "I've always been uncomfortable around Hollywood types."

"Then you should stay out of movie theaters."

"Such a bold tone isn't what I would necessarily call lady-like, Tracy. I'm not sure Mr. Steinke deserved such a peppy attack."

I hated it when my mother tried to reprimand me with words like 'peppy'.

Kyle shook his head, "So naïve."

I thought of James, and wondered just what I'd do to be in his arms at this very instant. Would I swim across raging rivers, crawl into a vat of teeming spiders, eat a barrel of bugs? And what I wouldn't give for his short script about a John Lennon hippie liberal at this point.

"This is just like you, Tracy – the nutty girl who rational people avoided in school. Fitting that you moved out to Holly-*weird*. It's such a shame, because your mother has always been the picture of what a *real* woman should be – a woman who cares about her family and her country."

Rejecting his movie-popcorn combo turned out to be a mistake I'd have to pay for – but I was pleased that he was glorifying my mother in a way that she would appreciate, something I was never really capable of. He was also lessening some of the guilt I felt at ruining her best-laid plans, although I really wanted to scold her for daring to understand me so little.

"You're calling my daughter *a nutty girl* under my roof?" my father asked. The veins on his forehead were bulging, a warning of things to come if the seas didn't settle.

"And what if I am a little nutty, Kyle? What would you like to do, point a big missile at me?"

"Tracy – enough!" my mother said – as though I were the only one having the conversation. But I suppose it wasn't polite to spook the gentleman caller in such an unpleasing way.

A vision of my parents' bedroom suddenly loomed in front of me. Something had changed between them – something they weren't telling me. And yet my mother still expected me to sit here and re-create a pattern that was fraying at the edges.

"Maybe we should bomb Canada for spending so much time watching hockey, or taking part in that laughable pastime known as curling. That way we could cut down all the trees even faster, and build more ridiculous houses like this one for people to imprison themselves in."

Shit. Crap. Piss.

I had stopped talking but the momentum of my words seemed to pummel everyone at the table. And it was too late to take it back.

"I didn't mean it like that at all," I said, unable to look at my parents. "That came out so wrong."

"No worries," Kyle said. "That's what happens when you think you're better than everyone else."

"But I don't."

"It sure sounds like it."

"I'm really just an aggressive pacifist." I tried to laugh but nobody joined me.

"That's what happens when you forget your roots and live out there with a bunch of deluded and self-absorbed twits," Kyle said. "But I'll take good old regular folk any day of the week."

I felt guilty and sheepish, and knew I'd have to endure his attacks unassisted. My mother's silence was especially grim, and I figured she was probably regretting her decision to have me in the first place.

"Just a bunch of left-coast loons, if you ask me."

I tried to ignore Kyle and focus on appeasing my parents, "I'm sorry. I'm just so tired from the plane, and the alcohol doesn't agree with me – clearly. Makes me say some very strange things."

"Snotty elites who look down on the rest of the country."

"Listen, Kyle," I snapped. "I don't even own a vacuum cleaner. So snotty elite is a bit of a stretch."

"As far as I'm concerned, Tracy – your take on things is pointless."

And that pretty much summed up my life.

I knew I deserved whatever it was I had coming – I just didn't want it coming from Kyle. I'd rather my parents take turns slapping me in the face with a dirty spatula.

"Have you ever fought for anything, Kyle? Other than your myths about the glory of fighting?"

He shrugged at me like I wasn't even worth acknowledging.

"I'm talking about a dream."

"I don't have your kind of dreams, Tracy."

"Have you ever wanted to create something?"

He bit a dinner roll in half.

"Challenge your boundaries or expand what you thought was possible for yourself?"

Now he was looking at me with such intensity that I was almost hopeful he was deeply engaged in the process of self-reflection – that he was sifting through his past and turning himself inside out. So I was surprised when he held out his hand in an almost aggressive gesture.

"You should give me back the pin."

It took me a second to remember what he was talking about. I handed him the appliance broach and he quickly gave it to my mother as if she'd more than earned the right to wear both of them.

"I'll stick to fighting the bad guys," he said.

Part of me wanted to make fun of him, and tell him that he'd just deprived me of a bona-fide source of self-importance. I wanted to wish him endless success selling new and used appliances and assure him that he was, indeed, the King of the Kitchen County – and that I would soon come to regret missing out on his generous discounts.

Another part of me wanted to make fun of my mother and declare it a relief that she hadn't set us up on a date or something, given our utter lack of chemistry, attraction, and philosophical compatibility.

But as I stared deeper into Kyle's eyes, I realized that his life probably hadn't unfolded like a celebration either. Maybe he simply dreamed of a woman who would love him.

"One day, Kyle, you might discover that the scariest bad guys you can conjure up are a creation of your own wounds." My voice was cracking, and I had to leave or have all of my own wounds exposed.

"And so – if you'll excuse me – I'm going to go and unpack my pajamas, and then sleep for at least eight hours. The flight from Los Angeles was a long one. Kyle, it was nice seeing you again."

"You too, Tracy. Let me know if I can help you with your vacuum cleaner issue – we have layaway plans."

"That's kind."

The evening had gone off like a bomb, and I contemplated what my mother could have been thinking to arrange it in the first place. Was she really so panicked about the state of my life? I stood abruptly and left the three of them to deal with the debris.

As I walked up the stairs to my old bedroom, I felt my guilt evaporating. It was an odd feeling of lightness, especially since I was so good at feeling horrible for falling so short of my mother's expectations. But tonight it was my mother's very expectations that felt so off and utterly divorced from reality, as if she were desperate to make a fish walk on land. And for the first time ever, I now realized that her desperation was more about her than me.

chapter 19

AT LEAST SHE'D left my bedroom alone.

The same posters were staring down at me: Bowie, Morrissey, Kate Bush, Annie Lennox, and Tina Turner. All of my high-school heroes were still here, and I stared at their powerful images. It was odd that my current fixations were such lighter fare compared to these icons I used to look up to – the ones who represented awesome strength and counter-culture. I imagined Tina Turner in the ring with McDreamy and knew she could deliver a wallop he'd never recover from.

Maybe I had lost courage over the years. Maybe it had taken these people to launch me out of here, and maybe I had gone soft in the aimlessness of L.A., a place where it was hard to know whose dream was whose. Dreams were generic there, and the city seemed to draw people *away* from something. Hollywood was the preferred destination for anyone fleeing the soul-sucking dread of the predictable mundane.

I closed my bedroom door and frantically tore at the bun – immediately relieving my tension headache. I wanted to call James and tell him all about my mother's attempt to normalize me, but I fell into bed instead. The sheets smelled freshly laundered, and I marveled at her knack for detail. Not one fine point of home management ever escaped her.

I opened my bedside table and pulled out a blank notebook and marker. I wondered how I could shrink the swelling heartbreak of my life into a tag-line, or a hook-line.

Dear Tracy,

You're drowning – hook, line, and sunk.

Tagline = Tag, you're it. Now get on with your failed life.

Tracy Johnston was ~~here~~ (but you wouldn't know it – because she failed to leave her mark;(

Beautiful boy comes to his senses and abandons Ms. Hopeless in the park.

I tossed the journal across the room and rolled over onto my side. I couldn't believe I lost out on the William Morris job. How was I ever going to get *Space Boy* into the right hands now – but maybe I should worry about that once it was finished. Besides, *Morbid City* was still simmering over at the Bloodhound Group – an executive assistant was surely reading it at this very moment. And it was probably only a matter of days before I got the call informing me that they were going to go ahead and shoot the damn thing.

If that didn't happen, I could always get a job at a posh eatery – and slowly ingratiate myself with the movers and shakers based on sheer charm. Just exactly like the kind I'd exhibited tonight.

The twin bed was too small for my large frame, so I bent myself up as best I could. I watched my kneecaps hang over the edge and understood that this room wasn't so different from the one in Hollywood. Finding a comfortable position was not easy, and I felt my skeleton creaking and popping as I shifted on the small mattress, an awful sign of my gathering physical mileage.

And to punctuate the thought, there were two grey hairs basking naughtily on my pillow. An existential gong must go off at thirty, reminding the cells to just throw in the towel. It was especially grim given the fact that I knew less about myself now than I did at fourteen, when I was so cocksure of whom it was that I was not.

Lucy emerged from under my bed and jumped up beside me to lick at my aching temples. I quickly fell into a light slumber where I remained until a gentle knock at the door alerted me to my father.

"Come in, Dad."

"How did you know it was me?"

"Because Stinky hates me and so does Mom."

"No one hates you."

"I'm really sorry about what I said – about people imprisoning themselves."

"No worries, no worries," he said, as if discussing such things might cause him to disintegrate.

"How's Mom?" I asked this like we'd all just survived a natural disaster.

"We had our dinner and our cobbler, and now they're having tea."

He studied the posters, "When did guys start wearing make-up?"

"Before we kept records. And you ask me that every time we're in here."

"Sorry."

"Did you guys talk about me?" I asked.

"I just said that none of us would've had the courage to ske-daddle to L.A. and make it on our own."

I wanted to admit that the only thing I could make on my own was a mess.

"Was that supposed to be a date?"

"I don't know. She just worries, that's all. Your mother wants what's best for you."

"With Kyle?"

He didn't answer.

"That wouldn't be what's best for me. I'd shoot myself."

"Me too."

"I mean – he's not that bad. But we're clearly not a match. And it irritates me – how she could arrange something so far off the mark."

"I'm sorry."

"Everyone seems to know who and what is best for me."

"She wasn't even planning on it until last night," he said. I could tell by his expression that he'd just let the bee out of the jar.

I sat up, "What happened last night?"

"Nothing, sweetie. Why don't you put your pajamas on and come and have a piece of cherry cobbler."

"What happened last night, Dad?"

"Jenny called and told us that she thought you might be a lesbian. Your mother panicked a little and called Kyle. And the only reason it was Kyle is because she just bought a second-hand microwave from him last week, so he was fresh in her mind."

"A lesbian?"

"As far as I'm concerned, it doesn't make a difference. You're my daughter and I love you."

"And who the hell buys a used microwave?" I asked.

He shrugged, "Your mother does."

"You think I'm gay?"

He nodded that he did.

A huge part of me wanted to come barging out of the closet, and force my parents to deal with the fact that my life trajectory could no longer be expected to parallel theirs.

"Give your mother time. She'll need some time."

I studied his face for signs of silliness but could find none. He was shifting his weight from side to side like a nervous contestant unsure of his answer.

"I'm not a lesbian, but tonight's set-up could have truly pushed me in that direction." I laughed at my mother's ludicrous attempt to ignite my already raging heterosexuality.

"Are you really sure you're not gay?" he asked.

"Not if Kyle's my only option."

"Well. I've opened that closet door."

"And it's empty."

"I wonder why Jenny would say such a thing then."

"Because I went on a date with a woman."

"Good reason."

"But only as a lark."

"A lark?"

"Yes. Now can we please change the subject?"

"Well? I mean – it's kind of a big deal. And I want you to know that I'd be okay with it. I'll just need a teensy-weensy bit of time. Oh – and by the way, Ellen's my favorite comedian, and I never miss Suze Orman's money show."

"Thanks, Dad. It's nice to know I have a supportive father. But I really like somebody, and he's definitely not a woman."

"Oh."

"Yeah. And I didn't even want to have to bring him up because things aren't going so good. So please don't tell Mom – I'd rather she think me a lesbian."

"But why?"

"Because I just can't live up to what she wants. And I doubt this thing's going to work anyway, and I'm not even sure I want it to. She'll just end up disappointed – like usual."

"She wants you to be happy."

"She wants me to be like her – the perfect idea of a woman and a homemaker. And I'm not an idea – I'm a person."

"Your mother's a person."

My father traced his finger along the edge of my dresser but all he caught was the slight residue of Lemon Pledge.

"So what's his name?"

"James."

"I like that name."

"Yeah – me too."

"Does he make you happy?"

"When he's not ditching me."

"Ditching you?"

"It's no big deal."

I nestled myself deeper under the covers and away from his earnest glances.

"You're way too big for that bed."

"I have been since grade eight."

He shook his head like he'd failed me in some indefinable way.

"Do you want to talk about him?"

"Not tonight."

"Why not?"

"I don't like using the past tense."

"You're not being very optimistic."

"Sue me."

chapter 20

I WAS IN no way prepared for the answer.

Still, I really wanted to ask him where he was spending his nights. And I wondered if his wife – my mother – had become some sort of a glorified roommate.

My father was stalling in my bedroom while Kyle and my mother reminisced about simpler times when people knew their place and loyalty was less complicated.

"I know about tomorrow," he said.

"What?"

"The anniversary thing."

"Oh shit."

"Your mother's sister accidentally called here to book the hall. She thought she was talking to the hall person but she was talking to me."

"Have you told Mom?"

"No, but I'm tempted."

"You can't tell her."

"I won't."

"Because Jenny would die."

"I know."

"Where are we having it?" I asked.

"The bingo hall – pre-decorated. I got all the details from Mertyl when she was telling me what our competitors were offering."

"Wow. The bingo hall? Really?"

"Yep."

"Are you sure Mom doesn't know?"

"I'm sure. She would have put me on a treadmill or something."

"Pre-decorated?"

He nodded.

"But Jenny wanted to decorate."

My father shrugged and looked mildly devastated, as if he was about to accompany my mother on an extended shopping trip.

"You don't seem all that excited, Dad."

He looked at me without saying anything, but there was a message in his expression. Something about old cans out-lasting their shelf life.

"Should I bring up the double wide air-mattress from downstairs?" he asked.

"I'll be okay."

"So you're not gay, huh?"

"Unfortunately not. But let that be our little secret."

"I guess I should go back down," he said. "They'll wonder why I've been gone so long."

"Tell them I was waxing your back."

After my father left the bedroom, I snuck into the basement.

The entire space, which had once been mostly unfinished, now sparkled with glossy blue paint and a gigantic leather chair facing a high-definition television. My mother's large hummingbird collection was no longer down here nor were any of her framed stitchings. He had covered the walls with the license plates he'd collected from his life-long trucking career. The musty basement smell had been replaced by the one conspicuously absent from the upstairs bedroom.

I studied his new sleeping quarters – Jenny's old bedroom. The closet was full of his clothes and ancient sports memorabilia. His old turntable sat in the corner along with a hefty vinyl collection of Waylon Jennings and Kris Kristofferson. The side table held a digital alarm clock and two Connelly paperbacks.

This was definitely my father's pad.

When I heard voices saying goodbye, I hurried back upstairs – my nostrils filled with the familiar memories of Old Spice, and my heart further emptied of its illusions.

I scrunched myself into the fetal position, but my little bed just wasn't working for me, so I made a makeshift mattress on the floor consisting of the folded linens in my mother's closet. It was risky and inconsiderate, but after this night it was either the linens or a cab to the airport.

I'd never know the fine print of the deal they'd struck, nor was I privy to the changing nuances of their union, but I now felt absolved of the crime of confusion. I was vindicated in my inability to so easily slip into the threads of a hand-me-down reality. And I could no longer allow my mother to shoot her angst-inducing arrows from her hilltop of hypocrisy.

But I still felt like shit. I remembered all the years she couldn't sleep without my father next to her. All the nights they had cuddled on the sofa watching wildlife documentaries and old Doris Day movies.

I opened my curtains and the bright sky fell into my room as silver light. My father was down in the yard, puttering in his vegetable patch. The big moon and porch light marked his outline, but I still couldn't see what he was doing. I walked to my closet, found my old binoculars, and returned to the window.

He was caressing a tomato the way one would a newborn infant's head. I focused in on his thumb – ever so gently rubbing the delicate skin, not unlike the way I had touched James. Then he pulled out a little ruler from his breast pocket and began measuring the vines. I zeroed in on his face and doubted I had ever seen him look so peaceful.

And that made me happy and sleepy. Floating away on my drowsy imaginings, I hoped not to encounter James and the all too inviting fictions of love. It was impossible however, as my head was filled with nothing but.

chapter 21

A SHIT-STORM WAS brewing.

The day of the anniversary had arrived, and breakfast was tense. My mother and I had not spoken since Kyle, and now I knew she thought me a lesbian. I was still almost tempted to let her stew in the anxious juices of what she may have done wrong as a mother, her most prominent identity. But instead, I looked directly at her and admitted the truth.

"I'm not gay."

She snapped her head toward my father, "Why would you tell her our private concerns?"

"Why keep everything under wraps, Joanne? Same as not telling the elephant that it's in the room."

"Thanks for that analogy, Dad."

"None of this is funny," she said. The tiny vertical lines atop her upper lip were especially visible today, and she'd only smoked for a year. She quit when she found out she was carrying a child, the only problem being that she was already four weeks pregnant with *me*.

Now I wanted to cough in her face and blame her for everything that had ever not gone right, including my perilous love life and inability to finish *Space Boy*.

And after learning of my parents' sleeping arrangements, I felt unapologetic about poking large holes in my mother's delusions,

"I would be perfectly happy if I was gay. Sometimes I really wish that I were."

She looked at my sloppy appearance, and I could tell she wasn't fully convinced of my heterosexuality. How could a straight woman start her day without a matching bra and panties?

"You were so rude to him last night."

"He sells ovens."

"So what?"

"You're right – I'm sorry. I guess I was just shocked that you invited him over here thinking that we'd somehow hit it off, and that you'd somehow save me from myself. And do you truly believe that if I *was* a lesbian, Kyle Steinke would be the remedy?"

My mother wiped her eyes with a cream napkin from last night, "I'm not saying that your life stinks, or that Kyle Steinke is the remedy. Is that what you *think* of me, that I would think your life stinks? Do you really think I think that?"

I wanted to scream that YES! I did think that's exactly what she thought. And I also wanted to let her know that she had – indeed – driven me to stress, hives, and a near ulcer. Instead, I sat quietly and managed a meager shrug.

"And my God, Tracy – Kyle's not a barbarian. He's just a man trying to make an honest living. Selling secondhand kitchenware is an honorable profession, and years ago it would have been right up there with all this fancy new computer stuff."

It was still very possible that aliens had long ago abducted my real mother.

"But no, you had to treat him as if he were a slug dropping on the bottom of your shoe. One lousy matinee wouldn't have hurt you."

I shrugged again, tempted to block her out with Colin Farrell. His rugged grunginess wanted to emerge, but who needed to fantasize in the midst of such vibrant melodrama.

"I just get a little concerned that my thirty-year-old daughter is living alone in a very strange place, far removed from her family and her church."

"There are all kinds of churches in California."

"Not the Presbyterian Knights for Christ."

Perhaps my mother should have been a stand-up comic, but alas, she took her solemnity very seriously.

My father poured all of us more coffee, happy to watch the infested waters from the safety of the shoreline.

"Do you have a plan for your life, Tracy? A woman's reality is different from a man's. Sometimes a woman's got to be thinking about other things, more practical things. I mean, don't you want kids?"

I took a large sip of coffee and tried to let her question float through me as though I were invisible. Watching my mother's emotional fragility, I knew this was not the time to let her trigger an avalanche of my own insecurities – I refused to explode in a reactionary fit.

"I don't know."

"How can you not know?" she asked. "You're thirty years old." Huge tears of frustration balanced precariously on the inside of her eyelids.

My father was fussing with a bent fork prong, and I could tell he wanted to defend my case.

I drank more coffee, wondering why I had to immediately know everything just because I'd turned a specific age.

"Are you just going to lollygag around Hollywood forever?" she asked.

"I'm not lollygagging."

"What are you doing?"

"Lots."

"Like what?"

I thought about *Morbid City* and *Space Boy* and all the rejections, false starts, and crumpled dreams – as abundant as the paper wads that used to blanket my apartment like giant snowflakes.

"You wouldn't understand."

"Just tell us what you *do*?"

I couldn't tell her how hard I'd tried to create something from nothing. Nor could I tell her that the only thing I really knew how to do was fetch coffee for people who had somehow managed to attain *my* dreams. It was just too humiliating to admit such a thing to these people – anyone else, but not these two.

"What difference does it make? I mean – how would it affect *your* life, Mother?"

I could feel the pre-show under my skin, warning that hives were preparing an entrance. Some sensible part of my brain was already counting blocks to the nearest Benadryl supply.

Her tears could no longer balance themselves and were now sliding down her cheeks; in an instant, I was filled with both guilt and bitterness. It was true, I didn't have the right answers to her questions – at least not the ones I could share – but that didn't justify her non-stop badgering. I felt like a helpless bug being poked in the belly with a hairpin.

"Maybe your emotions have more to do with what you're going through," I said.

"What does that mean?"

"I'm just saying that it's something you might want to consider."

The phone rang and I knew it was Jenny, eager to enact her top-secret, screwball festivities. The cruel part of me wanted to shout into the phone that her stupid cover had already been destroyed, but we all stared at the phone without answering it.

My father handed my mother his handkerchief, "Happy Anniversary, Joanne."

It seemed like the weirdest, most out of place statement ever uttered. Now I felt that someone really did have to warn her. She was in no way ready to receive a bingo hall full of relatives.

"Did it ever occur to you that I might want grandchildren?" she asked.

I didn't answer her, trying very hard to contain my anger.

"Did you hear what I just said, Tracy?"

I wanted to throw my scrambled eggs across the room and scream "Duh!" at the top of my lungs.

"So, it's all about you then?" I asked. "You already have a grandchild and yet you'd have me copulate with the used appliance prince in order to give some meaning to your life, a reason to live?"

"That is enough!" my father boomed.

It was a shock to have such a trusted ally turn on me, so I knew I'd ventured too close to the truth. In fact, I had landed smack in the bulls-eye.

"You don't need to be vulgar and you don't need to talk to your mother that way."

I looked at him as if he were the worst kind of traitor, one that sells you out to avoid exposing his own misdeeds, "I didn't realize I had been *vulgar*."

In the center of my hand was what looked like a large mosquito bite – white raised flesh on the inside surrounded by a circle of dark pink.

A hive.

It almost looked like a ghoulish little egg, sunny side up. The center of my bottom lip was on the verge of birthing a second.

"Your mother's just concerned, that's all. She just wants you to think about a family, that's all. She doesn't want you to miss out on your own fulfillment."

Gee, that's all?

I could not believe my father had taken over as her spokesperson, carefully regurgitating all the right talking points. It struck me as intensely cowardly, and I could no longer remain the target of their projections. I stayed quiet for a calculated amount of time – as if I were truly considering all of their helpful warnings – and then fixed my gaze solely on my father.

"So where exactly are you sleeping now?"

He looked at me as if I'd shot him.

"When I was changing into my dinner costume yesterday, I noticed that not ONE of your things was in the bedroom."

My mother immediately sprang to life, "Oh sweetie, your father snores something terrible. I just couldn't take it anymore, being up all hours of the night. He's in Jenny's old bedroom – downstairs."

"I know exactly where Jenny's old bedroom is."

"I tried the snore guards and the nose strips and the liquid solution," my father said. "We even had me checked for sleep apnea. I don't have it – thank gosh. You should see the masks people have to wear. Looks like a horror prop."

"Not very sexy," my mother added.

"I bet not," I said. "Not sexy *at all*."

They both tittered a little but my face did not move.

"Yes I remember, Dad. You've always snored. I used to ask Mom how she could stand it, and she said that it put her to sleep – that it was oddly soothing."

"Did I really say such a thing?" she asked.

I could not even believe these two, forcing on me what they themselves could no longer do.

"Besides, many couples move into separate rooms as they get older. It's a very common occurrence. Nothing at all shocking, Tracy."

"Who said I was shocked?"

She turned away from me, and my father took over, "Your mother always wanted more closet space. And now I can put my license plates up, you remember them? Mommy never wanted them upstairs."

Mommy?

"She never wanted them messing up her doilies and crochets. Right, hon?"

My mother nodded, "I never wanted grease on the wall."

They clasped hands to show me their love was secure, but it looked exactly like a false move made under duress. I felt like an immigration officer interviewing a very conniving couple – they were not going to scam me into signing off on some sort of happily-ever-after.

"What are you doing?" I asked them.

They both wrinkled up their faces like they had absolutely no idea what I was talking about.

"What game are you two playing?"

And then, as if they had planned it, the phone rang again. This time I yanked it out of its wall cradle, "Yes Jenny, what!"

My parents each scrambled off in opposite directions.

"Tracy?"

It was barely a whisper, but I knew it was James. And now was definitely not a good time, but I would've rather died than hang up the phone.

"Are you okay?" he asked.

A vivid scene unfolded before me – I was spitting dirt at my love interest, the one so intent on loping his way out of my life.

"How did you get my number?" I asked.

"I just tried your cell phone but you didn't answer."

"It's upstairs. How did you get my parents' number?"

I could hear him sigh as if the jig was up. "It was listed on the front of your script, along with their address, your cell number, and two email addresses."

"Script?"

"You forgot to add your social security number and bra size."

"*Script?*"

"I figured you wouldn't notice if I took Space Boy. And you didn't."

"You took Space Boy?"

"I just really wanted to read it. And I wasn't sure you'd let me."

"When?"

"The boxes. I'm sorry. I haven't read it yet. I feel really bad and so I'm calling for permission."

"Calling for permission to read the script you stole? How decent of you."

"I'm sorry. You have multiple copies."

"You dumped me in the park like a broken dresser."

"I know – it was a really bad night for me."

The tears were coming fast, but there was no way I could allow him access to such vulnerability on this particular day.

"So can I read it?"

"James — I really have to go."

"Tracy — "

"It's just not a good time."

I hung up the phone and cried for a pilfered script that was only half completed, and for a boy who was more than I could've ever hoped for. But mostly I cried for my old house, for it had surely become a place of broken dreams.

chapter 22

THE BINGO HALL had been decorated twice.

It was still plastered in Star Trek posters from a recent convention, and black balloons were slowly fading in dusty corners. I even found a plastic Spock ear on one of the tables. But instead of clearing out the old décor, Jenny had simply gone over it again – as she'd warned – adding light pink and peach streamers, bunches of white balloons, and a mountain of plastic dinnerware.

"Why are we *here?*" my mother had asked when we pulled in. "I hate bingo – and I hate smoky, tacky, bingo halls. I've always avoided this place like the plague. Where's the lodge, where's the lake?"

She'd only got in the car based on the pretense that we were taking her to a new lakeside lodge for lunch – and the additional fact that I was wearing another skirt, complete with full-length hosiery.

But now she was refusing to get out of the car. And standing in the middle of the empty party scene, I couldn't say that I blamed her. I texted a 911 to Jenny, warning her that she had three minutes to be here or I was taking them home.

A vision of James and me celebrating our thirty-fifth wedding anniversary filled me with both wonder and revulsion. This very hall was a dire warning of what my life could be if I gave in to anything too quickly – all the warmth that eventually freezes over and turns to ice.

The honking horn forced me back outside to the car. My father had been required to admit the obvious, and my mother was sobbing into her hands just as I had done earlier, "I don't want this, Tracy. Not now. Nothing's right. Everything is so off."

"I tried to tell Jenny that you didn't want a fuss, but she loves you so much and wanted you both to have a special day." My compassion startled me – especially given the fact that I was seconds away from filing for divorce from my parents and my sister.

"No," was all she could muster.

"Mom, it'll be fine. Auntie Mertyl will be here."

"Oh God, no," she wailed. Mertyl was her older sister, someone she hadn't seen in many years.

My father had both his arms around her shoulders in an attempt to steady the shudders. I put my head through the open passenger window, hoping to coax and coo my mother into some semblance of composure.

When my cell phone rang, I hit my head on the car ceiling and began cursing the car, the empty lot, and the entire heart-breaking scenario. I walked out of the earshot of my devastated parents, and looked through the window at Celebration Central. Never before had an impending party caused such outright and across-the-board misery.

"Jenny – where the hell are you?"

"It's James again."

I walked around the back of the bingo hall, and starting grinding dirt with the very pointy tip of my mother's ill-fitting dress shoe.

"This is a really bad time, James."

"That's what you said the last time I called."

"You stole my script."

"Can we talk about it?"

"No."

"Why not?"

"We're here at the bingo hall and nobody else has shown up yet."

"What?"

"They're sleeping in separate bedrooms on different floors of the house."

"Your parents are?"

"It's all crap. Plus, I'm wearing fucking panty hose to appease my mother. Oh, and she tried to hook me up with a used appliance salesman I knew from high-school."

"Should I fly out to Minnesota?"

"No."

"Why not?"

"You can't fix it."

I tried to block another image of him bee-lining it out of Griffith Park, but I couldn't, "It was cold and dark, James."

"I know. I'm sorry."

"There are cougars up in those hills. Lots of murders."

I couldn't believe I was acting like such a baby, but it was easier to whine than admit he'd so easily snipped at my heartstrings.

"Tracy – I'm really so sorry."

"And you stole my script."

"It's just that I'm so interested in you. In your perspective on life – how you feel. I was burning with curiosity."

"It feels like a violation."

"I just wanted to be closer to you."

"By stealing?"

"I know – I shouldn't have taken it."

Most of my mother's right shoe was now covered with a crusty coating of mud, thanks to my progress on a rather large hole that I was hoping to fall into.

"I miss you, Tracy."

"I've only been gone for a day."

"I know. But everything here... lacks you."

I wasn't sure how to respond.

Other cars were pulling into the parking lot, but I had zero interest in greeting anyone. The whole fiasco was Jenny's fault, so she could deal with it.

"Can I come and see you?"

"I just can't have you here right now."

"You're not making me feel so good."

I was silent as I watched my Aunt Mertyl try to exit Jenny's SUV with a large bouquet of flowers. She'd gained at least two hundred pounds in the years since I'd last seen her.

"It's not my job to make you feel good, James. I'm just trying to be honest."

I thought of my parents in the parking lot, "And it's not like we're responsible for each other. We can walk away anytime we feel like it. Right?"

He didn't answer.

"Well?" I asked.

"Maybe I should let you go."

No, you jerk! You should NOT let me go – that was the problem in the first place. You should get on your knees and beg me to forgive your lame and insensitive behavior.

I stared into the lush bushes behind the bingo hall. I could hide in them until the entire catastrophe was over – but where would I hide after that?

"Maybe you should," I said.

I wanted to add that between him and my parents, I felt like the filling in a nervous breakdown sandwich – but he hung up the phone before I got the chance.

And there was no way I could walk back into the bingo hall – not just yet.

The verdant world behind the hall was far more inviting than the anniversary greetings, and I made my way through it until I found a small clearing that opened onto a narrow footpath. I followed the little trail to the edge of a pond, and watched a family of ducks swim in endless circles – temporarily soothed by the small ripples that radiated from their plump little bodies. They weren't fretting over homemade problems or tossing insecurities back and forth. The swim itself was enough. And that's what made them so marvelous to behold.

I closed my eyes, and let my senses take in the blissful silence.

It was all shattered by the shrill voice of my sister. She was coming for me fast through the trees.

chapter 23

DOOM WAS CLOSING in like a heavy fog.

Jenny led me back to the hall, much like a prison guard might lead a death row inmate to the chair. She never released her grip on my arm until we were standing in the middle of what looked like a gathering of a local support group.

My mother's face was wet, covered in vertical streaks of black mascara. The effect was rather ghastly, but at least it matched her black funeral dress. Each of her wrists was covered in large noisy costume jewelry, so I could tell by the clanking sounds that she was shaking. Mertyl had an arm around her and was being very supportive, although the folding chair she was sitting on didn't look like it was going to support her through the night.

Next to her was her incredibly thin husband, Harley. He had one of those long grey biker beards without the mustache part, and reminded me of an undernourished gnome.

There was only one other occupied table. My father was sitting with his younger brother – Derek the dentist. He'd brought along his girlfriend-hygienist, Trina. It was hard to believe they were related at all because every feature on my dad's face was the exact opposite of his brother's.

"There are only four people here, Jenny," I said.

"Besides us."

"Why did you have to rent a *hall?*"

"People didn't get back to me until the last minute."

"We'd be better off at a restaurant."

"There's room here for dancing."

"But the place looks so empty."

"Listen, Tracy – they're just happy that their children are here."

"You can't be serious?"

She pushed a button on her portable stereo and Willie Nelson's sad voice drifted through the hall.

"You need something upbeat," I said. "To lift the mood."

"Dad likes Willie."

"Still – it's like a dirge."

"Don't bother taking an interest in anything *now.*"

"Where's the booze?"

"Behind you."

I turned around to a small folding table holding a few bottles of alcohol, soda pop cans over ice, and a bag of plastic cups. I poured myself a glass of gin – it felt wonderful in my mouth, nice and smooth and barely there.

"Mom's a mess," I said.

"I can't believe you were hiding in the woods, Tracy – that you'd leave them to wander around the parking lot like agitated pigeons. Dad was actually picking up plastic bottles when we pulled in."

"Good for the environment."

"You abandoned them and ran away like a baby. That's not what grown-ups do."

Just one more thing James and I had in common. And he could go choke on my script for all I cared. Maybe the two of them could live happily ever after – their development forever stunted at the halfway mark.

"Don't put all this on me, Jenny. You're the one who was late. I had them here exactly on time. We should have gone to a lodge or something."

"Why don't you go and offer people drinks," she said.

"Do you see me wearing a bunny tail?"

"You're in stockings," she said. "Never thought I'd see that again after Girl Scouts ended. Did you even get them a present?"

"I'm here, aren't I?"

"Well – three cheers and a big Yippee!"

I was so tempted to reveal that her picture perfect parents had a counterfeit marriage and that this whole production was therefore a con.

"So why were you late anyway?" I asked.

"Aunt Mertyl needed a Butterfinger blizzard."

"That's the last thing she needs."

"She'd been on a plane all day yesterday."

I looked back at the gathering. It was now so quiet that even a whisper could be overheard, "I can't believe this is it."

"Look, Tracy – I did my best. I made an effort. Have you ever made an effort for somebody else?"

I thought about what Tan had said to me at the spa – something about restless, bored, and selfish.

"If anybody needs me, I'm going to get the food out of my evil all-terrain vehicle," she emphasized each syllable, spittle flying from her lips to mine.

I wiped my mouth and let her go. My nerves weren't the only ones unraveling. I wondered if James had a back-up girl on the side. Maybe some poised little thing with a perfect family. The kind of family my mother wanted, but didn't get to have.

I gulped back my drink and poured another. The late afternoon sun was streaming through the windows, turning the plastic squares of bingo letters into light beams that criss-crossed the room like a laser show. It reminded me of The Matrix – and God, how I could use a Keanu Reeves right about now.

I walked through the beams to my father, "Would you like to dance?"

He looked shocked like I'd just stripped off all my clothes, "Stardust is my all-time favorite song."

"I know."

My father and I were the first ones on the floor. Clarice soon joined us, twirling around in a cluster of balloons. And then Derek and Trina were dancing elegant circles around our clumsy awkwardness.

Harley started clapping and whistling and I thought he was doing it for our benefit until I saw Jenny unwrapping large platters of deli meat, cheese, and pickles. Luke walked in behind her, loaded down with two pans of lasagna and a large box of red wine.

My mother was now mascara-free and engaged in conversation with her sister – they were slowly warming to each other, remembering the comforts of a familiar landscape. And my resentment toward my own sister was dissolving as I watched her busy herself with the work of organizing, serving, and making nice. It was amazing to me the way she could completely lose herself in such tasks.

Clarice had managed to wrap herself around my leg, and the three of us continued dancing our way around the room, tripping over balloons and trying to keep the slow pace demanded by what might be the most melancholy tune ever written.

The dancing ended when the balloon popped. The startle of it sent Clarice into a fit of wailing tears. But not ten seconds later she was giggling over a large feather that had floated down into her immediate vicinity.

I wanted to feel that way again too.

As I listened to her squeal with joy, I closed my eyes and tried to merge with the unedited yelps of delight – but my attempts to do so were blocked by the anxiety warriors that had embedded themselves in my brain. The ones that told elaborate stories of both my past and impending disappointments, and made cruel jokes about the failed writer who didn't even deserve such a title. And all too soon, the heroic cries of freedom were only the mad ravings of a bratty child.

All I could do was make myself a big cheese sandwich. As I stood at the table boozing down the bread lumps and obsessing over James, I thought it rather sad how food and drink could always be counted on to numb the agony of insurmountable odds and missing pieces.

chapter 24

THE MAN IN black was singing low about heartache.

But my mood was even darker. I was now directing a full-blown vibrational fury at James. How could he hang up on me when all I'd wanted was a large helping of reassurance.

I took my sandwich and gin and sat next to my mother. Clarice was now running circles around the bingo hall with a large piece of cheddar dangling from her mouth and two saucy sausages in either hand.

"Would you like another glass of wine?" I asked.

"I don't really like wine out of a box."

"Okay," I said, looking directly at her small pile of empties.

"But I guess I'll have another one anyway."

"The gin's good."

"How's your sandwich?"

"I put every type of cheese on here, but I still can't taste anything."

"Too much can drown out," she said, her gaze fixed on her granddaughter. It made me nervous when she spoke with such an economy of language. Giving up her niceties probably meant that she was still mad at me, but it might also mean that some new realization was stirring within. And I wondered why we all couldn't just get to the truth.

"Do you have a boyfriend?" she asked.

But then again, maybe the truth was overrated.

"Did Dad say something?"

"About what?"

"Can we talk about it later?"

"Why is everything always later? You keep postponing your life. Wouldn't you like to have one of your own children plan something like this for you?"

I couldn't believe this was the same woman who – only an hour ago – refused to get out of the car.

"Uh – not exactly."

I wondered if she'd even said three words to my father since they'd been here. A poster of William Shatner seemed to be mocking me, as if I'd crash-landed my spacecraft in the middle of a species I could never hope to understand.

Clarice was now frantically poking at the balloons with a plastic spoon.

"That child has a helluva lot of energy," Mertyl said. She had three gargantuan squares of lasagna heaped on her plate and was drinking a large bottle of Coke while her skinny husband ate a plate of pickles and sipped furtively at his beer.

"Wish I had that kind of energy," Mertyl said. "But the doctor tells me that I have a gene problem, get tired very easily. Hereditary thing, I guess."

"Diet and exercise help in that department too," I said.

My mother gave me a death look and pinched the top layer of skin off my thigh. The sting stung so bad I wanted to slap her and scream that it was such commonplace dishonesty that had ground her life to such an unfulfilling halt.

Uncle Harley – replete with leather vest, chaps, and cap – was trying hard to suppress a grin. He ended up smirking and looking away, the way Sam Elliott might in a similar scene. Obviously, any sort of truthful discussion with his wife regarding this topic had long ago ceased, and had probably never taken place at all.

"No, it's a *gland* problem," Mertyl said.

My mother nodded her head politely at her sister but looked quite uneasy, the way a person might if they were listening to an authority figure fart the national anthem.

"I think Pop had a thyroid thingy," Mertyl said, spraying ricotta cheese into our shared space. Her plastic fork broke from the pressure of trying to work through such massive three-dimensional pieces. Without so much as a sigh, she picked up the stubborn slice with her hand and forced most of it into her mouth.

"Is that true, Mom? About Grandpa?"

"Yes, I think so," she said — as cold as she could muster.

"I didn't know Grandpa had a weight issue," I said.

"It's not a weight issue," my mother snapped.

"It's not about diet or exercise, Tracy." My aunt spoke slow and deliberate, as if she'd just revealed a major secret of the universe. No way Earthlings, it was never about diet or exercise.

If I didn't act now, I knew I'd be banished to destination REALITY-WARP, and James and I would be forever broken somehow — together perhaps, but busted just the same.

"There's a lot of sugar in the Coke you're drinking. So if your glands are already having to work overtime, you're not giving them much assistance."

I angled my legs to the side so that my mother couldn't reach me.

"What you don't seem to realize, Tracy, is that I'm a heavy smoker. The only way I can stabilize my cough is with the Coca Cola." She still maintained her measured tone, as if she were the most rational person in the world.

"Okay," I said.

"Did you know that the fizzy bubbles cut through the phlegm build-up?"

"I know you smoke, Aunt Mertyl. I'm glad to hear you acknowledge that the smoking does *indeed* cause the cough."

"I didn't raise you to be this rude." My mother's face had turned a mild shade of blueberry, and I doubted that either of us would ever know what it would feel like to skip naked through a sunny pasture.

"I didn't realize I was being rude. Aunt Mertyl and I are having a conversation — that's all."

"It's okay, sis. Kids these days are short on manners. Not like when we were growing up."

Either I was the most insensitive person ever or chronic self-deception made for a very unhappy life.

"Pop would've cracked the whip by now. Anyway, Tracy — I didn't say that my smoking necessarily caused the cough. I'm sure it doesn't help, mind you. What I am saying is that I've been plagued by colds for the last ten years. Stubborn colds — more stubborn than most suffer. I've bought every flu remedy and cuckoo concoction on the market. Spent a forest full of Harley's money. I've even had those tiny needle stick-things poked in me by some little quack. I just haven't been that lucky in the health department. Lady luck deals the cards, and I play 'em as best I can."

As Johnny Cash crooned on about walking lines, I felt like I was straddling the one separating a mildly sane reality from the delusional brand practiced by my family.

I stared at the mounds of lasagna and Coke and cigarettes, and thought about the subjectivity of truth. Now I understood what Tan had meant by *stuck* — knowing something and pretending that you don't.

"Are you a creationist, Mertyl?" I asked.

My mother looked as though she might fall out of her chair, "You have had quite enough gin, young lady."

"Young? I thought I was past my prime, Mother. Only four paces away from hag-hood. Anyway, I was just wondering if she believes in Adam and Eve or if she thinks we evolved from monkeys."

"I do not believe we came from monkeys," Mertyl said. "And that's an awful thing to say on such a blessed day."

"It's called evolution."

"Where I'm from, it's called blasphemy."

"Why is there salt in our tears and our sweat?" I asked.

"From our food," she said.

"It's because we crawled out of the sea – single-celled organisms – without lungs, Aunt Mertyl. Imagine, no lungs – how could you smoke? Even without eyes."

"No more anti-Christian horror stories," she said. "I definitely need a smoke now – out of the sea without eyes, my left foot." She was seized by a violent coughing attack and I was afraid we might soon be inundated with regurgitated lasagna.

"Stop torturing your poor aunt," my mother whispered. "Now look what you've done to her."

"I never forced her to start smoking," I whispered back.

My mother scoffed at me like I wasn't even worth the bother.

Were we really this insane? Could my mother not see that Mertyl was torturing herself, and that I had nothing to do with it? I looked deep into my mother's eyes, into the welling anger and depth of sadness below. It sucked that she found it so difficult to really see *me* and connect, and my smart-alec approach wasn't helping. I had so many questions for her, ones that could never be asked with words. Sometimes it seemed like the words themselves were separating us.

I pulled my eyes away and decided that I would do whatever it took to make this night run a little more smoothly, "You're right, Mom. I'm sorry. I'm sorry, Aunt Mertyl. Still a little tired and obnoxious from the jetlag."

And just like that, I was able to do the *thing* – the cover-speak thing, the say-what-you-don't-mean thing, the keep-it-all-from-crumbling-asunder thing. It felt like I was erasing something vital, but I would do it for her – for my mother. I would do it for now, until we were both able to speak with our real voice.

Aunt Mertyl took my hand and held it in her own, "I understand sweetie, that plane thing can poop out even the best of us."

My mother finally exhaled, "Yes, those flights can be tricky, especially when you *lose* time."

We should all win Oscars for such performances.

But we'd be okay. All three of us would be okay for this moment, all three of us losing time and speaking our language of cover.

chapter 25

THE EVENING CLIMAXED with the painful croak of a trumpet.

Poor Luke had been instructed to blow his own horn – something he clearly hadn't done since high-school. Jenny closed her eyes and swayed her hips as though Miles Davis himself was standing awkwardly in the corner.

Meager applause followed the show and Jenny announced that she had a gift for our beloved mother and father. I'd only brought a card – something about the years being like sand in a breeze, or maybe it was a windstorm.

Jenny and Luke stood side by side, and only vaguely reminded me of my parents. She held her husband's hand and cleared her throat, "I just wanted to thank my husband for giving us such a lovely solo – which we dedicate to my parents – Herbert and Joanne Johnston." She said this like she was introducing them to a packed arena full of strangers.

"And I wanted to thank you all for coming from so far away, especially my sister – who flew all the way out from Hollywood."

More applause and soon I was feeling guilty about everything. I felt cheap and bare without a gift, especially given my hefty new account balance. And I'd also have to fix things with James – he didn't deserve such a generous offering of my jagged edges.

"Anyway, I just want both my parents to know how much I love them. How they've served as such a shining example to me." Jenny was near tears, "And my own little family would like to honor you both with a token of our gratitude."

Jenny handed my mother a key. I thought they'd bought another SUV, but it was quickly explained that the key unlocked the new version of yard shed offered by Home Depot.

Now it was my poor father's turn to suffer.

Every few years, my mother made it a point to not only paint the inside of the house a different color but also to change the upstairs carpet. She also enjoyed updating the garden shed every half decade. But most egregiously, she expected my father to share in her enthusiasm and be able to handyman the changes himself.

Unfortunately for them both, my father was not a handy-man nor did he have any real interest in construction or anything to do with my mother's brand of incessant décor. The non-stop home improvements helped to squelch her antsy thoughts, whereas my father was long accustomed to the ants and only wondered why she couldn't occupy herself with him.

"Does it require any sort of assembly?" my father asked. The edge in his voice bordered on severe.

Jenny looked at me with alarm, as if just realizing she'd poked at an open wound. She'd always been less adept at deciphering subtext, content to see her parents as a textbook case of storybook perfection.

"Yes, but it might only be tongue and groove," Luke assured.

"Tongue and groove?" my father asked.

My sister shot me a glance, as if just remembering that I was a lesbian.

"Of course it requires assembly," my mother spat. "It doesn't build itself."

"Right," Jenny said, reading from the descriptive flyer. "This shed requires nails and stuff."

My father shook his head and turned to me, "You know how much I hate assembly."

"I know. But Luke and I can put it together."

"No – I can put the damned thing together," he said.

My mother shook her head with disgust, as though erecting a shed should be the pinnacle of my father's desires.

Jenny continued to look at me with saucer eyes – like I somehow had to fix everything. I looked around slowly at the two tables worth of relatives. It felt like we were all actors on some strange set, and it was my turn to speak – to save the day somehow – but I was still waiting for someone to bring me my lines.

So it was time to improvise, "Mom and Dad, I love you."

I was shocked to feel the lump gathering in my throat, and was determined to avoid a crying scene. I tried to imagine everybody naked in the room, but it only made me want to sprint for the exit.

"Congratulations on a lifetime spent together."

Jenny started handing out large squares of vanilla bean cheesecake.

"And well, I do have a gift for you."

Eyes darted from the cheesecake to the scared thirty-year-old choking back an eruption of gin-soaked emotion. I almost started calling out bingo letters to ease the strain.

"You're both coming with me to Hollywood. We're going to go to the beach, and Disneyland, and maybe even a show taping. I know how much you love sit-coms. And don't worry about cost – it's all on me."

Jenny was instantly up in my face, scowling like I'd copied her wedding dress or something. Everyone started clapping and I could hear both my sister and my parents protesting that I couldn't afford such a gesture. I looked to Aunt Mertyl for support, but her eyes were already darting around for ways to devour her next slice of a hereditary gland problem.

The whole experience felt like some long experimental movie, the likes of which I could only discuss with someone like James.

I was eager to admit that I really did miss him, and that maybe he should fly out here. We could drive around the rolling hills of Minnesota, stopping to do God-only-knows-what in the back of my dad's Cadillac.

I hugged everybody and ran outside to call him. The air had turned crisp and fresh and wonderful – perfect for lovers. I fantasized us holding hands behind the bingo hall. He'd just presented me with a bulk supply of paper and ink; his strong hands were around my waist, kneading the small of my back. And then his mouth was on my ear and then...

The music died.

Something had crashed inside, and I assumed it was Jenny's ghetto blaster. I stood very still and waited until Patsy Cline started singing about how crazy she was for loving some putz that clearly didn't deserve her.

I closed my eyes, but James was gone. At least I'd allowed myself an extended fantasy over somebody I actually knew – a very encouraging sign.

I dialed his number, ready to cop to all of my mistakes.

"Hello?" The voice was weary, cautious.

"It's me – Tracy."

He didn't respond.

"James?"

"Yes, I'm here. I'm just tired."

"I'm outside, behind the bingo hall. Things are going a little better."

He only yawned.

"Dusk here is really beautiful," I continued.

"That's good."

"Are you okay?" I asked. "Because you sound distant."

"I am."

"I don't mean miles."

"Neither do I."

I really wasn't expecting this much ice from him, "I just wanted to tell you that I'm missing you."

"You'll change your mind in five minutes."

"I'm sorry if I hurt you."

"It's not your job to make me feel good, remember?"

"It's just that I'm going through a lot, and you know that."

More yawning.

"I'm afraid to be in a relationship. There – I said it."

"Is that so?"

"And you are too."

"Really?"

"Stop being so smug. I don't want to lose myself, James. But I don't want to shit on my own joy either."

"And?"

"And every time I've ever felt anything for anyone, I've started to feel my own selfness fade away. And I'm still fumbling about for myself. I'm fumbling. And I'm craving real intimacy."

"What kind is that?"

"The kind that comes from self-acceptance. That's where it has to start."

I was pretty pleased with the way in which I was expressing myself – maybe the bucket of gin was helping.

"Listen, Tracy – I really do have to go."

"You've been calling me all day."

"This is a really bad time."

"It is not. You're just saying that because I did."

He was silent.

"James?"

"I'm on a date."

Bingo.

I hung up my phone and turned off the power.

chapter 26

I WOULD HAVE sworn to it in a court of law.

That my heart was nothing more than a cold black stone.

The three of us were driving home in silence. My mother was sleeping in the backseat and my father was flicking at the wheel.

I was trying hard not to think about James, but it was once again impossible. He'd lived up to all of my expectations by letting me down so quickly - but maybe I'd even hoped for it. He had confirmed the accuracy of my theory about romantic love – that nothing in this world was more conditional.

The sweaty crevice behind my knee started to itch and I knew I was on the brink of another outbreak. I had to breathe deeply and try not to think about the fact that I was lonely, unemployed, and without a single inkling as to what my next move should be.

"Piss on the leprechaun," my father spat.

I reminded myself to find the humor in the insanity, because it often had the effect of an antihistamine.

"Excuse me?"

"I'm not assembling that damn thing."

"You don't have to, Dad." I hadn't spoken for a while, and my booze breath surprised me.

"If I never see another shitty Home Depot, I'll be a happy man."

"Luke and I will do it. We already said we would."

"You don't know *how* to assemble it. It's a big shed, Tracy."

"I'm sure we can figure it out."

"You've never hammered a nail in your life."

"It's not rocket science." I was sorry as soon as I said it, and watched as he gripped the wheel for dear life.

"The instructions are never right. You always need to make adjustments. And there's always some bloody important piece missing."

"A screw loose?" I asked.

"Every time I turn around there's another home and garden center going up. Fucking cock-eyed shed."

"What's wrong with you?"

"I don't want that damn thing going up at all. Not at all."

"Well then, don't put it up."

"Your mother will be miserable if it's not set up just exactly so."

"Then let her assemble it. If she's miserable about it, then that's her business."

"Believe me, it's my business if your mother's miserable."

"Didn't you enjoy the party at all?" I asked.

"That's not the point. We already have a shed – a perfect shed."

I turned around and looked at my mother crunched into the corner of the backseat. Her face was criss-crossed with the gentle shadows of the trees we passed. She looked almost angelic; I pretended she was a sweet little cherub sneaking a break from her crazy day job as my mother.

"Anything bigger will crowd the whole place, ruin the light, and destroy my vegetables."

"Dad, it's almost midnight. We can't keep talking about the shed."

I couldn't believe the amount of struggle that occurred over such trivial matters. My parents were the Masters of the Mundane and I was once again confined in their Realm of Humdrum.

I desperately wanted James and our impressive struggles against the world. But he was dead to me now – or at least in the process of dying.

"What are we going to do?"

"For the love of world peace, Dad – don't put up that blasted shed. If it's causing you this kind of anguish, just return it and they'll replace it with a store credit. You can get a couple of those plastic gnomes you like so much and just stick them somewhere."

"Are you making fun of me?"

"No. I'm just saying return the stupid thing."

"It's not *his* thing to return."

The voice was like a hot poker and I heaved against my seatbelt – sleeping beauty had definitely flown the coop.

"It's *ours*," my mother said. "Plus, this new shed is a thousand times better. It will probably even increase our property value."

My father stared so hard into the rearview mirror that I was certain we'd drive right into the ditch.

"It's nicer wood, Herb – doesn't look as cheap." Her voice had turned steady and methodical – the way it always did when she was set on getting her way.

"Doug Branton next door put up something similar, and he did all the labor himself. He had no help at all. It only took him a day – one day. I never heard a single complaint out of him, and I was in the backyard the whole time."

I could see the life force leaving my father, and wondered if my mother was really that determined to get us killed in a head-on collision.

"We haven't even seen the shed, Joanne. Why don't we wait and see it before we make any rash decisions." He sounded like the lead negotiator in a hostage crisis.

"It's *new* – it's got to be better. That old one's had to contend with the weather."

"But I've stained it, Joanne. It's weather-proofed."

"I have *seen the flyer* for the new one, Herb."

Quibbling over a garden shed is probably something that James and I would have never done – if given the chance. We'd be satisfied arguing over the grand unifying theories of the cosmos.

I turned down my parents' banter and watched the future images from a life I'd never have: James and I were doing yoga on the beach, eating pizza in the tub, napping in a hollowed-out tree, planting flowers with soiled hands, philosophizing in a pagoda, and marching for peace in San Francisco.

We could never do such things now – not after tonight – but maybe he would do them with *her*, whoever the hell she happened to be. She was probably better behaved than me – far more refined, polite, and deferential – less of a mouth on her, and far less threatening to his manhood. But he'd soon tire of such monotonous deference and would want his little firecracker back.

I could never go back.

We finally pulled into the driveway of our house. My mother went straight to bed, but my father walked alone into the dark of the backyard. I watched him from my bedroom window. The porch light illuminated a skeptical man, hands on hips, staring at the perfect patch of space separating his cucumber garden and tomato vines from the current shed.

I watched my father but thought of James – allowed myself to conjure his hands and shiny purple hair.

I turned my phone back on, and was delighted to see that wonderful blinking light – the one informing me that I had at least one new message and therefore some semblance of a life on this strange and lonely planet.

Surely it was James, and he would admit to me that he'd only been kidding about the date. That of course he would never do that to me – to us. He would tell me that he's just scared because he is, in fact, crazy about me. And I would call him back and admit that I'm scared too because marriage and love only hurts us in the end. I would tell him all about the proof I was gathering out here in the mid-west, the place of my earliest impressions.

I called my voicemail and listened as the lovely lady told me that I had one new message. Of course I did. I smiled and braced myself for the miraculous sound of his voice.

But it wasn't James at all, and I hadn't even prepared myself for such a crushing possibility.

It was Lila.

Lila – who works as a receptionist for the B-movie production group known as Bloodhound – my last hope for redemption. She apologized that it had taken so long to get back to me and admitted that the only reason she was calling at all was because she'd accidentally doodled over my email address – and my cell number was the only contact still visible.

Lila went on to say that *Morbid City* was not a proper fit for them at this particular time. She reminded me that such opinions are highly subjective and that she and the entire team at Bloodhound wished me luck elsewhere.

And she said all this with the most chipper of tones.

It was time to admit that loss was very real, and that I'd always been surrounded by it. It was like an abyss, teasing you towards it but still patient – simply waiting for the inevitable fall.

chapter 27

THE NEXT MORNING started with a literal bang.

It sounded like someone had shot a gun in the basement. My father was screaming something about roots and pipes. I groggily walked down the stairs in a jogging outfit and my fuzzy featureless Tweety Bird slippers.

My mother handed me a mug of coffee, "Your grandmother is here."

Grandma Mary was my father's very spunky mother – the only member of my family that I truly considered cool.

"Why didn't she come for the anniversary?" I asked.

"Because she's a very wise woman, but her official story is that she had car trouble."

"She drives a new Camry."

"Exactly."

"Where is she?"

"Helping your father with the plumbing."

My mother placed a large stack of French toast in front of me, "Try the nectarine-chunk syrup – it's homemade."

"Who made it?" I asked.

"I did – who else ever would?" She seemed to genuinely resent the fact that no one else under her roof was interested in making nectarine-chunk syrup.

I wondered if James had slept with his date. Maybe they'd even read my script in bed – making fun of how blindingly awful it was. It didn't matter because from this day forward I would never write another word again. It was simply time to do something else. Be someone else – *with someone else.*

My grandmother walked into the kitchen, kissed me on the cheek, and sat down across from me, "The washing machine is full of poop."

"What?" my mother asked.

"Well – poopy water is more accurate."

"How?"

"Blown pipes – tree roots got at them."

"Maybe we should call Kyle," I said, looking at my mother.

"The problem is with the *pipe*, Tracy – not the machine."

My father's curses rang through the house and I felt awful for him. In the space of a day, his life had become consumed with unwanted sheds, ruined pipes, and shitty washers.

My grandmother turned to me, "Your sister tells me you're a lesbian."

"Not true, Granny."

"Too bad," she said.

"Please, Mary – Jenny said no such thing. Try to be appropriate." My mother was back on autopilot.

"I wouldn't know appropriate if it sat on my face."

I covered my giggles with both hands.

"So how have you been, kid?" she asked.

"Just turned thirty. Not so good."

"Add forty years and get back to me."

"I guess so, Grandma."

"Call me Mary."

"Really?"

"Yes – really."

"She should call you Grandma," my mother said.

"Call me Mary," she whispered.

"Okay, Mary."

"Oh my God, I forgot. Wait right there." She rushed out of the kitchen, and even though she was almost three-quarters of a century old, her breezy attitude easily translated to her feet. She returned with a white paper bag and placed it on the table in front of me, "Open it."

It was a book entitled, *The Second Sex*, by Simone de Beauvoir.

"A feminist classic," she said.

My mother retrieved a cloth from the sink, and began wiping the sticky dribble from the mouth of the syrup bottle, "I can't believe you're encouraging her in such a way."

"Encouraging her to find the truth."

"What truth is that?" my mother asked.

I shoved a large slice of French toast into my mouth in an effort to stifle myself.

"Truth is personal. Isn't that why you're a writer, Tracy? Trying to express yourself?"

"I'm really not much of a writer."

"Nonsense – I've read your poetry."

"You're not helping."

My father walked into the kitchen with very long and very soiled tube socks on his arms, all the way up to his elbow.

"No one can use the washing machine today – or the toilets. You'll have to go to Seven Eleven or drive over to Jenny's hotel."

"What's wrong with the toilets?" I asked.

"They'll continue to flood the washer."

"Just scoop out the poop, Herb – and call the root people," my mother said. "And then after that you can deal with the new shed."

"But Joanne – "

"I want the new one up. Luke's got all the pieces."

My father's expression changed and he had to wrap himself up in a hug – I assumed he forgot about the shitty socks on his arms.

"Go take those reeking stockings off, rinse out that machine, and wash yourself with a decent soap."

I had to wonder what other kind she thought he'd wash himself with.

My father left the room with my mother hot on his heels.

I turned to Mary, "Thanks for the book."

"You're looking really good, Tracy."

"Really? I just plucked ten more grey hairs yesterday."

"No, it's not about any of that – it's about you, your energy. You remind me of myself a little."

"When you were my age?"

"No – now."

Mary's hair was short and silver, and she was wearing a navy blue blouse that was two sizes too big and covered in homemade bronze stars; long orange fish earrings swam whenever she spoke. She seemed much younger than her actual years and was filled with an odd light, almost extraterrestrial – she reminded me of Shirley MacLaine.

I could hear cursing and banging coming from the laundry room – it sounded like he was actually washing himself inside the machine. Maybe my mother had muscled him in and sprinkled him with Tide.

"They don't share a bedroom anymore," I said. "Dad lives in the basement like some sort of troll."

"Your grandfather lived in the basement – after his accident. It was cooler for him down there."

"Do you miss him?" I asked.

"Yep," she said, and looked away. I thought I saw her wince.

"So what should we do today?" she asked. "Sky-diving, dirt-biking, strip club – what?"

"Really?"

"Why not?"

I didn't answer.

"Because I'm old? No. Aging has been very beneficial to me."

"In what way?"

"Other people's opinions matter less and less."

My grandmother felt like a soft and refreshing breeze after years spent in a mildewed box.

"I wish I'd felt this way earlier on, but most people live things backwards," she said. "It's only the rare ones who don't."

She looked deep into my eyes, as if she needed me to absorb every vowel and consonant, "Most people do only what others expect, and they fail to ever really know themselves. And when they can't live with the boredom, they think themselves a failure. But the only failure is in the succumbing."

It was as if she could read my mind, and I was suddenly scared that I was fantasizing all of this too – conjuring up a matriarch who could confirm my very best hunch.

"No *succumbing* to any truth other than your own." Her words had trailed off to a loud whisper just as my mother entered the room. She gave us a very suspicious look.

"What?" I asked.

"I thought I heard something."

"You mean *suck or coming?*" Mary asked.

My mother could only stand and shake her head, and I wondered when exactly she'd lost her sense of humor.

"I said *succumbing,* for goodness' sake – warning Tracy of the dark side."

"You're going to make her even more confused."

"I don't think she's confused at all, and maybe that's where all the confusion comes in."

I felt a ping in my gut, and figured she may be on to something. And if that were truly the case, I'd have to reconsider *Space Boy.* My very own grandmother was reminding me that I did indeed have a point to make.

My mother grabbed her car keys from their hook, "Help yourselves to the fridge, ladies. Turkey cold cuts and lots of bingo leftovers."

"I don't eat meat," I said.

"That's your issue."

"Where are you going, Mom?"

"To inspect the shed."

chapter 28

No more life support for my baby.

I would coax my dream right out of its coma.

I needed to compose a list of all the possible and impossible leads for *Space Boy*. I was so sick and tired of breaking my own heart, but something in me refused to listen to reason or be tamed by logic. Success, like gambling, was a numbers game; every rejection was like a breadcrumb leading me one step closer to the big jackpot.

And I was actually receiving phone calls from Hope's executioners — they could have thrown my scripts in the garbage, used them for kindling, or simply ignored me forever. One of them even told me to keep writing. So it all had to mean something. In a town full of near desperate hopefuls, I could almost see myself as the chosen one.

My father entered the kitchen with the cordless phone.

"I was about to make a call when I heard a voice on the other line," he whispered. "I think it's a boy."

"Thanks, Dad."

He handed me the phone and left the room.

"Hello?" I asked.

"Hi, it's me."

"James?"

"Yes. Is it a bad time?"

A long pause followed as I tried to decide what I should do with him – a fly that had voluntarily trapped itself in my web.

"How was your date?" I asked.

"It sucked."

Luckily, I was so depleted from the last three days that I no longer possessed the mental speed to throw the appropriate poison at the situation. The normal barbs, passive-aggressive jabs, and lightning-quick comebacks would not be coming with their usual alacrity. Or maybe I just didn't want to ruin my own chances for peace by turning against someone I cared for.

"Why did it suck?" I asked.

"Because she wasn't you."

"Oh. So who was she?"

"I'd rather not say."

"Why is that?"

"Because you may never speak to me again."

That meant only two possibilities, and I very much doubted he'd bother with Ann Coulter.

"Sheila?" I asked.

"How did you know?"

"Who else could it be?"

"You're furious, aren't you?"

I wasn't exactly sure what I was – all I knew was that I had to get off the phone. Now.

"James, I have to go."

"But we really need to talk."

"Maybe we're just not cut out for this."

"Yes, we are."

"I don't think so."

"Just promise you'll call me back in an hour... or two. Please promise."

"Okay, James – I promise."

Story Girl

I hung up the phone thinking that I might need to puke. I looked down at the piece of paper I'd been writing on: **_POSSIBLE LEADS FOR A SPACE BOY LAUNCH – WELCOME TO THE STRATOSPHERE!_**

Maybe I really did have a lead. I dialed Sheila's cell phone, surprised that I'd ever bothered to remember the number.

"Hello. This is Sheila."

"Hi – it's Tracy."

"Oh. Hi. Tracy." I could hear the fear in her voice and wanted to bring her to a slow boil.

"Is this about James? Because it was just a friendly dinner – emphasis on friendly. We talked about – you know – nothing much."

"Listen," I barked.

"Okay."

"I have a favor to ask of you."

"Sure, whatever you need."

"I'm finishing up a script about space."

"Space?" she asked – her voice balancing precariously on the edge of sarcasm.

"I remember you mentioning some guy you know over at Creative Artists."

"Mitch."

"Yes, that's right. Mitch."

"Okay."

"I'd appreciate the chance to pitch the script to him."

"A pitch for Mitch," she laughed.

"Listen here – I'm serious."

"Well, he only deals with big names – established writers."

I was stone cold silent.

"Tracy?"

"I'm here."

"Did you hear what I said?" she asked.

"No, I was thinking about the conversation I just had with James."

She was quiet, silently calculating what I was worth to her.
"Sheila?"
"How long would this pitch take?"
"Give me ten minutes with him."
"I'm sure he could spare that – especially if I agreed to that coffee he's always begging for."
"Good thinking, Sheila. When will you know?"
"You're not even finished the script yet."
"Doesn't matter – I'd be pitching the idea."
"What if he asks for the script?"
"They never do."
"But, Tracy."
"You literally have to force the script on them – and then, God willing, one of their assistants might read the first few pages."
"But – "
"Just set it up and call me back with a time."
"How's it going out there anyway?"
"Gotta run, Sheila – late for a double root canal – just call me back when you have a time."

I hung up the phone, and stared down at the piece of paper that didn't look quite so blank anymore.

Mary drove us out to our favorite pond, the one she used to take me to when I was small. It was not unlike the pond behind the bingo hall. She'd made us a picnic out of the anniversary remnants, a huge basket of cheese sandwiches and cheesecake. We sat near the marshy edge of the water and watched a family of ducks glide along the surface.

"Are you in love, Tracy?"
I thought about James and shrugged my shoulders, "What difference does it make?"
"It makes all the difference in the world."
"My mother thinks I'm wasting my life."
"Do you?"
"I don't know."

"Maybe she's just never seen such luminosity."

I had to blink at the bright new picture she was painting of me, "Luminosity – really? I'm sure she'd have a different opinion."

"How do you feel?"

"Nothing I try for ever turns out."

"Maybe that's because what you're trying for takes courage and heart and perseverance."

The tears actually felt nice against my cheeks.

"It's okay to cry, Tracy."

"I know."

"We're allowed to muddle about – to play a little bit."

"But I'm tired of it."

"That's life. Just hold on and try to find your own joy – not someone else's attempt at it."

"Are you talking about my parents?"

"I'm talking about conformity."

"Oh."

"The kind that comes from conditioning."

"Weren't you conditioned?" I asked.

"Of course I was."

"And you conditioned others?"

"Yes."

"So – what gives?"

"I just finally started listening to the deepest, most buried, most under-appreciated part of myself."

I cracked open a soda pop and pent-up fizz erupted all over our picnic blanket, "Don't worry about me conforming. I don't want to, and I wouldn't even know how."

Her eyes narrowed to slits, "Conforming can lead to pretending."

She spoke as if she were a spy, passing on vital information. It felt like we were in a scene from *Julia*. I checked the woods for movement, just in case.

"And pretending creates a world of secrets, Tracy."

A tiny breeze was gathering force, but it was her words that made me shiver. And I grew cold wondering at all the secrets – the ones that stirred restlessly behind the perfect veneer of what was expected.

chapter 29

WE WERE TAKING comfort in the countryside.

Like two figures left in peace at the far edge of a pleasant watercolor.

"But doesn't everybody want to belong somewhere?" I asked. "Isn't that just a normal part of being human?"

"Let me ask you a question – would you rather erase yourself in the presence of others, or be fully drawn and alone?"

"That's a hideous choice."

"Some people slip through their own fingers – but at least they're not alone."

"I don't think I could ever erase myself."

"Good – you can't stay forever attached to anything anyway."

I thought about how much I'd like to be attached to James. He would come home after a long day of dodging his angst, and I would be there to rub his shoulders and his feet. Then we'd sip tea and nibble raisins until the moon was full over the platinum sprawl of our city.

"Tracy?"

"Yes?"

"You were day-dreaming."

"Sorry."

"The young man?"

"Yes."

"Do you want to call him?"

"No."

A mother duck led a procession of her babies through the tall grass.

"I pushed him away a little and last night he went on a date with someone else."

"That happens," she said, matter-of-factly.

"With a friend of mine."

"Oh."

"I guess he was trying to hurt me or get my attention, because sometimes I can be cold."

One of the smaller ducks had left the procession, and was wandering toward the tree line – a rebel stray that I could relate to.

"Real relationships are never going to be perfect – not when they involve two living, breathing individuals. Besides, perfect is dead."

"So when did you become a Zen master?" I asked.

"Zen Master I am not," she said, in her most perfect Yoda accent.

We both started giggling which started the ducks quacking.

"Since your grandfather died, I've been doing a lot of stuff – meditating, reading, walking for miles by myself. But mostly I've been excavating the rubble, trying to salvage what has value."

We took turns sipping tea and brandy from a large thermos. Her honesty freed me of my acrimony, something I automatically reverted to when overwhelmed by fables.

"You never would have done this twenty years ago," I said.

"Done what?" she asked.

"Shared a thermos. You would have considered it germy and you would have insisted on separate mugs, or shall I say, cups. Tea is properly served in cups, and preferably china cups for formal occasions. Isn't that what you taught me?"

"Yes, and I apologize. If it pleases your spirit, you can drink your tea out of a boot."

"So you're unlearning?"

She studied the sky, searching the clouds for a sign of that which I wasn't sure.

"Sometimes the unlearning can be a very painful process, Tracy. All those years wasted on such nothingness – like trying to dust a beach. When you come to realize it, there is sometimes a lot of anger."

"I can imagine."

"But then something magnificent happens – a grace, and you realize that no time is ever wasted, and that it all gets us to exactly where we need to go."

"I've never been able to talk this way with my mother."

"Because you're her reflection. And when she looks at you, she sees all the parts of herself that she couldn't trust."

"So she looks in the mirror, and I'm the flyaway strands?"

"She looks in the mirror, opens her mouth, and speaks with a different voice."

"You're sweet, Mary."

"I'll also say this, Tracy – you've been thinking that she wants you to change, but you're also hoping that she'll change. Just mirrors."

"If that's how it works, then I need to be careful," I said. "Because I want to see my own freedom reflected in James and vice versa."

"Is that why you're afraid?" she asked.

"I just never want to force him into any sort of mold just to make me feel safe. I want to feel safe on my own."

"Me too."

I nibbled my Swiss cheese square into a circle, "Remember the time you were babysitting Jenny and me, and you woke us up in the middle of a school night to take us driving along the lake – all because the moon was so huge?"

She nodded as if she only half remembered.

"It ignited all that was unknown. You told us that all the mysterious creatures of darkness would be cast in silver, and that neither of us would ever have to fear the wolves or the boogeymen again – because they were all really friendly, just woefully misunderstood."

She looked amazed, "You remember so well."

"As soon as we came home, I went upstairs and wrote my very first short story."

"Really?"

"Yep – so I have you to blame."

"What was it about?"

"It was about all the monsters that live under beds and in closets – how they really aren't so bad. It was called, The Bagman."

"That was the one you were most afraid of."

"Until I looked underneath."

"I'd love to read it."

"It's probably up in the attic somewhere. Might actually make a pretty good script today – like an anti-horror."

The breeze had suddenly turned to wind and the ducks were gone. We carried our picnic remnants to the car and I realized she wanted me to ask her something.

"Mary?"

"Yes?"

"Do you have secrets?"

She lifted her head to the darkening sky and exploded with a laughter that was filled with irony.

"I have demons."

chapter 30

I WAS FEELING bad about a million things.

Mary and I were sitting in the new lodge by the lake – the same one used to lure my mother to the bingo hall. The restaurant overlooked one of Minnesota's thousands upon thousands of lakes.

I was heavy, but the weather had lightened up.

Looking out at the green glass water suddenly made me feel like a jerk, "I wish we'd had the anniversary here. I should've helped Jenny plan something."

"So bring your mother here for dinner sometime."

I watched the shadow of a floatplane make its way across the lake.

"Maybe you should call him."

The smell of fresh cut timber filled my nostrils. I ran my hand over the smooth log wall beside me, "Why?"

"Because you've been thinking about him all day, and at the very least you could practice your communication skills."

I carefully dipped a fry in mayonnaise and then twirled it in ketchup. James was the first and last person I wanted to call.

"His parents have a ton of money."

"Good for them."

"I can't relate. What if he never has to work?"

"Free as a bird – remember?"

"Right."

"Stop putting so many roadblocks in your own way."

I thought about *Space Boy* and the fact that I hadn't even finished it yet. How could I ever pitch something that wasn't complete? Would I just trail off in the middle of a sentence?

"Are you okay?" she asked.

"I don't know."

"It's gonna be alright."

"But what if it's not?"

"Life moves, Tracy – that's the theme."

But I wasn't so sure it was the theme of *my* life.

"Sometimes I fantasize so well – it's like I don't even need real life."

"You're probably not alone in that."

There was just no way she was going to be able to pick up my pieces.

"I really *really* suck, Mary."

"Where the heck did that come from?"

I was shocked that I'd ever admit such an excruciating tid-bit to a family member, especially one that I admired so much; but I was disappointed that my fears were back in the driver's seat.

"Because it's true. All I do is sit around in a room and pretend that I'm some sort of writer."

"You're not pretending."

"There's been nothing but a solid wall of rejection, and I keep banging my head on it."

"That's part of the process – doesn't mean that you're not a writer. All it means is that you have tenacity."

"I can't even sell a B movie about zombies who get stoned."

"Well, that's okay."

"To a production company that purchases B movies about stoned zombies?"

"All it means is that you're not meant to be writing about zombies. I think you want to go deeper."

"I have gone deeper," I said. "I've written about people who screw-up their suicide attempts, children that go to war, the final days of our sun. I've gone deep. I've stayed light. And how is this for deep? I'm knee-deep in rejection letters — I could wallpaper my apartment."

"Maybe you *should* wallpaper your apartment. Every day you could stare at your walls and remind yourself that you're not a quitter — that you're committed. Every letter is like a badge of honor."

"I don't know."

"You're like the Energizer bunny — you just keep on going. And if you run into an obstacle, you just pound your drum, turn, and move off in another direction."

"How do you know all this?"

"The determination is carved right into your face — it's there between your eyes."

"So I need Botox too?"

She didn't answer.

"I shouldn't give up is what you're saying?"

"How would you feel if you ever really gave up?"

"I don't know, because I'd be dead."

"See — that's the only thing you pretend at — you pretend that you give up. But it is your distinct reality to never give up."

"What if I end up homeless?"

"You won't."

I stared hard at my grandmother, wondering how she could be so sure of everything, "You're the only person I can admit this to. So will you promise me something, Mary?"

"Yes, anything."

I tied a knot in the stem of my maraschino cherry.

"Will you give my eulogy?"

"Your *what*?"

"I mean, if I should die before you do. If I should finally succumb to my disappointments?"

"That's a little outrageous, don't you think?"

No, I didn't think it was outrageous at all – and I really had to make it through this request without breaking down.

"It's just that – "

"What?"

"You seem to get me. And I'd want you to say something specific."

"What's that?"

I looked out the window and all I could see was the face of my mother.

"Here lies what was once Tracy Johnston. And she was a dreamer. But she was a person who tried – and then tried again."

"My goodness."

"Maybe you'll even be able to say that she tried her heart out."

Mary stared down at her beer, "You bet I can say that. But I very much doubt that I'll have to. And you know what, Tracy?"

"What?"

"I just spilled a tear in my beer."

And then laughter brought all sorts of tears, as if all emotions were actually only one. She handed me a man's handkerchief and I wiped my eyes and blew my nose.

"Was this Grandpa's?"

She nodded.

"You must really miss him."

Her eyes lit up as though she'd been slapped, and I watched her hand tighten and release around her mug.

It was an uncomfortable moment and I felt strangely guilty, "I'm sorry."

"Don't be."

"I've upset you though."

"It's okay. You never knew him, Tracy. He died when you were still a baby."

"Farm accident, right?"

"Initially, but he didn't die from that. He lost his hand and part of his arm under that horrendous machine – like giant razors. But it was the infection afterwards, and his leg never got better. He never really gave up though – just slowly wore out. And those last years between us were nice, in a very odd way."

"Weren't they nice before?"

"They were just different. I was a farm wife – the work was never-ending. And there was never enough money – especially when the weather didn't turn out and the crops failed. It was stressful and he didn't always handle it well. Neither of us did."

I looked back out at the lake – the green glass was darkening.

"But after the accident, all he could do was be still. And it changed him. He was a very forgiving man, Tracy."

I nodded my head and put two more fries through the condiment routine.

My grandmother looked as though she was struggling to tell me something.

"What's wrong?" I asked.

"Nothing at all," she said. "I was just... I guess I was just debating."

"Debating what?"

"Remember when you asked me about secrets at the pond?"

"Just don't tell me I'm adopted. On the other hand, that might not be so bad."

"Of course you're not adopted. Besides, you look exactly like your mother."

"Was my *father* adopted?"

"No one was adopted."

She closed her eyes tight, either conjuring or fending off the images of the past. My nerves were waking up – one by one. I pulled the cocktail menu out from behind the napkin rack, wondering which martini would best complement a chocolate shake.

"It's so hard to talk about this," she said.

"Maybe it's too personal."

"I think it's meant to be – you know – that we've come to this."

The familiar tingling had started ever so slightly, warning me to settle down or risk the revolting splotches in a public place.

"As crazy as it is, I feel that you should know this about me."

While she stared at the now blackish water, I scratched violently at the palms of my hands. The soles of my feet were starting to burn and my eyes were watering. My pores were portals for the coming persecution.

"What's wrong, Tracy?"

"I'm sorry, Mary – my immune system's ridiculously sensitive."

"Tracy?"

"I'm getting hives. We have to go home."

"But – "

"Now."

She put a fifty-dollar bill on the table, and led me by the hand all the way to the passenger seat. She sped home while I practiced holding my breath. I couldn't even look in the visor mirror because touching anything made the itching so bad I would have happily scraped off my skin with a vegetable peeler.

We pulled into the driveway, and I leapt from the car before it stopped moving. I raced into the house and up the stairs and locked myself in the bathroom. These suckers felt far more determined to crack me open, something inside hell-bent on escape.

I started a freezing bath after discovering that hot water only helps them spread. I'd already gobbled up my Benadryl supply – as a precaution against any possible feeling that might ignite this suicide-craving itch – but as a small miracle would have it, my mother's ancient box of cornstarch was still under the sink.

I slowly sat in the icy water and dumped the box of powder over my head, hoping to at least alleviate some of the agony, but all I really managed to achieve was a coughing fit.

As I coughed, I could almost see James in the dust. He was watching me hack my lungs dry in a glacial pool of gooey paste – just one more vivid reason to steer clear. But it didn't matter anymore.

All that mattered now was that I didn't scratch. That was all that had ever mattered or would ever matter again in the future.

chapter 31

IF MY SKIN could speak, it would beg me to set it ablaze.

Worried voices were shouting at me on the other side of the door. I had to clamp my teeth over a thick bathroom towel to keep from fainting. My swollen eyes were shrinking my vision; my tongue was expanding at the back of my throat. I bit down as hard as I could and watched my eyes and veins popping in the faucet reflection. If I didn't clamp, I would scratch – and if I scratched, I just might have to slit my wrists with one of my father's razors.

"Tracy, are you alright?"

It was my mother's voice.

Nails on a chalkboard.

"Tracy?"

The same voice again. The voice of the woman whose face I'd inherited. Maybe these were her fucking hives; she was the ventriloquist and I was the dummy. I'd just bet that was the karmic deal – her mountain range of angst was somehow fighting through my epidermis.

I heard my grandmother recounting our day in pained detail, promising ever so absurdly that we hadn't done any acid, grass, or 'shrooms.

My mother tapped on the door with what sounded like a wooden spoon, wanting to know if we'd injected anything illegal.

"I'm fine, Mother! Just some hives. Might be allergic to baby ducks. Can't talk now."

It killed me to yell after exerting so much pressure on my jaw. It felt like it might break, but I knew the pain was less than if I started scratching.

"Let me in," my mother said.

I had to ignore her now, and focus on the repetition of my desperate mantra:

Scratch and die, scratch and die, scratch and maggots will consume you whole. Don't you dare scratch!

And while you're at it, Tracy, don't think about your grandmother's awful secret, the new shed, your utter failure as a writer – and for God's sake, don't you dare think about James and the petite little thing he's surely screwing by now.

From a galaxy far *far* away, I could hear my father vowing to bust down the door.

Fine, Buster – bust it down! And for the rest of your life, you'll have to deal with the image of your naked adult daughter, covered in starch and sickening blisters.

I was breathing through my nose, alternating nostrils, 1-2-3 in and 1-2-3 out; my hands were balled into tight fists, and my toes were ballerina points.

The voices outside were loud and clear, threatening to use force and pick locks. I didn't care about any of it. A swat team could barge in and stare at my flabby stomach and sloppy breasts that had now fallen off the sides of my chest into the frigid bath water.

I wondered if each hive somehow represented one of my characters that would never have a voice on the screen – the scared mother who overdoses on valium, the pilot who flies blind, the doctor who moonlights as a thief. In my head, they were all fifty stories high and begging to be born – somehow – through me.

And then the screen went black. The itching had stopped.

I wasn't sure how much time had passed. All I really knew was that the itching had stopped. I'd been sleeping in my mother's big bed, wearing her silk pajamas. My skin smelled like oatmeal and there was a cup of cold tea and a bowl of red grapes on the bedside table. Candles in glass jars lit the room in a very gentle amber glow. No one was here to nag me with questions about what the hell my freaky problem was. I was gloriously alone.

But someone had taken exceptional care of me. I opened the bedside drawer where she stored her alarm clock; glowing red numbers informed me that it was 5.07 am. I studied the inner sides of my arms, gentle and smooth. There were no battle scars on my skin indicating what I'd suffered through so many hours earlier. Only the pulsing ache in my jaw proved that my ordeal hadn't just been a nightmare.

I had no clue how I made it from the tub to the bed. The last thing I remembered were faces coming at me. I wondered if my father had burst through the door or if it was still secure on its hinges. I considered getting up and checking it out, but damn, if I wasn't the most comfortable I'd ever been in this house. I rolled over and sank back into the cool heavy warmth, hoping that no one – real or imagined – would ever disturb me again.

When I finally made my way downstairs and into the kitchen, it was early afternoon and the three of them were seated patiently around the table. The euphoria I'd felt at being alone instantly died. I poured myself some coffee, and devoured the lemon cupcake that had been offered at my place setting.

"You look much better, sweetheart," my mother said.

"I feel better."

"Should we go to the doctor?"

"No. I just need to rest."

"What was all that about?" my father asked. "You looked like you were in so much pain."

I ignored his question, hoping to God he hadn't seen my naked gut flaps.

"You looked so incredibly bad, Tracy."

"Thanks, Mom. Who got me out of the tub?" I asked.

"You don't remember?" my father asked.

I shook my head.

"Your mother eventually unlocked the door with a paper clip. She gave you some medication, bathed you, and put you to bed."

I was rather embarrassed that she had witnessed me in such a state; I was also a little annoyed, considering that a viable argument could be made that the panic pimples were more or less her fault – and part of me wanted to say so. Instead, I just asked if there were any more cupcakes. My mother handed me a ruby red one with butter cream topping and baby jujubes.

Now that I was sick and dependent and no longer a threat, my parents were both comfortable spinning around in their caretaker orbit. My mother had firmly re-established a familiar dynamic with me, and there was relief in her expressions – relief that had come at my expense.

"Your mother went and bought you those from Chips and Sprinkles," my father said. His tone was eager and needy, like he felt responsible for my affliction.

"Thanks."

"Do you like them?" he asked.

"Are you putting up the shed, Dad?"

He leaned back from the table, and stared at me as though I'd just taken a chainsaw to his Cadillac.

"Not yet. Why don't you try the banana swirl?"

"I thought you wanted to keep the old one."

I was well aware that I was risking the pampering I'd earned with the hives, but there was no way I could stop myself.

"The new one is better," my mother said. "It's *new*."

I never took my eyes off of my father, "But Dad says that the new one will ruin his garden."

"Let's not be paranoid," she said.

My father started to fiddle with his pager that hadn't beeped, and had probably never once beeped in all the time he had owned it.

"Did you get a page?" I asked him.

"No, but I think this thing's busted."

"Are you *trying* to break it?" I asked.

He sighed and put the pager down.

I knew I was pushing him, but I wanted to bust the dam and let the floodwaters burst and flow and maybe even heal the thing that had turned me into a big ugly allergy ball. And if he was going to continue to be such a wimp, I would show him no mercy.

"Why don't we start working on it then. I'm feeling a little better so maybe I could start counting screws and keeping track of them. We wouldn't want any screws on the loose, now would we? Didn't that very thing happen with Mom's big bookcase?"

"Okay fine, Tracy. Thanks for the offer. Maybe you should go lie down upstairs. You've suffered quite a medical fright. Let me know if I can take you to the emergency room."

"The emergency has passed, let me start on the shed."

"You must rest. We'll bring you an early dinner – whatever you want. Just go and rest. Please!"

My father's urgent tone was immensely funny.

"I can't rest until the new shed is up. Then everybody can go back to their normal lives."

"We're not going anywhere near that *thing*," he seethed. "So I suggest you get to bed."

I felt six years old again, being scolded after taking my pocket-knife to Jenny's giant doll head – the one she practiced make-up on.

"Go rest, sweetheart," my mother said. "And I'll bring you whatever you need."

Even though she sounded sweet, I knew she was on to me – aware that in challenging my father to stick up for himself, I was threatening the whole power structure, including her reign as the undisputed queen of 1221 Petrie Lane. But if she was bothered by any of it, she wasn't letting on.

"And take my room again, sweetie. Much better mattress."

That was a point I wouldn't argue with her.

chapter 32

THOUGHTS OF THE shed were scattering my wits.

I tried to burrow back into my mother's bed, but I was stiff with aggravation. My father was actually going to decimate his own needs once again.

I called our home line and my mother answered. She asked me if I needed anything. I told her I needed a well-toasted feta cheese sandwich and extra crunchy pickles on the side – nothing soggy was to touch my plate.

Twenty minutes later she entered my room with a full tray of my demands, along with tea and another cupcake. She sat on the edge of her bed while I quickly chomped away at my snack.

"Are you okay, Tracy?"

I nodded and crunched.

"I was very worried about you last night."

"Where did you sleep?" I asked her.

"On the couch in the living room."

"You took the plastic off?"

She scowled at me, "That plastic's been off for ages."

I sipped my tea, "Not even with Dad when you're out of a bed, huh?"

My mother looked away from me, and stared at the wall.

As I peeled away the wrapper of the cupcake, I figured I'd indeed begun the perilous descent into eating through my woe. It would be just typical if I was destined to follow in Aunt Mertyl's house slippers. Still, the unexpected sour cream center nearly had me in a full-blown swoon. Who needs love or sex or fulfillment of any kind when chocolate cupcakes explode sour cream in your mouth?

"I used to get hives exactly like that," she said. "Same exactly."

"You did?"

"Yes. I was quite a bit younger then, of course. But they finally went away, after I had settled in with your father."

"I can't believe they haven't returned."

"What do you mean?" she asked.

I could only shake my head.

"The doctor said it was onions, salt, heat, and sweat – or any combination of those."

"What exactly did you settle into with Dad?"

"A family, a home, a life – exactly what you'll have someday."

She started re-folding the square doilies that were already perfectly folded on the rectangular table at the end of her bed. I knew by the abruptness of her hands that her defenses were operating at full force. I didn't care.

"My hives are caused from *stress* – not from onions, sweat, or an invading army of ear-wigs. They come from not having a clue where I belong or what I should be doing in the world. I don't want a husband and I don't want kids and I'm not gay and I don't want to be alone when I'm old. There – got it? Nothing fits. So I guess they just don't have anything in my size."

My mother looked shocked and ridiculous at the same time, with her handful of faultless doilies.

"Nor do I want to fold doilies or ever even *care* about doilies. And I'm tired of you trying to tell me what I should want or how I should feel because quite frankly you and Dad don't seem all that thrilled with what you have."

I could see the tears in her eyes and knew I had landed in the vicinity of somewhere important.

"What has Mary put in your head?"

"This has nothing to do with her and you know it."

"I just want you to be happy."

"Is that really true? Or do you want me to be happy only if it gives you a sense of validation and reinforces your *own* choices? What if my happiness looks like nothing you've ever seen before? What if I want to go to Botswana and swing in a hammock or spend a year in Hawaii learning how to barbecue coconut?"

"Tracy?"

"What if I'm content to live in the moment and not have a clue about anything at all and not be trapped in any commitment where every day is identical to every other day, and any sense of freedom or creativity has to be banished away for the rest of my life on Earth. Aside from, of course, folding doilies, painting walls, or putting up a different fucking shed when it's completely unnecessary."

My mother sucked in her breath and I knew that I had hurt her, but I had never felt more liberated – like a wounded critter dragging itself out of some dank hole into the curative radiance of sunlight.

"You said you wanted to be a writer, but so far I haven't read anything. Not one thing for us to read since you were in school here."

"Please don't go there right now."

"Why not?"

"Because."

"Because why?"

"Because I have to pitch half a script to some hotshot jerk who's going to decide that it sucks bricks, and then I'm going to be blackballed from a town that doesn't even know I exist."

"It sounds horrible."

"It is."

"So why bother?"

She asked me this with such genuine sincerity that it finally dawned on me how much I'd been withholding from my parents.

"Because I can't seem to stop myself."

"But how are you going to earn a living?"

"I don't know exactly, but I guess I've been doing it continuously."

"I don't want you to end up broke and alone."

I wanted another cupcake.

"Does that really make me such a bad person, Tracy?" She dabbed at her tears with one of her dusty-rose doilies, and suddenly I felt like something close to a monster.

"No – it doesn't."

I wanted to hold her tightly in my arms, but I couldn't.

"I'm sorry I haven't given you anything to read."

"Why haven't you?"

I shrugged.

"Well, if you have a good romance stashed away – I'll take it."

"I do have one – called Happy Hour – about a wealthy old man who falls in love with his male gardener."

"Anything more traditional?"

I started taking a mental inventory of all the stories I'd written.

"Nothing about a boy and girl in love?" she asked. "You must have something."

It was just the crack James needed to slip back into the front room of my mind.

"I don't do Harlequin, Mom."

"And I don't read them."

"I do have a story about a general who falls in love with a draft dodger."

My mother sighed.

"Well, Mom – stories need drama."

"I know that. Regular people – extraordinary circumstances?"

I nodded my head like she'd just revealed herself to be Cher, but I was still more concerned with extraordinary people drowning in the shallows.

"I used to love your little sagas – the ones you wrote in high-school."

"You did?"

"Of course, Tracy – you remember? I even had Golden Frog framed."

We sat together in bewildered silence until she did something wonderful. She tossed the entire stack of doilies high up in the air, a la Mary Tyler Moore, and watched them land all over the room as if a powerful wind had blown in and displaced their very neat and predictable existence.

"I think I'm going to go make us some homemade tapioca pudding. It'll take the edge off of everything, Tracy. And I'll pop us some corn in the meantime."

She was behaving like the most wonderful person who'd ever existed, and I was suddenly certain that she would never rip out my father's heart by tearing down his shed.

"Mom?"

"Yes?"

"I'm going to write you a traditional romance."

"Really?"

"Something nice – I can do that."

"I will consider it my Christmas present."

I was touched by her loyalty, even in spite of everything. She might be the only person on the planet who'd consider such a thing as a gift and not just a tedious part of some pile.

Unless I was counting that guy in L.A.

chapter 33

WHEN SHE'D LEFT the room, Lucy attacked the doilies.

I was debating whether I should scold her when my cell phone started vibrating. It was probably another rejection – this time from a non-existent production house that I had yet to even send a script to. Maybe they just wanted to get a cosmic jump on things.

"Hello?"

"You never called me back – you promised you would."

"I was with Mary, who happens to be the most awesome person in the world. And I had another outbreak – so I've been sleeping it off."

"I'm sorry."

"Listen, James – I've been dealing with major family issues."

"I wanted to talk to you about the Sheila thing."

"It's not necessary."

"It's so necessary – I have to explain."

"What for?"

"I mean, I ran into her at a Coffee Bean right after you and I had another botched phone call. Can you believe it – in a city this big? It was like the universe was testing me. We went for Chinese food, and I was barely there. I felt like such an ass the whole time."

As I listened to him unload his conscience, I realized that a change had taken place within me. Instead of the usual fireworks that would accompany such a disturbing conversation, I once again possessed absolutely no desire to wound him. The knowledge that he'd gone on a date with my friend didn't even cause me stomach or chest pains — let alone any murmurs from the band that cued the awful skin show.

"But I was stung, Tracy. I'm weak and needy, I guess. And you're right, you're not the one to decide how I feel, and it was so shocking to hear that from you because it runs counter to the whole mythology of love — which I didn't even realize I believed in. But I do."

I rubbed gently at my temples.

"Tracy — are you there?"

"I'm here."

"I do believe in all the ridiculousness and craziness of romantic love — all the wacky insanity. I believe in it because I want to believe in it — and that's what I discovered. That's what you've helped me discover."

I wanted to warn him that my parents had believed in it too.

"I was trying to hurt you, Tracy. But I only ended up hurting myself."

"I understand."

"You do?" He sounded sort of amazed, as if witnessing the flesh of my very own hand coming through his phone.

"You're not my own personal trash heap, James — so I don't want to dump my junk on you."

I could almost hear him thinking, trying to cross-reference my words with my tone of voice. The rhythm of his breathing made me wonder what it would be like to fall asleep against him.

"So I'm off the hook?" he asked.

"It's not for me to put you on the hook or not."

The breathing stopped. He was probably afraid of what I'd say next. But I said nothing.

"You're not mad?"

I didn't answer right away. It was such an important question, and I had to check every corner of my scared little ego to come up with an honest answer – it also helped that imagining him with Sheila was just a little too far to stretch.

"No."

"Why not?"

"Because I care about myself."

"What does that mean?"

I wasn't exactly sure.

"It means that I can care about you. And I want you to live your own truth. That's what I want for you because that is all I've ever wanted for myself. All I've ever wanted is to be loved without conditions, but I guess I have to be the one to start."

"Oh, okay," he said – as if I'd just decided on pepperoni pizza.

I picked a chunk of super-sized sleep out of my eye.

"Are you gonna stay out there with your family then?"

"For a bit."

He held his breath again and I knew he wanted to ask me something.

"What, James?"

"Do you have any real interest in getting to know each other better?"

"I don't know. It scares me because I don't want to get trapped in my old patterns."

"You don't want to lose yourself?"

"I just can't do it, James."

"Why do you have to lose yourself?"

"Because that's just what I do."

"But, Tracy – "

"I just can't give up my freedom. I'll need room to grow and be left alone and make mistakes or whatever you want to call them. And then the other person – you – will inevitably think I'm cruel – and then I'll think I'm cruel."

"Okay, so you don't have any interest in getting to know each other?"

"I didn't say that – I'm just trying to admit in advance what I'll need."

"From me?" he asked.

"No, *from me.*"

"And it'll work both ways?"

"I would think so."

"What will this look like, Tracy?"

"I have no idea."

"Maybe it will look just like this phone call."

"Maybe it will," I said. "I hear people talking – where are you?"

He didn't answer.

"James?"

"I'm in the bus traveling north on La Brea, and a couple of women in front of me are arguing about citrus fruit."

"Why are you on a bus?"

"I wanted to see what it was like."

"So what's it like?"

"It's okay. A little exhausting."

"You're not doing this to impress me?"

"Maybe three percent."

"Do I have to give the money back?"

"No, and stop asking."

"Good. I promised my parents I'd fly them out to L.A."

"Will they come?"

"I don't know."

"Why not?"

I yawned and tried to come up with a reasonable answer, "The shed."

"Huh?"

"Long story."

"I searched the want ads today. Lots of jobs available in the restaurant industry, but I'm not sure how well I'd do balancing trays."

"You're searching the want ads?"

"Are you impressed?"

"I'm surprised. I thought you'd be writing."

"My muse told me to search the want ads."

"Sounds reasonable."

"Can we hang out when you get back?"

"I hope so."

"I'd like to go for a bike ride with you, or maybe a hike somewhere. Whip up some sprout sandwiches... and we could sit up in the hills and watch the ocean."

"That would be really nice."

I could feel us both smiling over the phone.

"I think I'm getting the hang of this honesty thing – especially when I don't get in trouble for it," he said.

I suddenly saw his face at the end of a leash, and it was me who was tugging at him – pulling him this way and that until all he could do was pant and beg and follow me around.

"I can hardly wait to see you, Tracy."

He started to say goodnight, but I stopped him.

"James?"

"Yes?"

"I never want to end up as the warden."

"What?"

"Nothing."

"Tracy – "

"I can hardly wait to see you too."

He hesitated only for a second, "Good then."

We said goodbye, and I stared at the ceiling until the intercom buzzed – my mother informing me that another snack had been prepared. It was a comforting idea, but this time I wasn't willing to stuff an empty space that no longer felt so empty.

chapter 34

IN MY NIGHTMARE, James and I were mannequins.

Our lives were firmly set in fiberglass – not even the tiniest allowance for wiggle room. All I could do was plot getaways in my head, but there was nowhere to go because I couldn't move. James tried to reassure by reminding me that it was our job to stand in the window and look pretty – to show people what they wanted. Everything else was simply a heartbreaking impossibility.

The new morning was coming at me through the eyes of my lousy old stale self. I wanted to be the person from last night – the one who'd been so sensible and understanding in the face of such gut-wrenching adversity.

A headache started in my right temple, probably triggered by the tension I felt drifting up the stairs and into my mother's bedroom. I rolled out of bed with trepidation, wondering what might be in the works – but even more concerned with my own heaviness.

I sauntered into the kitchen as casually as possible, and nodded in response to the chipper greetings from my family – although everyone's body language suggested that something awful was about to happen. My father and grandmother were tense while my mother looked as though she were about to march onto some bloody battlefield.

The last of my serenity evaporated with the steam from the boiling kettle. After graciously handing out mugs of tea, my mother announced that this would be the day the shed was *coming home* – much like a demonic child that only she wanted around.

This was bad.

By jeopardizing her husband's garden patch in such a careless way, she was threatening the very fabric of her current existence – and I had to wonder if it was deliberate.

My father quietly stood and placed his cup and half-eaten donut on the table in front of him. Without a sound of any kind, he gently picked his keys off their brass rack, left the house, and backed his Caddy down the driveway.

His serene demeanor and lack of protest were very worrisome. Stories of super calm people who erupt in a postal rage were rolling through my head, and I wondered if he would return to the house armed to the teeth with death-inducing weapons.

Fifteen minutes later, Jenny strolled through the door and announced that the shed had arrived. Luke would begin the assembly immediately. I looked out the window and watched him scramble up the driveway with Clarice in one hand, and an armful of shed shingles in the other. Clarice was drooling over a Ziploc bag of small, medium, and jumbo nails.

I didn't have a clue what to do – so I decided to blame everything on my sister, "Jenny, I really can't believe you'd put such added strain on our parents' marriage – they don't even sleep in the same room anymore. Dad doesn't want anything to do with the new shed."

She looked at my mother with astonishment, "Is that true?"

"Oh for heaven's sake, your father snores like the devil and I needed more closet space."

"Mother?"

"And that new shed is a much nicer wood and will hold far more of your father's tools – and maybe even more tools in the future. You know how he's been going on about that new deluxe paint stick.

The paint comes up through the stick right onto the brush. Far less mess."

"No, Mother – I haven't EVER heard him mention any sort of paint stick. He's never mentioned wanting any kind of tool – at all."

My divide and conquer strategy was working very well, although it sucked to see Mary watching me with such palpable disapproval.

Jenny never took her attention off my mother, "But what I really want to know, is why you never told me about your new sleeping arrangements?"

Now it was my mother's turn to feel the heat of the expectations she so vehemently helped to create, "Because I never thought they were anyone's business but our own."

"I could have saved myself a lot of hassle and expense, Mother – packing a small child across the country."

"Are you referring to the bingo hall deal?" my mother asked.

I could hear pained hammering coming from the backyard.

"It was not a bingo hall *deal*. It was an anniversary celebration – attended by your close family and relatives."

"Had I known of your plans earlier, dear, I would've clipped them like a dirty toenail."

Ouch.

"Then I'm sorry I went to the trouble," Jenny said – sorrow spreading across her face like wildfire.

"I didn't mean it like that, Jenny."

"Dirty friggin' toenail?"

"No. It's just that your father and I weren't prepared for such a fuss."

"Don't speak for him!" Jenny snapped. "He's not here. I'd appreciate it if you'd speak only for yourself."

Despite Mary's between the teeth protests, I was still rather pleased with the way things were going. I was watching the most natural of allies – who'd always been indirectly united against me – turn on each other based solely on my clever machinations.

My mother's convenient delusions and Jenny's naïve fairy tales were about to be made over.

"I don't think this is the time or place to discuss this," my mother said.

"You've been lying to me!" Jenny barked. "And I won't stand for it."

"Do not take that tone with me, young lady. I did not raise you to speak in such a way."

I yawned. My mother's dialogue was straight out of the stale script on what to say when one's uppity yet harmless daughter protests. But I guess that was the best she could do with her precious little duplicate.

"Maybe you two would like some privacy," Mary said.

Clarice wandered into the house carrying a ball of dirt. She looked up at us, felt the tension, and started to howl. Jenny picked her up and started whispering to her, but no amount of cooing could soothe her.

Having now trashed the feelings of even the tiniest member of my clan, I was beginning to feel just a tad wicked. And to make matters worse, my father was still out there somewhere, probably at the guns and ammo shop by now.

I offered Clarice the box of cupcakes and she started to giggle. At least one of us here was incapable of holding a cumbersome grudge – or in this family's case – a cucumber one.

"Thirty-five years is a really long time to be together, Mother – kind of a landmark," Jenny said.

"You mean milestone?" I asked.

Everyone ignored me except for Clarice, who was picking at the cakes with a very stiff little index finger.

The hammering outside sounded bad, even worse than my father's, as if Luke were blindfolded with one arm tied behind his back.

"I think this project should stop," I blurted. "Luke's gonna lose a finger."

"Luke is doing just fine," my mother said, as calm and in control as I'd ever heard her.

"I think it should stop too," Jenny said. "My husband shouldn't have to do your dirty-work."

"You're the one that gave me that damn thing as a gift, and now you're accusing me of some awful scheme. Are you trying to say that I'm a bad person?"

"Of course I'm not saying you're a bad person – but you obviously didn't want the *dirty toenail*, and Dad apparently wants the shed he already has."

"Your father doesn't really care about that old shed."

I imagined my father walking zombie-like into a bottomless lake.

"How can you say that?" I asked. "He's obsessed over it. This new shed is too big for the garden, and will *ruin the cucumbers!*"

"Wuin de kukes!" Clarice screeched.

"Oh, Tracy – now you sound just like him," my mother said.

And out of nowhere, like a laser beam of much needed precision, Mary spoke, "What's really going on here? This is like squabbling over a toothpaste cap or toilet seat when there are perfectly visible crooks making off with the real treasures."

Clarice and I were open-mouthed, and I watched as a long string of drool – which had been connecting her finger to the cupcake – was now working its way to the floor.

"So – until all the facts are in – we should probably suspend all building," she continued. "Plus, Herb should be here."

My mother ran out to the backyard and the rest of us followed. She hollered at Luke to drop his hammer, although it was quite evident that not much had been accomplished, aside from a board accidentally being nailed to a beam.

He looked up, confused, as Clarice threw tiny fistfuls of garden dirt in his face. *She's starting early*, I thought.

"Stop building!" my mother screamed.

Luke nodded and coughed up soil.

"Herb's turned a very simple little thing into a monumental issue – and now the entire family has turned against me."

Grateful that my grandmother was on the scene, I ran out of the yard and started a slow jog around the block. I needed a breather from my family before I completely cracked. Thankfully, I soon found myself in the place of my effortless childhood meditations.

chapter 35

HE WAS WAITING for me in the park.

The little boy version of James.

I watched as he wandered around the perimeter of the playground. His brow was wrinkled; he was looking for something. He stopped to pick long grass, and sucked the dew right off of the stem. After tiring of the honeysuckle, he carefully placed stones on top of each other, creating elaborate designs embedded with hidden codes.

Codes that were somehow meant for me.

There was no one else around, not a single child of any description. The teeter-totter and old-fashioned swing set that accompanied my early days had long since been replaced with a state-of-the-art jungle gym. I sat deep inside one of the colorful fort lookouts and waited.

The playground remained still until he looked up and spotted me. His smile told me that I had been the object of his earlier search. He waved at me till all the remaining traces of loss were gone from his expression. And with a face like the sun, he began running toward me.

But now there were many variations of James coming toward me – child, teenager, even old man. I stared down at the gathering – into the face of each and every incarnation. I knew they had something important to tell me.

I closed my eyes and listened.

"Here you are."

At first, I thought little James was behind me; when I turned around, I saw only my sister.

"Why did you take off like that?" she asked.

"I needed to get some air."

She sat down next to me – as close as possible, and we let our feet dangle over the edge of the fort.

"I didn't mean to cause problems," she said.

"I know. And I didn't mean to blame you for all that," I said. "I just needed to get it all out without attacking her directly."

It was odd, but she didn't seem pissed off by my questionable tactics.

"I feel like I'm always the last to know," she said. "How long have you known they were sleeping in different rooms?"

"Just since I've been back."

"That sucks."

"But does it really, Jenny? Are people always supposed to feel the same way? Are we really meant to stop the one constant in life?"

"Which is?"

"Change."

She looked a little annoyed, or maybe scared was more accurate.

"Are people really supposed to be in charge of each other's fulfillment when they can't even manage their own?"

"Maybe you get things that I don't," she said. "You're the smart one, you're the daring one, you're the fearless one."

Apparently, no one had clued her into the hives or the sweeping saga known as, *My Never-ending Discontent*.

"And you get things that I don't," I said.

"Like what?"

"Like how to care for others, how to remain open and un-cynical. I think I'm a cynic, Jenny. Even when you were a baby, you had such a sweet optimism. All I had was colic."

"You really think so?" she asked.

"Have you ever seen a violent film in your lifetime?"

"No."

"Why not?"

"What for?"

"See what I mean – you don't pollute your atmosphere."

I thought of their new vehicle, but quickly put it out of my mind. Jenny seemed perplexed.

"I'm trying to compliment you."

"Oh."

"I know it doesn't happen often."

Jenny stared down at her dangling toes, and I could tell that she felt sorry for me.

"What?"

"Doesn't it get lonely out there? In that place?"

She made it sound like I was living in a garbage dump on some distant moon.

A sudden flash caught the corner of my eye. It was little James, peeking around a large tree and holding a sparkler. I watched the jagged little spurts of electricity until he was gone. My fantasies seemed to be creating themselves now – as if I were just a convenient host.

"I'm fine."

"But don't you want a family? A husband at least?"

"Would I be a space alien if I didn't?"

"No – but you might be a liar."

"Then I guess it's not a clean-cut yes or no answer. Things just haven't worked out that way for me."

"Yet," she said.

I looked up into the sky and could almost see the faintest glow of the space station. I knew it was looking back at me, and so was the audience I'd so longed for. Everyone was looking down – wondering at my next move. Only little James was looking up at me, still holding his sparkler for dear life. He smiled as though he already knew my next move, and the next hundred after that.

"We'll see, Jenny."

"I think you ran away."

I knew exactly what she meant, but such detection coming from her made me uncomfortable.

"What are you talking about?"

"I think you ran away from us, your family. But no matter how far you get, we'll always be a part of you."

"What are you talking about? I mean, you live out in Colorado."

"We're only there because of Luke's practice. We'll get back here. I want to."

The thought of moving 'back here' gave me such a spasm that I almost fell out of the plastic fortress. I remembered what I'd said to James, *just a mad dash scramble to get out of Bumble Fuck.*

"I did not run away."

"You did so – because part of you is ashamed."

"Not true."

"You expect other people to be honest, so now it's your turn."

"I'm not ashamed, Jenny."

"Yes, you are. You look down on the people who stay in one place and live ordinary lives. But how do you know what their lives really are?"

"I don't look down on people here."

"Just be honest with me, Tracy. You'll feel a whole lot better."

"Okay, Jenny. Fine. I never want to be comfortable with the mundane. I never want to sell any sort of new or used appliance. I never want my crowning achievement to be a broach in the shape of an old crappy oven. Happy now?"

I so desperately wanted to come clean, and reveal that I was chasing a dream that I just couldn't give up on yet. How could I possibly finish what had never even begun?

"See! You think our lives are mundane. Our father was a truck driver and our mother was a homemaker."

"I've never had a qualm about that."

"I don't believe you."

"If they're happy with their lives – I'm happy for them. And if your life works for you, I'm overjoyed. But one size does not fit all, and I don't want to live here. Ever."

"But now you don't want to leave." She had an odd smirk on her face that gave me the instant creeps.

My baby sister was unearthing me with phenomenal skill. I felt like a fat and sluggish worm that was being toyed with for kicks, "I do so want to leave – I frantically want to leave, Jenny. Why would you say such a rotten thing?"

She laughed at me, "You must be so tired of spinning around like a hamster wheel."

"I am not spinning – what's wrong with spinning, anyway?"

"What's out there for you, Tracy? In Hollywood? You don't network, and I doubt you even go to parties."

"Why does something have to be out there for me?"

"And you don't write anything."

"I'm working on something."

"I bet you couldn't write your way out of a wet paper bag."

"I said I'm working on it, Jenny."

"Work on it here."

"No."

"Why not?"

"Because I hate it here."

"Why?"

"Because I do."

"You only think you do."

Luke and Clarice appeared out of nowhere, and I was spared the rest of her horrendous inquiry.

"Your dad's back," Luke informed us. "I think he's moving out – moving into some motel or something."

Clarice started kicking at her father's leg.

"He walked into the house with a very large suitcase – the price tag still on. Probably just bought it today, I bet. I think his mom's talking to him now."

Jenny couldn't get out of our fort fast enough, practically spraining her foot on a plastic cube.

"Aren't you coming?" she asked.

"What can we do?"

"We can hog-tie him if we have to."

"But what if leaving would be best for him?"

"It's not."

"How do you know for sure?" I asked.

"It wouldn't be best for us."

"How can something that isn't best for him possibly be best for us?"

"He doesn't really *want* to leave."

"How the heck do you know what he really wants?"

She looked up at me and her eyes smoldered, "He wants to stay. And that is final."

"You sound exactly like your mother."

"You just want him to leave so that you can feel better about your own life."

She turned away from me as though I were some strain of a deadly virus, gathered her family, and started running in the direction of our house.

"I think you're being selfish, Jenny!"

She stopped and turned back to me; she said nothing.

"What?" I yelled.

"You're like the washing machine. Full. Of. Shit."

chapter 36

MY FATHER WAS definitely moving into the motel.

At least that's what Mary told me when I walked through the door. I heard bunglesome bustling on the stairs, and figured he was about to pack his life into the Cadillac that was now parked on the street. This was the first time I'd ever seen it anywhere other than the meticulous safety of the garage.

He finally managed to heave his new suitcase up the stairs.

"What's going on, Dad?"

"Hey, you – taking a little space, that's all."

"Where are you going?"

"Bud Jarkinson's giving me a good deal on his little motel – eighty-five a week, including ice. You remember old Jarkinson – used to give you quarters when you were growing up."

"You're leaving because of the shed?"

"Partly yes, partly no."

I looked at Mary, "I thought we were gonna talk about this."

"Listen, Tracy – if your mother wants to dismantle the back-yard, and ruin all that produce, that's her business. I'm just not gonna stick around to see it."

"So you're gonna live in a motel forever?"

"Maybe I'll get a cabin somewhere – you know I've always wanted to live by a lake."

"What about the winter?"

"Wood stove, down blankets, and fleece jackets."

"You've given this a lot of thought."

My father shrugged as though I wasn't wrong.

I could feel my fear turning to anger, tightening my jaw, and switching my loyalties, "Just how long have you been planning this?"

"I haven't been planning diddly. You know I've always wanted a cabin."

Jenny, Luke, and Clarice entered the house just as I was about to call for backup. When Jenny saw her father lugging his belongings across the linoleum, she dramatically flung herself across the counter.

"Daddy's not going far," my father said.

"That motel's at least ten miles away," I reminded him.

"Which motel?" Luke asked.

"Old Buddy Jarkinson!"

"Why not just prance around and click your heels together?" I asked.

"It's not like that," he said. "But listen to this, Luke – you can catch fish right from the deck of your room. Plus, he's got ESPN hooked up."

"I'll have to bring a couple of cold six-packs over," Luke gushed.

Jenny punched him in the arm, "You won't be taking beer anywhere – especially to my father's getaway pad."

"Careful, Jenny," my father said. "That husband of yours may discover he has a little something called a backbone."

Luke guffawed like a circus clown which, for whatever reason, prompted me to look at his feet. He was wearing a pair of garden-variety sneakers – appropriate for the occasion – but I was convinced he was being assisted by a pair of hefty arches.

"Well, I should be off before Bud leaves for the day – don't want to miss out on that special rate."

My father tried to get out the door too fast and ended up wedging his massive suitcase in the doorframe. The nasty side of me wanted to point and laugh, but my idealistic side was rooting for him to escape before my mother descended from her post.

It occurred to me that my mother might actually be waiting for him to leave. Maybe this is what they both wanted.

Luke pried the oversized suitcase loose and carried it out to the car. He struck me as an eager accomplice – desperate to live vicariously through my father's courageous act. I watched as my dad practically galloped after him – they looked as though they'd just escaped a wicked labor camp run by sadistic hags.

I heard the jangle and click of my mother's heavy jewelry, and braced myself against the dining room table – not at all sure what to expect. The situation she was about to encounter would not be a familiar one.

"What's all the commotion about?" she asked.

"Dad's moving into a motel," I said.

My mother looked at me with genuine surprise, as if she'd had no inkling of the shaky ground beneath her very own kitchen, "Was this your idea, Tracy?"

"Why me?"

"The timing's a little odd, that's all – you come home with all your fancy ideas and all of a sudden your father's moving out."

"Have you been sniffing glue?"

I didn't mean to be so rude, but her accusation ignited my guilt and subsequent defenses.

"It's just all a little too convenient. Your father was perfectly fine a week ago."

"Was he *really*?" I asked.

"Yes, he was."

"So, what exactly are you saying? If I wasn't around, you guys would be enjoying a storybook marriage? Or better yet, if I'd started dating the oven man and wore nylons on a regular basis, you'd both somehow morph into master communicators?"

My mother didn't answer, but Jenny was moaning in the corner.

"I cannot believe you're blaming me for your own crappy marriage."

"It does seem a bit of a stretch, Joanne," Mary said.

"Of course you're going to side with her," my mother said. "You probably put her up to it. You never liked me anyway."

"That's absurd."

"No – it's not."

It was as if every single member of my family felt compelled to pass the buck of responsibility, including myself.

"I see myself in you, Joanne," Mary said.

My mother gulped back her pent-up emotion; she opened and slammed a random cupboard door.

The guys came back inside the house and reluctantly found seats at the table. My mother stared at my father like he'd just been caught pissing on her bulk supply of silk, "So, we receive an anniversary gift from our youngest daughter, and you decide to move out?"

My father could only twiddle his thumbs. I looked at my grandmother, but she was deeply engaged with her mood ring. Her maharishi skills seemed to be a little hit or miss. I really didn't want to be the facilitator now – given my inability to be neutral – but it seemed there was no other option.

"I don't think it's quite so simple, Mother."

"Nothing's ever simple with you."

She looked at me with uncertainty – perplexed as to how I could do this to her after she'd granted me life, and nurtured me so carefully into the super brat I had so clearly become.

I felt especially guilty given that she'd so recently nursed me back from the skin inferno, given up her bed, and even tossed her doilies in the air to show me what a maverick she was.

It was almost impossible not to run over to her and wrap my arms around her, tearfully admitting my gratitude – no matter her particular genius for driving me nuts. But I sat frozen – suppressing an impulse to stand on the table and scream that I was not against her, that I loved her, and only ever wanted what was best for her and my dad.

Instead I said, "Stop blaming Dad for your unhappiness."

I waited for his usual race to her rescue, but it didn't come. I looked at him and knew in an instant how much he longed for the freedom of Bud's motel room – the freedom to watch sports, drink beer, be alone and do nothing.

"I've never blamed your father for anything, and I am not unhappy."

Nobody budged, breathed, or believed her.

And she looked so forlorn that Jenny finally came to her aid, "Maybe Dad's the one who's unhappy."

"Maybe we should leave," Luke said.

"Leeeeeeave!" Clarice screamed.

At this point, I was ready to get in the car and drive over to Bud's motel myself.

"This is a little dramatic," my mother said. "All because of a shed?"

"It was a bad gift," Jenny said. "I didn't know it would cause this."

"I didn't realize our marriage was so rice paper thin, Herbert."

My father shrugged his shoulders, and I was annoyed that I would have to translate his body language.

"Maybe he's just tired of feeling unimportant," I said.

I looked at him to see if he would dispute me, but he said nothing.

My mother's jaw tightened and her bangles hit the table hard, "What on the great plains are you talking about, Tracy? You don't even live here and now you're declaring your father unimportant? He's the one who had the damned income all those years. I'd say he had all the importance."

Luke picked up Clarice and informed us that he was taking her back to their hotel. Everyone nodded and said goodbye, even Jenny didn't protest. My grandmother poured us all a mug of coffee.

I put way too much sugar in my mug and saw that I was shaking.

"I'm so sick of feeling like the bad guy," my mother said. "And what do I do to deserve it? Cook, clean, iron people's clothes – make sure everyone's comfortable."

"You're a domestic goddess, Mother."

"I'm not fishing for compliments, Jenny."

I gulped back my coffee and shot Mary another silent plea. Couldn't she do something – quote from a book, give a sermon, light a candle? Damn.

We were in way over our heads.

Maybe it was time to sink.

chapter 37

HE'D WANTED HIS license plates upstairs.

My father was in the middle of making a case for himself and – like hearing from a favorite actor who'd retired long before – I had never been so riveted. The entire family drama was unfolding like some sort of peculiar miniseries.

"That's all I ever really wanted up here – and I've wanted it for decades. I didn't even mind all the doilies and the stitchings, and the potpourri, and knick knacks and the bric-a-brac, the pumpkin carpet, the pastel walls, the dried flowers in every corner."

He turned to my mother who was sitting directly across from him, "I asked you if we couldn't just incorporate the plates somehow. Maybe frame a couple in the kitchen – something classy. Even put them in the little bathroom that nobody ever used. You just said no, time after time. It didn't matter to you what I wanted. It mattered to you what you wanted."

My mother looked rather stunned, as did Jenny – but Mary and I had been waiting for this.

"And let me tell you something else, Joanne – I hate painting and building and installing. I'm not good at it – I've never been good at it, and I'll never be good at it. I hate it. And anything that I love – like my cucumbers and tomatoes, you just scoff at."

Now I could feel her eyes penetrating me as though I were speaking the words and not my father.

"And anytime I wanted to do the things I love – like fishing, you'd make me feel like a bum or a jerk. And I'd have to make up for one lousy trip with a long list of horrible chores."

"Is this pity party over, or do you have more?" my mother asked.

"See how you belittle me? I tell you the honest truth and you reject me. You're not interested in how I *feel*. Not now – not ever."

"Well how about this for honesty, Herb? For years I've dealt with ugly specks of paint on the wall, shelves that would collapse at random, crown moldings that were crooked, an entire entertainment unit that sits lopsided, and a basement that now resembles a truck stop. In a one word summary – tacky."

My father started to stand, but Mary held his forearm.

"If you wanted to marry a goddamed handyman – then why didn't you? You married me, Joanne – what did you expect? Did you think you'd wake up one morning and I'd morph into Bob Vila?"

"Maybe I was hoping."

Emotion was cracking her surface like the cold on a windowpane.

"Hoping you'd learn some class – appreciate manners and stuff. Be accepted by such people. People who have real taste – people that are admired in the world. I wanted you to know about wine and opera and travel. But no – you wanted license plates on the walls of our home. You wanted bacon dinners at four in the morning for you and your greasy truck driver friends."

My father passed her his handkerchief, but she only swiped at it.

"I at least expected you to understand the art of being a man, which normally involves building things and fixing cars. Like the way I've been saddled with the art of being a fucking woman."

"Okay, Joanne," he whispered.

"All a man has to do to have a child is orgasm. But women need to work miracles from that very second forward. You get release; we get bondage."

What fiends of the pits had I set free?

"It wasn't what I'd hoped for, Herb."

Now she was choking on her sobs, and it was clear that none of this was really even about my father. This was all and only about herself. I watched my mother literally fall across the table, bangles jangling, mascara tears pooling in the creases of her hand-stitched tablecloth.

My cheeks were hot, and I was sure I could feel the hives readying their attack.

"I'm a retired truck driver, Joanne."

"I know full well what you are," my mother wailed.

"Do you know what it's like to close your eyes and see nothing but road in front of you? Sometimes it was just torture. But I'll tell you what, those endless miles paid for a lot of stuff around here. And that truck paid for this house and raised two healthy daughters."

"But I mean, is that all you were content to do? Drive a big dirty truck back and forth?"

I had never witnessed such nerve – blaming him for all of her unrealized potential.

"Yes, as a matter of fact. I was very content, Joanne – with my job, with my greasy buddies and bacon dinners, with my wife and children. I'm sorry that I haven't measured up in your eyes. But maybe you should be asking yourself these same questions – you've never even mentioned *opera* before. I thought Tim McGraw was your favorite?"

Super Bingo!

"Who do you think has taken care of you all these years?" she asked.

"We've taken care of each other."

It was such a defining statement that nothing else really needed to be said. So I barely heard him remind us that he'd be at the motel – if we needed him.

His car started up with Tina Turner screeching splendidly about rivers deep and mountains high, and we all listened as he sped off out of audible range.

My mother looked up and around the table with a wet black smudgy face, announcing with finality that my father's departure was entirely my fault.

Jenny immediately concurred.

"How is it her fault?" Mary asked.

"It just is," my mother said.

"She's the one that had to dig all this shit up," Jenny said. "Instead of just letting people be a little bit unhappy – which is totally normal – she had to blow the whole thing sky high."

"Why couldn't you two just let me be?" I asked. "I'm like a wound that wants to heal, but you just keep picking at me."

"Do you even want us in your life?" Jenny asked.

"All I ever wanted was an example."

"Of what?" my mother asked.

"People who are comfortable in their own skin."

"Then maybe you should be that example for us, Tracy. Did you ever think of that? Maybe you should show us how to do a relationship."

A horrible image of James speaking at a Republican National Convention flashed through my mind. He was standing next to his picture-perfect wife who was proudly beaming by his side.

"Me?"

"Yes, you. Why don't you be the example?"

"Well," I said, rather flummoxed. "What do you think I'm doing? But you've never liked my example – not one bit. I'm trying to feel my way, based on my own stuff – not someone else's. I just want you to let me find my way without all the pressure. And now I come home to see that what you want for me doesn't even bring *you* happiness."

"Try to raise a child and keep it fed and protected and alive and healthy to the very best of your ability – and then all *this*."

"But all this is *real*."

I looked at my mother whose watery green eyes were the precursors of my own. Now they appeared to be melting. I'd never really considered the strength of our resemblance before, although from time to time people remarked that our left profile seemed an identical match.

And I could see exactly what I would look like at her age. It was true; she was my mirror – just as I was hers – perfectly reflecting the future of my features and probably my unhappiness too. But it wouldn't be the same kind of unhappiness – I'd risk it all to create my very own brand.

As if she had so easily read my mind, she turned to me while speaking to my sister, "Jenny – go and get me the biggest hammer you can find."

Oh shit. I wondered if she was finally going to bash in my ungrateful brains.

"Why?"

"And call your husband."

"But – "

"That shed is coming down. *Now*."

chapter 38

As a DETECTIVE hunts for clues, I needed to re-visit the underground.

I ran downstairs and looked around at his large and controversial collection of license plates. I'd never really asked him about them, having no idea that they'd meant so much. Some of them were custom, but most were standard issue. Over half were from the mid-west, with a couple of really neat ones from the south. A vertical column of plates started near the ceiling with North Dakota and ended at the carpet with Texas. He had one from every state – except Alaska.

The plates reminded me of my scripts – symbols of a difficult journey. My father and I had traveled far and wide, but somehow I'd ended up lost while he'd arrived at the very place he'd probably started – at ease.

My mother's hurt had turned back to anger. She was pounding around upstairs like an obstinate queen who'd just discovered a major betrayal within her inner circle. Jenny was echoing her distress – at least my mother hadn't lost the loyalty of her best princess. It wouldn't be long before they were trash-talking the gargoyle under the stairs, surely even more Machiavellian than the one who had fled.

A pot smashed against the wall, and I could only hope that Mary wasn't in any immediate danger. But then intermittent bursts of a measured voice broke through the wailing and moaning, and I knew that she was trying to talk sense to the temporarily insane.

As a frying pan came crashing down the stairs, I realized I should probably get out of the house. I could almost see the headlines now: *Woman – who tried to write about the awesome magnitude of inner and outer space – perishes in dispute over backyard garden shed.*

But then again, I reminded myself – who'd really care?

I wiggled out a basement window and scurried to the old shed itself – a true monument to the Johnston family power struggle – just a modest rectangular structure of light wood and shingled roof. It was locked, but I knew my father kept a spare key buried in the soil of the bonsai plant that sat on a tiny table beside the door.

Inside was a vision to behold. Everything twinkled in the most meticulous of condition. Boxes were stacked from heavy up to light, and everything had a square label printed in neat block letters. Golf clubs, fishing rods, and skis were placed in their own hollow columns of bamboo. Fishing tackle was organized by color; screws and bolts were organized by size. The lawn mower sat in the corner beside the infamous red toolbox that opens up like a staircase – the one my mother gave him for his fiftieth birthday instead of the horticulture book series he'd requested.

But the most beautiful things in here were my father's plants – big and small, dark green and lime. There was also a small shelf of books, arranged in alphabetical order, describing plants and seeds. The walls of the shed were covered in special shots of vegetables – the ones I assumed were from his very own garden. The largest picture was a blowup of a superstar tomato – ripe as heaven, as he would say.

A beige curtain covered the back wall, perfectly blending with the interior. His ability to coordinate was not a big surprise, as he had often matched the fabrics for my home economics class. My mother was always delighted with my color choices; nobody ever let on that it wasn't me who was making them. Left to my own druthers, I would have happily sewn myself a wardrobe of straw colored sacks.

I doubted my mother had ever bothered to explore in here. She might have discovered that while he failed at construction, he could organize his heart out. And I would defy her to find a more passionate green thumb.

Lost in appreciation for my father, I almost forgot what I had come for – but quickly spotted the wheel under the curtain. The Lindsay Wagner Streak was my truest companion between grades four through nine.

Lindsay was the total bomb, and I was quite sure I still had a bionic woman shirt or two in my mother's old trunk – the kind that was both undershirt and over-shirt combined. Removing the Streak from her secure spot took some time, but I finally pried her free. I was about to maneuver her outside when I heard something stir.

I was being watched. Perhaps my mother was standing outside with a meat tenderizer. I turned my head slowly to the small window that served as the shed's only natural light source – nothing but my overactive imagination.

But then I saw them: two eyes peeking at me over the rim of a large orange plant pot.

A lizard.

"Are you the keeper of this shed? Master of the cucumber and tomato world?"

He ducked below the rim of the pot and coiled his tail around the stem of a geranium.

"This place stands only to be flattened."

I stared out the window and saw the new shed strewn about the lawn – boards, ladders, measuring sticks, and bags of nails littered everywhere. Poor Luke – having to spend most of his trip in some silly hardware store.

"So be careful you don't scuttle over a nail and spike yourself. And take care of my father then, when I'm not here. You alone are the ancient guardian – a throwback to a different time. A prehistoric time – when everyone accepted his or her place without confusion."

"There was always confusion, Tracy."

I spun my head from the window to the pot – nothing but a miniature reptile cozied up around a plant. The scaly little thing probably didn't even have a voice box, although I was most certain I'd seen his green skin turn yellow.

"I'm finally and completely ill. I guess this is what happens to a screenwriter without a screen, a writer who is never right, a woman who..."

I thought of James.

"Never-mind."

I wheeled my bike outside, locked the lizard in the shed, and put the key back in the bonsai – underneath a small wooden character I'd never noticed before. A very old Japanese sailor was sitting on the bank, fishing. His line was made of dental floss – gently skimming the tiny watery hole my father had so carefully dug in the soil. The little tree cast the sailor's face in shadow, but I could tell he was otherworldly. Perhaps it was he who had spoken to me about the past. I peered closer at his tiny figurine features – minuscule lines had been carved into the wood of his face.

"Did my father carve you?"

He was lost in bonsai shadow again, forever engaged in his own contemplation.

Perhaps my dad was a secret craftsman after all, but only when he got to create little spectral fantasies of his choosing. I thought about the hordes of my own little toothpick people.

The vines outside the shed were rather beautiful. I studied the elaborate way in which they'd been wrapped and twirled and looped. They seemed fragile but they were strong, having to hold the weight of heavy sustenance.

I left the lizard and the sailor and the vines, and set out for my father on a bike that was, like my childhood bed, two sizes too small.

chapter 39

MY KNEES NEARLY circled my cheeks.

But oh well, I was riding Lindsay Wagner and that's what mattered. The pink banana seat was a little faded, but still wore remnants of the gold speck glue I had slathered on two decades prior.

I swerved along my old street, thinking it remarkable how little a neighborhood could change in twenty years. Aside from an updated version of mid-sized sedan or mini-van, it was as though I was riding through 1985.

My legs started hurting, so I had to stand and pedal. I also had to roll my right pant leg up to the knee to keep it from getting caught in the chain; the side of my rather saggy calf muscle was soon streaked with old grease.

Dark clouds were moving in from the northeast, so I decided to take preemptive shelter in a donut shop. I bought my dad and I some old-fashioned ones with the sloppy pink glaze, along with some chocolate donut holes for myself.

Luckily, I had never removed the big white Easter basket that would now carry the deep-fried dough to the motel. To my own childhood credit, I hadn't buckled under the peer pressure that demanded I either remove the basket or spend the rest of pre-pubescence exiled to Geek-Ville. I couldn't even remember where I'd found the strength to ward off such an onslaught of ridicule.

I liked to compare that challenge to Ms. Streisand and her unwillingness to screw around with her nose; she never had it chopped, shaved, or otherwise beautified in any way – and consequently retained the greatest voice in the history of popular music.

The rain never came, but my knees felt like cement balls by the time I rode into the motel parking lot. I leaned my bike on its kickstand next to my father's car, and then knocked on his ground-level door.

He was startled to see me – so much so that a tinge of shame crept through me. I shouldn't have come so soon.

"Did you really ride your bike all the way here? That old thing?"

"Yep."

"The Wonder Woman?"

"Lindsay Wagner."

Since he still hadn't invited me in, I pushed past him with my donuts and sat on one of the two double beds that were facing a large mirror, an ancient television, and a garish painting of fluorescent yellow fish splashing around in an aqua blue forest stream. The carpet was a marmalade shag, and the bed quilts were a yucky variation of brown.

A very beautiful couple was making out on the screen; they seemed so perfect – so profoundly meant for each other. It was almost funny the way such un-reality created an impossible standard for most people to live up to. And yet, my particular reality seemed to be dedicated to adding my own contributions to that same world of make-believe.

My father quickly turned off the couple.

"You were in the shed?"

"Yes."

"So it's still standing?"

"It was when I left."

My father offered me a beer, and I gave him a donut.

"That shed is really something, Dad. That curtain you picked really matches the walls."

"It was an old boat cover I found at a flea market."

"So you sewed it?"

"On the sly."

"And the tomatoes look incredible."

"Did you try one?"

"I'll let you give me one when you think they're ready."

"A bigger shed would block out the sun, shadow those vines, ruin the math, ruin the angles, ruin the fruit altogether."

"I thought tomatoes were vegetables?"

"Technically, they're fruit. Didn't you know that?"

"No."

He looked so disappointed, as if I'd never learned anything of real value.

"The cucumbers?"

"They're fine, Dad."

My father looked at me like he was calculating a very difficult math problem in his head, but I knew he was just trying to brace himself for such an enormous loss. It occurred to me that I'd never taken much of an interest in my father's interests – I'd really only seen him as a digit in the equation known as ME.

"I hear you make one heck of a garden sandwich," I offered weakly.

He looked at me as though I'd just dismissed a year's worth of parking tickets, "Who said?"

"Word on the street."

"There's nothing like a cucumber and tomato sandwich – nothing like it in the world. The marriage of the two – between bread – is perfection. People are always squawking on about the tomato with the damned bacon but really it's the union of the garden dwellers – the health of the two."

I nodded as though he were describing how to perform a surgical incision.

"You cut them into cubes and soak them in a bath of oil, vinegar, and salt. And if you use the coarser salt, use less of it. Your mother enjoys it when I add a hint of red onion, but I like the cukes and tomatoes alone yet intermingled."

That's what James and I were now – alone yet intermingled. His presence was like an echo on the ether, and I could almost feel him in the next room.

"Make sure the olive oil is the good stuff – same with the Balsamic. Then you toast dark brown bread, and add a little bit of mayo and more olive oil – and then you load on the perfection."

"I won't let her take it down."

My father looked at me as though the entire endeavor was hopeless anyway, as if the invading army was already outside our door.

"She could be taking it down now for all you know."

I couldn't tell him about the big hammer she'd requested.

"Why don't we just haul the new one away – all those pieces? Just dump it somewhere, Dad? Like a body in the night."

I imagined us as two shadowy figures laying low, eating bad food and waiting for the law to come down heavy.

"Don't you get it, Tracy?"

"What?"

"Your mother doesn't respect me."

"That'll change now that you're here."

"No, it won't," he said, spewing bits of pink-iced donut.

"Why not?"

"Because she's not happy with herself."

"It's my fault," I blurted.

"How's it your fault?"

"If I'd stayed in Hollywood, you'd still be in the basement."

"Yeah, right. I'd still be living in the basement with my life stored in the backyard. Your mother would still be unhappy."

"She projected her stuff onto me, and then I had to come out here and project all of my problems onto you guys."

"What problems do you have, Tracy?"

"Aside from the ones she thinks I have?"

"I'm asking about what you think. Anything to do with this James person? How did you meet him?"

I shrugged and ate another donut hole, "Car crash – I rear-ended him."

"You date the guy you rear-ended?"

"Uh – that sounds really bad. His old clunker just stopped on the freeway. Anyway, his parents have loads of money. That's how I can afford to bring you to Hollywood."

"They gave you money?"

"For the car and lost wages."

"You lost your job?"

"It wasn't stable or anything."

"But if they have money, why was he driving an old clunker?"

"Trying to prove a point."

"What point?"

"That he can take care of himself."

"Apparently he can't."

"Yes, he can. He will. Eventually."

I went out onto the patio, and looked down the hill at the narrow stream that was flowing swiftly, "Can you really catch fish from here?"

"Bud swears he's caught a wild brown trout every year for the last thirty."

We stood side by side peering into the dark grey water.

"Why don't you come home now?" I asked.

"I just got here. I haven't even watched a football game yet – not even a lousy bowling tournament. You wanted me to be honest and stick up for myself, so here I am."

"I just wanted you to resolve things – that's all."

"And that's always meant resolving them your mother's way."

"What about your produce?"

"God's hands."

We went back inside the room, and I threw myself across one of the beds.

"Can I ask you something, Dad?"

"Anything."

"Do you think I should be married with children?"

"I think life is short and you should try to be happy. Whatever that means. And by the way, you really haven't known this guy very long."

"So?"

"So maybe you should relax."

"I am."

He sat on the edge of the other bed with his chin in his hands and his elbows on his knees, "If those hives have anything to do with him, then you're looped, kiddo."

"I was breaking out before James. But yes, I really do like him."

"I know."

"You do? You can really tell?"

"Yup. And your grandma kind of filled me in."

Despite some mild embarrassment, I was happy that they'd discussed it.

"It's like something mega, Dad. Half the time, I can't breathe. I mean, I can't explain it at all. It's so weird. It's actually a relief to be out here."

"Hiding out a little?"

I nodded and hid my face under a pillow – one that was far less than a Joanne Johnston kind of fresh.

"I understand. That's how it was with your mother."

"Really?"

"Of course – do you really think we started out where we ended up?"

I sat up and looked at my father in the motel mirror; something in our expressions matched – like we could play the leads in a script I really needed to write entitled, *The Outcasts*.

"Mega, huh?" he asked.

"Yeah – but please don't make fun of me. I just feel like such a late bloomer."

"Do you love him?"

"I really want to."

My father sighed, "It's not something you necessarily have a choice in."

"I guess not."

"But he's a lucky guy."

I looked away from the mirror and turned to face him for real, "Remember that Christmas years ago when you got so mad at me? Freaking out in front of everybody like a madman?"

He nodded, "Sort of."

"All because I lugged firewood into the house and got a bit of dirt on her new carpet. It was a light pumpkin color meant to match her sherbet orange drapes. Everyone had to call it a stupid tapestry instead of a carpet. Remember?"

"Yes."

"You were so mad, and the worst thing was – "

"That I was the one who loved a fire in the fireplace."

"Yes! You were the one that got me excited about fires and marshmallows and a family sitting in front of a roaring hearth. It was your idea. And then that ugly carpet came – an entire month's paycheck – and no one was even allowed to walk on it. Nobody was allowed to walk on the carpet, imagine? What were we supposed to do – levitate?"

"I do remember that, Tracy."

"Well it *hurt*," I said. "You hurt me."

"I'm sorry. You can kick me if you want."

"I don't want to kick you. And I really don't want to kick the spirit out of James."

My father twisted the tab off of his beer can, "You won't."

"But it just kind of seems to happen. What if that's all I know how to do?"

"He won't let you."

We sipped more beer and ate more donuts and listened to the movement of the creek below.

"Listen, Tracy – your mother put up with a lot of stuff. We didn't have much money. Times were stressful. Her home was her castle. It's okay. I could never do half of what I did without her help."

"So you do love her?"

"I've always loved her – more than you could ever know."

"So it is possible for two people to love each other – for real?"

"Of course it is. Things don't have to be so complicated. God knows I'm a simple man, Tracy. I love the simple things because they're really not so simple. And if you're still for long enough, you'll feel what I mean."

I wondered if my very own father might possess all the answers to all of the riddles that had ever stumped me, "If I had the power to grant you anything – right now – what would it be, Dad?"

"A raspberry bush."

"That's it?"

"Yes."

My father waved me over and I fell into his warm embrace, thoroughly enjoying the combination of Old Spice and fresh beer.

"You need a ride tonight?"

"No thanks."

"The sun will shine tomorrow, Tracy."

"It's supposed to rain."

"Trust me. Tomorrow will be absolutely incredible."

"How do you know?"

"We know stuff like that around these parts."

"And you're really sure you're not ready to come back? You have a better television at home."

"How about you come ask me tomorrow."

"I'll do that."

I went outside and took my sweet time rolling my pant leg. The green trees behind the motel looked black against the moon.

Lindsay creaked under my weight and I slowly peddled away from my father; I knew he was watching me go. I made a wide loop in the parking lot so that I could see him – for what might possibly be the very last time, although I knew I was being dramatic.

He was standing in the doorway, moving his arms like he was signaling a mayday, and maybe in his own way, he was. It seemed we both shared a knack for the theatrical. And in the sweetest region of my crazy head, I knew that whatever happened, my father would forever be known as the mighty gentle cucumber king.

chapter 40

THERE WAS NO such thing as a perfect marriage.

I rode my bike back to the safety of the donut shop thinking that maybe fruits and vegetables could pull it off, but humans most likely couldn't. Like my grandmother said, perfect is dead. I tried to watch the road but James was blocking my view, taking up my entire mind's eye.

I ordered a coconut tart and a large coffee. The visit with my father had been a disgrace. I was as needy as Jenny. My father didn't have to return, ever.

An elderly couple was cuddling in a booth across from me. They were a curious pair, actively listening to each other instead of incessantly barking their own point of view. They had an array of fattening treats in front of them. I wondered if they were celebrating an anniversary – perhaps their fiftieth. Exactly how I'd want to celebrate my own fiftieth anniversary – something as romantic and unfussy as holding hands in a donut shop. Maybe they could explain a straightforward blueprint for living that I could actually follow.

I took my cell phone out of my pocket and dialed his number, smiling at the couple whenever they smiled at each other.

"Hello?"

"Hi James, it's me."

"You don't sound well."

"My father moved into a motel."

"What?"

"He's gonna fish off the balcony."

"What have you been drinking?"

"Donuts."

"Huh?"

"My mother basically told him that he's a complete loser. But he's not a loser at all. It's more like he's on the brink of some kind of fulfillment. And that reminds me, I really need to start eating more vegetables and I need to find a good olive oil and a complimentary vinegar and I must learn how to prepare something other than – "

"Tracy!"

"What?"

"You're rambling. I'm sorry. It's just that I have to tell you something."

"What else is there to tell?"

"I'm not sure how to say it."

Oh God. I suddenly wished I'd hit him harder on the freeway – a full-blown crash at top speed, "You had a second date with Sheila?"

"Of course not."

"What then?"

"I finished your script."

"Oh. So what do you think?"

He was dead quiet; I felt my tummy curdle.

"Was it really that hideous, James?"

"It wasn't hideous at all, but that's not the point."

"What are you talking about?"

"I finished *writing* it – forty pages. I figured it out."

And just like that, my head was empty – I'd become the most vacuous person in history.

"It's about seeing yourself from a different vantage point – a wider perspective. Like the way the characters see Earth from the space station. Things become new with such a sweeping panorama. And the boy – well – he blew me away."

"You finished writing my script?"

"Just one version of it, Tracy."

"You couldn't write something of your own? You know, like, come up with your own ideas?"

"I just sat down with it, and my only intention was to read it – but then I couldn't let it go."

"You couldn't find anything else to do?"

"I didn't want to do anything else."

"Job search?"

"It hasn't been going well. I'll ride the bus, but I'm not gonna *bus* tables for six bucks an hour."

"First of all, James, lots of people have to bus tables for six bucks an hour – that's just how it is. Secondly, it's a collaboration without my consent. I never gave you permission to finish off my idea. I never even gave you permission to read it. Those are *my* people – I gave birth to them."

"I know you did."

"So I get to decide how they develop."

"I know."

"How the hell did you finish it so fast?"

"It kept me close to you. It was only forty pages and they just flew by. That's all I wanted to do. Minute after minute, hour after hour."

"And what else are you going to steal from me?"

"I don't want to steal anything from you."

"Right."

"I was thinking about you and me and about everything you're going through out there. It all just came to me somehow. I don't know. Sometimes we can't see it all. Sometimes the mystery is so big that the simplicity part eludes us."

"Simplicity, huh?"

"Yes."

I thought about my father and his raspberry bush.

"I had to write it down, Tracy. You can throw it out – burn it if you want to. But just read it first."

"I need to think."

"I won't be mad if you throw it away."

"Yes – you will."

"I really won't."

"Did you at least move the protagonist along his journey – visually?"

"It's more about symbols and signs and metaphysics."

"Great. I think we're both fated to the restaurant industry."

"Why?"

"Well, it's a movie, James – not a book."

"It's not like we'll have a budget."

"Somebody might buy it."

"Studios never buy from a nobody."

"Who said anything about a studio?" I asked. "And I don't appreciate being called a nobody."

"We can make it ourselves."

"A movie about *space* by ourselves? Hello – a green screen?"

"Blue screen."

"Green – blue – gentle mahogany. Whatever! Do you have any idea how much the effects alone would cost?"

He didn't answer.

"Oh, I get it now. With your parents' money, right?"

"You weren't even gonna finish it."

"That's none of your fucking business."

"Well maybe you would have, but you would have taken your time getting around to it."

"Fuck off," I said, completely lacking conviction.

"And there's something else."

"There couldn't possibly be something else."

I brought the tart to my mouth.

"I want to make love to you."

Coconut shavings fell from my lips.

"I want to share a meal with you – I'll cook – and then I want to read you the script, and then I want to make love to you."

"In that exact order?"

"No."

"I can only make love to bakery treats."

"We could make love in a wheat field or something."

"I'm packing on a lot of weight. My hamstrings need shoes of their own."

"I don't care."

"You will."

"I want to make love to your soul."

"Do we really need to discuss it?"

"Yes."

"I'm not sure I can accept what you're offering."

"The reading or the loving?" he asked.

"Isn't it all the same, James?"

"It is. I'll take my time with it – deep and slow."

I choked on my coffee. Suddenly something was lodged in my throat.

"Tracy? Are you alright?"

"I need air."

The elderly couple was leaving now, headed back to their happy home. I had missed my chance to make contact.

I could hear him asking if I was okay – so many people had been asking me that lately.

"Can you just try to live in this moment, Tracy? With me? And without trying to make sense of it completely?"

"I don't know."

"Just try."

"I really need to go."

"Why?"

"I'm in the middle of a gluten overdose."

"Think about what I said."

"Goodnight, James."

I hung up the phone and nestled my face in my hands. The man I was in love with finished writing my script and wanted to make love to me. I wasn't sure if I wanted to kill him or ask for his hand in matrimony.

What would it be like to let James cook me dinner, let him read me a completed version of my work – touch me in vulnerable places? Would it do odd things to my brain – impair me with silly delusions? Would I end up moving into a motel thirty-five years later?

I tried to remember the little boy version of James in the park – there for me in my distress – the one who didn't seem like a threat.

But I was still a threat to myself.

I looked out the window to the waiting night – so uninviting compared to the fluorescent warmth of the bakery. But I could no longer loiter here and pack my ass with more sugar – especially after such a mind-altering phone call.

Perhaps my mother had recovered from her meltdown. I got back on the bike and tried to rub some life back into my legs. My shins felt like soft fruit embedded with spikes. But the minute I gathered some significant speed, I allowed myself to feel the excitement of his words – instead of the fear. And all too quickly, the pain was gone.

The park was too dark to sit alone in the jungle gym. So I sat on a swing and thought some more about James. The idea that he existed in this world – with such wonderful thoughts of me – made me want to run through the streets singing arias. I almost considered it until I heard something that sounded like a werewolf bellowing nearby. And even after everything – I'd rather take my chances with the she-wolves in my own family.

I left Lindsay Wagner leaning up against the jungle gym – an uneventful goodbye. Some kid who was a lot smaller than me could put her to better use. I patted the banana seat and whispered thanks.

It was true what they said. All good things do come to an end.

But then again, they also have to start somewhere.

Part 3

The Cucumber King,

A Lonely Space Boy,

and a Totally Rad Hollywood Ending

chapter 41

PETRIE LANE SCARED the living crap out of me.

My heart-rate quickened the second I walked onto my old street. The house loomed like an intimidating fortress in the moonlight. It was my mother's fortress, just as it had always been. As I stood shivering and watching for signs of movement, I figured it might be best to sneak into the basement and sleep in my father's bedroom closet. But I was too tired and cold for any further physical discomfort.

The door handle was my last warning; I wondered if the entrance was booby-trapped with glass bottles strung together with ribbon. Or maybe I would open the door to a spritz of Windex in the eye. Kyle could be waiting to strangle me with an oven cord, and then he'd gleefully plaster my bedroom in Toby Keith posters while my mother baked him an apple pie.

And I deserved it all.

I'd ripped Herb from her clutches and nearly turned Jenny against her. But worst of all, I'd ripped away the polished surface of her life to expose the underbelly of dissatisfaction.

Just who in the hell did I think I was?

I could only hope that my mother would be brave enough to deliver all that I had coming – that she wouldn't once flinch as I begged for mercy.

"Hello, sweetheart."

The words were clear, coming from the black kitchen.

It was my grandmother who'd spoken.

"Why are you sitting in the dark?" I asked.

"Your mother and I have been sitting here awhile and our candle just went out."

Figured.

"Is she still mad?"

"Everything's okay, Tracy." My mother sounded fine, as if her raging tantrum had been nothing more than a deleted scene from a discarded script.

"Is Jenny with you?"

"No – they're already headed back to Colorado."

"But I didn't even say goodbye to them."

The kitchen was silent again, except for the breathing.

"We took that new shed back, Tracy," my mother said. "You know the one?"

No, Mother – what shed could you possibly be talking about?

"Your father's current shed will remain standing – just as it was. We got him some seeds, and the rest he can use as a credit."

"Did you get anything for yourself?" I asked.

"Peace of mind."

"Can I turn on a light?"

"Of course."

I turned on the light and took a seat at the kitchen table. A box of donuts sat ravaged, along with an empty pot of coffee.

"We had some donuts too," I blurted.

Thankfully, my mother didn't bristle, "Yes – that bakery does the best business in town."

I smiled at Mary only to notice she'd been crying.

"What's wrong?"

"Your mother and I have been having a very long overdue talk."

"About what?" I asked. "Me?"

"Not you."

"Your grandma's been very courageous tonight."

Doublewide shit stack.

"The secret?"

"She's revealed it," my mother said.

The donuts were coming up hard and fast, "I guess I should get to bed."

"Don't you want to talk about this?" my mother asked.

"I really can't risk another outbreak."

"Of hives?"

"No, Mom – of the happy wiggles."

"You think that you're gonna get hives from the truth?" she asked.

"Seems about right."

"Isn't that a defense mechanism?"

I shrugged my shoulders.

"Why don't I put the kettle on?" she asked. "You look like you've been wandering around Antarctica."

"No thanks – I'm fine."

"Would you like some edamame beans? We went out for sushi."

"*Sushi*? How did that happen? You've never eaten a living thing – unless it's been seared into charcoal."

"Given how the day unfolded, I wanted to try something – you know – current." My mother said this like she was the new poster girl for the twenty-first century.

"No thanks, Mom. I don't really need anything."

"Probably best – you don't need the salt at this hour."

I had to blink a few times, but there she was – the woman who'd given me life, and was currently concerned with my sodium content. I guess that's just who she was – sushi or casserole, husband or not.

"I think the two of you should talk about this together," my mother said. "I'm going to go read in bed. It's been an endless day, and my back is sore."

I nodded at her.

"But if it's not too late when you're done, I'd like to speak with you, Tracy."

So – a trap had been set.

"Okay, I'll be there."

My mother squeezed Mary's shoulder and left the kitchen.

"Break it to me gently," I said. "I'm not well."

"Of course you are."

"My body can't take it anymore."

My imagination was in turbo charge, wondering what this sweet woman could possibly reveal. She was like a cool piece of shade on a sweltering day, and I hoped her revelations wouldn't throw us both back on the coals.

"How is your father?"

"He likes it there."

"I'm not sure that they've ever been apart."

I slouched in my chair, trying to keep the little guilt bubbles from rising.

"You sure you don't want a piece of eel, Tracy?"

"I'm sure."

"Did you talk to your guy?"

"I don't know."

"What does that mean?"

"I did. But my head feels scrambled."

"How so?"

"He stole my script, then he read it, and then he finished it."

"Sounds like you have a lot in common," she yawned.

I placed my forehead on the edge of the table, stared down at the polished floor, and talked into the tablecloth, "I just feel like I've been waiting forever for my life to start."

"You're not alone."

"I guess I'm just scared."

"It's okay."

I really felt like I needed to throw up, but all that came out were confessions, "I'm afraid that if he gets too close he'll see that I'm actually quite… gross. He'll see the uneven skin – the globs of cellulite that look like they've been hurled at me by someone wearing a blind-fold. He'll notice that I wake up with bad breath and frizzy hair. He'll be witness to the birth of my double chin – the faint trace of jowls. He'll see that my feet are wide and one leg is slightly longer than the other. When we sleep, he'll hear me fart – and there will be nothing I can do to stop myself. And each time we wake up together, the sparkle will grow just a little more dim – until it's out for good. And worst of all, he'll come to realize that I have no talent, no confidence, and no depth. He'll see all this with the clarity of proximity and experience. And he'll know that I'm just a cynical terrified little girl who pretends to be above it all – for lack of knowing what else to do."

I looked up for Mary's reaction, wanting to pass my fears to her like a top – hoping she could give them a different spin.

But she was sleeping.

I started laughing because sometimes the irony was too obvious. Instead of losing sleep over her secrets, I'd put her to sleep with a list of my own.

chapter 42

SHE WOULD'VE CHOSEN strep throat over the bingo hall.

My mother made the announcement shortly after I entered her room. We'd been sitting on her bed, in silence. The moonlight from the open window fell across her face like she'd been framed and lit by some old-time cinematographer.

"Is that because things weren't perfect?" I asked.

She moved her head only slightly, but her eyes were fixed on something in the night sky.

"It's just that I was expecting something different. At this point."

"Yeah, sometimes life can feel like a let-down," I said. "That's why I try to keep my expectations reasonable."

I nudged her but she didn't move – just kept staring out the window, probably transfixed by something within.

"Do you think I was hard on your father?"

"What do you think?"

She didn't answer me, so I took it upon myself to elaborate.

"It's like you fought so hard for what you settled for. And then I wonder why you'd try to force it on us – as a lifestyle?"

"You really think I'd want you to be unhappy, Tracy?"

"I guess not."

"I loved raising you and Jenny – it brought me great joy."

"I know."

"My frustrations are my own – nothing to do with you. It's just that a person does everything they're expected to do and – well – I've just always sort of felt alone. We struggle out of the womb, perhaps get a happy blip of childhood, and then move into a – what did you call it exactly – it was the title of one of your short stories?"

"A World of Masks."

"That's the one."

"And?"

"And then we die alone, after all the years of togetherness in between. And even when we're together, sometimes we're really just alone – wearing a mask."

"But it doesn't have to be that way."

"But wasn't that the point of your story – that that's the way it is?"

"Not if you show up as yourself – completely."

"I'm not really sure who that would be."

"Why don't you do all the things that you want to do, feel what you feel, do whatever it is that moves you?"

"I don't know."

"You do."

"Maybe my imagination is scarce, Tracy. But I think everyone's imagination is weak, compared to what we may or may not be capable of. Let your mind wander – can you really visualize a new color? A color you've never seen before? I try to, but it's not possible. We can only see what we already know – whatever's firmly established. So nothing is ever really new. Only re-mixed, re-arranged, and re-conditioned."

Ironically enough, she was studying me as if I were entirely new to her.

"And then there's you. The story girl."

I sat very still in the cold room, allowing her recognition to warm me like a sunbeam.

"Always so full of possibilities."

"But, Mom – all I do is re-arrange and remix. And I never thought your life wasn't cool – I just wanted you to think mine was okay too."

"I know."

"I never wanted to screw with your head."

"Don't be silly."

"Because maybe I could have tried harder to wear nylons and blouses and lip-gloss. I could have read more chick-lit and smiled more."

"You're being ridiculous."

"Not had my hair cut at the stupid barber shop."

"Barber shop – really?"

I nodded my head.

"This has nothing to do with you. It's my own stuff, my own restlessness. It's just part of me – regardless of anything. You wanted me to own it, so here it is. I'm owning it."

"But why are you suddenly owning it now? You never owned it before?"

"A lot has happened today – tonight."

Mary must've unveiled a whopper. And whatever it was – combined with my father's mad dash to the motel – delivered quite a jolt to my once familiar mother.

"Do you love him?" I asked.

She turned back to the window.

"Do you, Mom?"

I held my breath, but she said nothing.

"Have you ever even been inside his shed? Ever seen the way he holds a tomato?"

Still nothing.

"The way he strokes his cucumber?"

She looked at me like I was about to get scolded, but only shook her head and smiled, "Did it ever occur to you that I might just be jealous of that damned garden?"

No, it hadn't.

"It's the only thing that ever lights him up. Imagine having to compete with a pile of dusty vegetables."

"You could have rolled around naked in the soil or put a mattress in the shed."

"Tracy — my God."

"What? You could share in all that together — help him prune the vines or something. And then he could take an interest in something that you love. It could be so wonderful."

We both realized that I was pleading.

"Settle down, sweetie."

"I always wanted to break away from your patterns, Mom — and have you love me anyway. But I don't need *you* to break away from them. Not if they work for you. I just wanted you to know that you have options — that I have options. And it's okay to be an individual."

"Instead of a cardboard cut-out?"

"You know what I mean."

I assumed a fetal position and tipped myself over into her lap, "I really need you to love Dad."

"Tracy — "

"I can't love James if you don't love Dad — because you used to. You used to love him."

"Who the hell is James?"

"It's too risky."

"Is he real?"

"Too big a waste."

"Have you been drinking?"

"I really want you to hear me!"

"But I don't even know what you're saying."

I wanted to tug on her silky sleeve until she made the world make sense, and everything in it less scary. Instead, I just pulled at a thread on one of her displaced doilies.

"God, Tracy — it's not up to you. It's never been up to you. So there's no need for you to be scared."

"I'm not scared."

"Then why are you shaking?"

I wanted to deny it but my teeth were chattering, "Because it's glacial in here."

"Your life will work out."

I wasn't so sure.

"And I do love your father."

"You do?"

"Of course."

"In what way?"

She didn't answer.

"Mom?"

"Just please – chill out, Tracy."

"*Chill out?*"

"Yes, chill. You're the most dramatic person I've ever known."

Lucy stalked into the room and stopped abruptly – gawking out the window much like my mother was. They were both mesmerized by some enticing energy that I was clearly oblivious to.

"What are you looking at?" I asked.

"The sky."

"That's it?"

"What else do you need, Tracy? Invading Martians?"

"That'd be cool."

Maybe she was looking for a space station, and maybe it was my job to find it for her. And maybe I'd been working for the both of us all along.

chapter 43

THE THREE OF US were snug, basking together in our separate worlds.

I was curled into my mother's lap and Lucy was curled into mine. My existence had settled into something slightly manageable, and all of my own jitterbugs had finally scurried off.

"Did your grandmother tell you her secret?"

Crap.

"Tracy?"

"No – she didn't."

"Why not?"

"She fell asleep."

"Mary has a great deal of respect for you."

My mother took a deep breath, about to pick up where Mary had dozed off.

"I don't need to know, Mom. I mean she had a great life, a solid marriage – a perfect story, really."

"Tracy – "

"And she's still evolving into this whole, spiritual being. So I don't need to know. Actually, I think it's best not to know because – "

"Your grandmother was a prostitute."

Lucy looked at my mother before I did. And suddenly, staring out the window became the most crucial thing to be done.

"By necessity – not choice," she continued. "Your grandfather had that awful accident and could no longer work."

"You mean when that tractor ran over him?"

"Yes, of course. What other accident would I be talking about?"

I tried to shrug but my shoulders felt heavy.

"Anyway," my mother sighed, "they didn't have insurance. And the wheat crops had spoiled. So after a couple of months of terrible stress, and living off of now and then charity, she explained her hardship to a couple of people, hoping to get cleaning work or childcare. Well, one of the men offered her a very large sum of money and..."

"And?"

"You *know*."

I shook my head that I did not know.

"And anyway, Tracy – I'm not going to spell everything out for you... or position a key light."

"Wait – you know what a key light is?"

"Well, I wasn't hatched. Plus, last time I was at the library, I borrowed their book on film production."

"Wow."

"Yeah. But let's not change the subject."

"I was kinda hoping we could."

"Tracy, please."

"Fine."

So my grandmother reaches out for help, and some jerk decided it would be the perfect opportunity to exploit her. I wondered when the tingling would start, and what I'd have to slather myself with this time – I remembered seeing a jumbo jar of Miracle Whip in the pantry.

"It must have been terrible for her – I can't even imagine it," she said. "There were so many questions I wanted to ask, but they all seemed so inappropriate."

Horrible prehistoric birds were getting ready to crash through our window. They would lunge first for Lucy but I would sacrifice myself to protect her, allowing whole chunks of my flesh to be ripped clear off the bones.

"Just imagine how hard it must have been, Tracy."

No, I didn't want to imagine it – Mother! Didn't want the visions of my beloved grandmother in a tangled mess of sweaty limbs, servicing men like they were on a conveyer belt.

"Are you listening to me, Tracy?"

No, no, no!

More birds were gathering outside – that's what we'd been watching for, waiting for all along.

"Tracy!"

"Well, Mother – was she a street walker, a call girl, or a member of an escort service?"

"This isn't funny."

"I know. What else do you want me to say?"

"Just be serious for a minute."

We both exhaled something akin to a gasp, and I wondered how my skin would react to the mayonnaise. Maybe a teriyaki marinade would better quell the coming prickle.

"Just hours ago, if you had put a whore in front of me, I would have judged her harshly."

"Mom!"

"What?"

"Grandma's not a whore."

"I know that – sshhh, for God's sake. That's my point exactly, if you'd let me finish. I'm trying to say that I would've judged that person harshly. But not after listening to your grandmother's story."

Lucy and I didn't move, silent witnesses to my mother's off-the-wall attempt at empathy.

"I even have to admit something else."

"What more is there to admit, Mother?"

"I felt what she did was rather *heroic*."

"Really?"

"Yes."

"Are you being serious?"

"Very."

Outside, the birds were changing course.

"Mom?"

"Yes?"

"Was Grandpa's farming accident after Dad was born?"

"Yes."

"After Derek?"

"Tracy, relax – Derek's a dentist."

"So what?"

"He was able to buy his gal a new face."

"Are you gonna tell Dad any of this?"

"Of course not."

"Jenny?"

"No."

"Probably best."

She inhaled the skin on my forehead – an instinctive move from our early years – and I knew there'd be no hives tonight. I could only hope that my father was half as safe and warm as I was this instant.

"Tracy?"

"Yeah?"

"Nothing."

"What is it?"

"I don't want to fight with you anymore. It's like bickering with oxygen."

"Maybe you should be the writer."

Lucy's purring increased in intensity. It was the most soothing sound I'd ever heard. She was offering us her cat approval, born of deep feline wisdom, assuring us that everything was still okay – just as it had always been.

My mother smiled at me triumphantly, "I'm glad you have a man."

I smiled back, "Doesn't mean you win."

"How about a tie?"

"I can live with that."

"What does he look like?"

"A Rob Lowe-Patrick Dempsey cross – with a subtle hint of Rick Springfield."

"The gorgeous one who used to play the doctor on General Hospital?"

"That's the one."

"Good grief, Tracy. Wow."

"I know, Mom – I know."

I was dreaming before I fell asleep.

And in my dream, my mother and I were waking up. Waking with each other's watery green eyes, seeing life through the other's perspective. Back and forth we would pass the eyes, seeing it all again for the first time.

The world that anchored my dreams grew darker; somewhere on the outskirts of my consciousness, I knew that she'd just closed her bedroom curtain.

But soon the world consisted only of Lucy – she was a giant menacing stalker, but there were no more scary birds to chase.

chapter 44

I SIMPLY COULDN'T see my granny as a hooker.

The silver hair and worn hands kept throwing me off.

And that was a good thing. It meant that she'd neatly stuffed the last of my remaining pigeonholes.

The three of us were sitting around the kitchen table eating scrambled eggs, fried potatoes, and things that looked like spongy English muffins. I was trying not to stare at the woman I now considered a bohemian sage, but the latest revelations only strengthened my curiosity. I tried to imagine her as someone other than the pretty dame who was content to sit and meditate beside duck ponds.

Such an intriguing character deserved a script of her own — someone who shatters all pre-conceived notions of, well, everything, and manages to save the universe in the process.

She would be the greatest anti-hero in cinematic history.

"Tracy, why are you looking at me like that?"

"Like what?"

"You've either got one eye closed or you stare at me at an odd angle from the side – using your peripheral vision."

"Oh that. I was just trying to imagine you fighting everyone's demons."

"Everyone's demons?"

"Yes – you help to slay them – because you've had experience with your own. It's a new script I was thinking about writing. The Demon Slayer – metaphorical, of course."

"Your mother told you about my past?"

"Yes."

"Are you mad?" my mother asked, holding a dripping spatula of egg.

"No." She turned to me, "What do you think of me now?"

"You did what you had to do."

"You did exactly what you had to do," my mother said. "You paid for all your husband's needs, and you paid for your kids' needs, and the mortgage and the utilities and the groceries."

My mother shook her head in amazement, "You did it all, Mary. And I can't even comprehend how you did it. How you managed to give away what, you know, what you had to give away. You're like some sort of superwoman."

As my mother lavished her former rival with genuine praise, her entire presence seemed to lighten – as if she'd just unloaded a huge burden of invisible bricks.

"Did you have regulars?" my mother asked.

"Yes, I had a very small roster of repeat people."

"People?" I asked.

"Men, Tracy – I never had any lesbian johns."

It was such an astoundingly absurd statement to hear – from the same woman who'd once powdered my belly – that I had to pull at a hangnail to keep from erupting in a wild dance and tearing out my hair.

"Where did this happen?" my mother asked.

"There was a local truck-stop. It was very clean, safe. I know you don't want to hear this, Tracy – but they actually served decent cuts of meat. Fresh vegetables – nothing canned. The owner of the place understood my jam. Kept my cover discreet."

"Did they all pay the same rate?" my mother asked, as if inquiring about a currency exchange.

"Most did, although one man in particular paid triple. He would also bring fruit baskets and tickets to hockey games and horse shows. He even bought that pram I gave you for baby Tracy."

"He bought her *pram?*" my mother asked, in awed wonder.

"What the hell's a pram?" I asked. "It's not like a prom, is it? Because I never went to mine."

"We know you never went – you had that tummy upset thing," my mother said. "Your grandma's talking about that beige buggy of yours. You slept away half your babyhood in it."

"That thing with all the ladybugs?"

They both nodded.

"What else did he buy me, Grandma?"

"He bought you a month's supply of formula when your mother was having a hard time with her nipples."

"He bought all that *milk* too?" my mother asked. "And here I always thought you were secretly wealthy."

"What happened to your boobs?" I asked.

"They broke down for a bit, Tracy – too much stress."

"Why didn't Dad buy the formula?"

"We had no money that year. Countless problems with the truck."

I had to wonder what Peter Republican would think of my entire cache of infant needs being so generously supplied by the Christian kindness of my grandmother's trick.

"Sounds as though he loved you?" my mother asked.

"Oftentimes we would only make conversation. His wife was also very sick – a hardening of the lungs. We had all that in common. And he was so emotionally consumed by her condition that he had odd looking marks all over his body."

"Were they hives?" I asked.

"Perhaps."

"He loved her greatly," she continued. "But when she died, I knew that he relied on my companionship."

"Is that what you considered it all?" my mother asked. "Companionship?"

"Sometimes, but sometimes it was just sex."

I was actually starting to feel a good sort of tingling – almost the light, airy feeling one gets after a strenuous cardiovascular workout.

"And he left me a considerable amount of money when he died."

"Did you ever love any of them, Mary?"

"No, not in that way. My husband was always the one."

We all took a breather, and I realized I needed to re-create this entire scene – beat for beat.

"Could you pass me a crumpet, Mary?" my mother asked.

"A crumpet from a strumpet," she said. I watched in amazement as she put a hand over her mouth and adjusted her false teeth.

"I'm so impressed that you can be self-deprecating about all of this."

"I try to hold things lightly. It's just life, Joanne. When you see your own curtain preparing to drop, you either find the humor or slog out your final act with Mr. Despair."

"Exactly," I said. "Your character – the demon slayer – would bring light to the shadows and depth to the one-dimensional."

"I can hardly wait. Who'd play me – Vanessa Redgrave?"

"I was thinking Shirley MacLaine."

"Okay, ladies!" my mother said. "I'm gonna do a little grocery shopping – make us all a big spinach salad and some beet tacos."

"I think I'll go with you," Mary said. "We can try that new coffee shop – heard they have a mean butter roll. We'll go in my car."

"Awesome," my mother said. I had never once heard her use that word before.

"Do you want to come with us, Tracy?"

"No thanks, Mom. I think I'll just stay home and do some writing."

"Well then, by all means – we won't keep you."

I watched as they gathered their sweaters and purses, bubbling over with a laughter only they could really understand.

"And Tracy?"

"Yes, Mom?"

"Make it a block-buster."

My deconstructed mother closed the door before she could see a smile the size of a crater crack my face wide-open.

chapter 45

SHRILL RINGING STARTLED me out of the space station.

And I plummeted to Earth with a thud. I'd torn myself away from writing preliminary notes on *The Demon Slayer* in order to plot my own possible endings for *Space Boy*. James was not necessarily going to have the last word – or the **FADE OUT** – as the case may be.

"Hello?"

"Hey, Tracy – it's me, Sheila."

"Did you talk to Mitch?"

"Yeah, and I have good news."

"Did you set up the pitch meeting?"

"Well, it turns out he's going through a really bad break-up – I think it's even humbled him a little. Anyway, he's looking for distractions and wants to see a copy of your script immediately."

"But, Sheila – I'm still in the mid-west!"

"So attach it in an email."

"You were supposed to set up a pitch meeting – period."

"Well – this is even better."

"No – it's NOT! I haven't finished the damn thing yet – remember?"

"Oh shit – I forgot. I'm sorry. Can't you just quickly finish it?"

"In a couple of hours?"

"I don't know. I asked him about it, and this is what he suggested. I did the very best I could."

And then it hit me — *there was a completed version.* The James version.

"Is this all some sick conspiracy between you and James?"

Three seconds passed before she answered.

"What does any of this space script nonsense have to do with James?"

I wanted to accuse her of being the worst person in the world — a boyfriend stealer and a career saboteur.

"You know James is a writer."

"I do not know that."

"Yeah, sure."

"What's wrong with you?"

"So what did you two talk about on your *date?*"

"Not much."

"What the fuck did you talk about?"

"You're completely unraveling, Tracy."

"Sheila!"

"If you must know, we talked about YOU!"

"In a good way?"

"Yeah — you, you, you. Glorious fucking YOU!"

I couldn't help but feel the ends of a smile creeping up, lifting the entire geography of a face that wanted to remain skeptical.

"Got it?" she asked.

"Yep."

"So — should I just cancel this entire absurdity? Tell him that it was a false alarm?"

I suddenly saw my life flash before my eyes. And there I was — the old stooped spinster without a man or babies, but I'd be damned if I'd be without a career.

"No — do no such thing. Just give me his email address and tell him that he can expect one hell of a script."

"But you don't have a script."

"Well then, that would be my problem, wouldn't it?"

"I guess so."

"Just give me his address."

I wrote his email address on my hand and hung up the phone. But how could I email him a script I didn't even have?

Unless – of course – Sheila and James were sleeping together, and she well knew that he had finished it. And once it became clear that I had nothing to send – they would slide his version across Mitch's desk.

I poured myself a cup of coffee, and stared at the microwave clock. Part of me wanted to make a mad dash for the bakery, where I could lose myself in donuts, rolls, croissants, and crullers – but I couldn't just give up before I'd even hunkered down. I had to begin the ending.

First, I had to call James.

The phone rang until I was almost ready to hang up.

"Hello, this is James."

"It's me. Listen, I have to ask you something."

"Okay?"

"Are you and Sheila working together – against me?"

"What?"

"You heard me."

"No, I'm not sure I did."

"Do you know who Mitch is?"

"Mitch who?"

"Come on, James."

"I haven't a clue what you're talking about."

I set my jaw and considered my predicament.

"I asked Sheila to set up a pitch meeting with this agent named Mitch. She knew the script wasn't finished but went ahead and promised him he could read it. So I wondered if maybe you two were in cahoots or something."

"You think I'm in cahoots with Sheila? Do you really think so little of me?"

"You're the one that went on the date with her!"

"And I haven't seen her since."

"She doesn't call you?"

"No."

"Does she know where you live?"

"Of course not."

"She's probably watching you from the street as we speak."

James was abruptly silent.

"James?"

"I have to tell you something."

"You always have to tell me something."

"I'm not even in Los Angeles. I'm not even there."

My heart dropped into my stomach, "So – where are you?"

"I'm not sure."

"What do you mean you're not sure?"

"I mean, I know where I am. I'm just not sure I should say."

"James!"

"Why don't you look out your window?"

"James?" I whispered.

I ran over to the window and nearly ripped my mother's hand-sewn curtains off the rod. At the far end of the street, I could make out a lone figure walking in the direction of the house.

My house.

Me.

I hung up the phone and looked down at my ratty apparel. My hair was knotted in clumps, and I still had bike grease caked on my skin. But despite all this, I couldn't move. For a split-second, I fantasized that future explorers would find me here – frozen on the spot – waiting for the prince I never thought I believed in, and still rather suspicious of the ever after.

chapter 46

I WASN'T SURE I'd even existed before the doorbell rang.

Then I wondered if maybe I was just playing tricks with myself, lost in another interesting – yet pointless – reverie. There was no way James was *really* standing at the door, pressing the doorbell – it must all be in my head.

But when it rang again, I opened the door.

He was standing there – holding a script – with his purple blue hair shining in the sun. And suddenly there was a majestic symphony piping itself through my senses.

"You're here."

"Yes, Tracy. I am."

My hands scratched at my sides, but my eyes never left his face.

"Can I come in? This back-pack's a little heavy."

I moved out of the way and watched as he looked around at the place I'd always feared was some sort of white picket prison – one I'd surely end up in if I wasn't careful.

"How long have you been in town?" I asked.

"Not very long. Just putting some final touches on the script – and walking around. And I wasn't riding a bus in L.A. – I was on a bus from Minneapolis."

"So not a lot of job searching?"

He shook his head, "I fibbed about that."

"Why didn't you tell me you were here?"

"I wasn't sure how. You weren't exactly warming to any of my suggestions."

I stiffened against whatever it was that had just started to melt inside me, "So you got a room in town?"

"I did – checked out this morning."

"Maybe you could bunk with my dad over at Bud's motel."

"Yeah, wow," he laughed. "What a trip."

"Yep."

"Tracy?"

"So how's the weather out there?" I asked.

"Tracy?"

"Well?"

"It's sunny."

"That's wonderful. Cup of tea?"

"Sure."

I hurried to the kitchen and tried to get a grip on myself, but everything was loosening into shapelessness. My senses were betraying me; I felt like I might faint. I struggled to put tea bags and water in large mugs, and then I struggled some more with the buttons on the microwave.

Stick your head in the freezer and get some cold air.

But instead I discovered a miniature bottle of Kettle One vodka and promptly guzzled it. I came back into the living room with the tea and sat on the sofa.

James was sitting in the exact same chair that Kyle Steinke had occupied not so long ago; it was amazing how dramatically a scene could change given the right player.

"I'm sorry about Sheila," he said.

"I know."

"The date consisted of a bowl of chow mein and a twenty-minute chat about how awesome I think you are. And I booked my flight the minute I left the restaurant."

I stood and hid behind my oversized mug, completely unsure of my bearings, "Is your tea okay?"

He nodded that it was.

"Do you want some honey?"

The look in his eye assured me that he did indeed, but he said nothing.

"I'm also sorry I just left you in the park that night."

I shrugged my shoulders as if it had meant absolutely nothing.

"I'm a big girl."

"Are you okay, Tracy?"

"Yeah, why?"

"You seem a little – "

"Yes – I sort of am."

"I understand. It's not every day that someone just sort of drops in on you like this."

Not a particular someone like you is what I wanted to say, but didn't. Instead, I looked at him over my tea mug, "No – it's not."

"Your parents have a nice place."

"I guess – when pipes and marriages aren't exploding."

I sat back down on my mother's sofa and stared at her latest carpet – a color that could only be described as heated bran muffin. Part of me was still waiting for this fantastic new reality to fade into thin air.

"I haven't exactly been honest, James."

"Okay."

"There was something I wanted to say – that night in the park. Something I wanted to tell you. You sensed it, but I was too scared to admit it."

"Was it something about me that you couldn't confess?" he asked.

"No – it was something about me. Something I realized."

"What did you realize?"

"I realized that you were right."

"About what?"

"About how much I really do love writing."

James dropped his gaze into his lap as if this was a pivotal moment for me, and he should give me my privacy.

"How much I do miss it, and how much I hate myself for not allowing myself enough of – I don't know… whatever it is that allows for it."

He kept his head down.

"Remember that song by Prince – When Doves Cry?"

"Of course."

"I think I was ten when I first heard it. Remember how he screams and screams at the end – and the guitars are wailing?"

"Yes."

"Everything was purple and electric for me – for weeks after. And I wanted to be able to write even just a fraction of the way he played – make someone feel just a touch of what he made me feel. Does that make any sense?"

"It makes total and absolute, uncompromising sense."

"I knew you'd get it. You can look at me, James. It's okay."

He looked up and into my eyes.

"It's just that all the rejection got to be so painful. I couldn't deal with it anymore. So I pretended it didn't matter – just like you thought."

He nodded and let out a sigh of relief.

"I am a writer, James."

"A what?"

"A WRITER!"

"I know you are."

"And while I'm alive – so help me God – I will build, shatter, and re-build people's lives… no matter what becomes of it."

I didn't realize I was crying until James was telling me that it was okay to let it all out – which took me a while since I was crying for so many reasons. He went to the kitchen and brought me back a paper towel.

"Do you want some privacy?" he asked.

"No."

"Do you want to talk about it?"

"No."

"What would you like?"

"I'd like you to read me the script."

"Now?"

"Yes."

I rested my head on the pea green pillow my mother had stitched when I was just entering elementary school. James sat back in Kyle's chair, and watched me for at least a minute.

"Go ahead," I said. "Don't be afraid."

He cleared his throat and slowly began introducing me to the beginning of my quest – and all of my dusty imaginings were soon roaring back to life. I listened as he described the journey of the boy – the one who longed to find some meaning in a world that seemed so random. He wanted answers where there were no questions. And no matter how much space he managed to cross, he could never get past what was infinite within himself.

When James finally finished reading me my script, I felt something that I wasn't really sure I'd ever felt before – utter relief. My transmissions had somehow been received... and understood.

"So?" he asked.

I stared at the shadows on the carpet, waiting for them to change their shape.

"Tracy?"

"I can't talk about it just yet."

"You hate it?"

I stared at him, wondering how he could say such a thing.

"No – I don't hate it. And you know I don't."

Children were laughing in the street; their dreams were still intact, because to them, everything was a dream. But for me, my dreams had started to fade – and this guy was so casually handing me back their brilliance.

"You finished it, James."

"I just followed your lead – you laid the foundation."

"But it was trapped in that concrete. I was stuck."

James got out of the chair and stared out the window, "Maybe you couldn't finish it because you were terrified of how good it would be. Maybe you were afraid to go to the next level in your own life. So it was easier to stay stuck in what you knew – in what was familiar."

"Maybe."

"And maybe I was afraid to begin anything again because of what happened last time. So it was easier for me to finish... rather than begin."

"Maybe."

"So can we talk about it, Tracy? I mean, really talk."

"Not right now."

"Why?"

"I just can't."

He sat back down.

My eyes wanted only his face. It was like the chemistry between us had grown into an entity that was threatening to swallow us whole.

"I'm overwhelmed, James."

We both sat very still and very quiet until I knew what had to be done.

"It's time to send it to Mitch."

"Now?" he asked.

"Did you bring your laptop?"

He nodded, "It's all ready to go."

"So add your name to it, and I'll show you where the Ethernet cable is."

"You're really ready to send it now?"

"It's already gone."

"But we haven't even discussed it."

"We will."

"When?"

"I don't know."

"Tracy?"

He followed me into my mother's sewing room – a place that doubled as my so-called writing office when I was home. Neither of us spoke while he set up his computer on the floor. And when he finally hit the send button, I'd never felt so fired up – but when he turned around to look at me, I wondered if I'd simply die of exposure.

chapter 47

OLD SCRIPTS WERE being re-written all over the place.

The idea of success – in all its forms – was gathering speed through zones that were once restricted. And with *Space Boy* zipping through cyberspace and James right next to me, there was absolutely nothing I could do to stop it. I didn't want to stop it.

We were walking in the direction of Bud Jarkinson's motel, our arms casually interlocked. The sky was as blue as I'd ever seen it here, and children and dogs were out in full force – along with a variety of people who I'd never once noticed before. The sun was handily sweeping people outside, demanding that the day be witnessed.

Or maybe I was just seeing with fresh eyes.

I could hardly wait to tell my father that his shed would remain standing, certain that his vegetables could lure him back home. Thanks to Mary's generous sprinkle of shock dust, everything might soon be back to whatever it had been.

When we sauntered past the donut shop, I wondered if we'd ever end up like the elderly couple I'd watched the night before.

"Tracy?"

"Yeah?"

"I'm nervous."

"About Mitch?"

"About meeting your father."

"Just be yourself."

"He'll think I'm a psycho for just showing up like this."

"He'll be flattered for me."

When we finally arrived at the Creekside Oasis, there were only two cars in the parking lot – and one of them belonged to my father. I heard the laughter before we got to the door – the kind that emanates from unfiltered and boisterous joy. I wondered if he might have a woman in there – some random stranger he picked up in a bar, or worse yet, a long-stashed mistress who could finally be aired out.

"It's just Bud," I said, out loud to myself.

"What?"

"The guy who owns the motel."

We stood outside and listened as they yelled excitedly about the past – about all the gargantuan fish they'd caught in the little creek beside them.

I knocked on the door and my father answered it with a beer in one hand, and a pizza slice in the other.

"Tracy?"

"Can we come in?"

"Get your pretty little rug-rat butts in here."

We walked into a room that was littered with beer cans. There was a bucket on the floor containing a tiny fish draped over ice.

"Dad, this is James. He flew in from L.A. – we just finished collaborating on a script."

"Well – that's terrific news. It's a pleasure to meet you, James."

My father scrutinized him as best he could through his booze fog, and then tossed him a can of beer.

"Give it a second or it'll explode all over you, son."

I couldn't help but cringe inside.

"A script, heh?" Bud asked.

"Yeah," I said. "You know, a movie blueprint."

"A Hollywood thing?"

"Yes – wouldn't that be nice."

"Bunch of nuts," Bud said.

James gave me a look, and I was disappointed to feel the embarrassment on my cheeks.

"You want some pizza?" Bud asked.

"What kind?" I asked, although the room reeked like a greasy mix of pepperoni, sausage, bacon, and beef.

"Meat lovers."

"No, thank you."

"Why not?" Bud asked.

"I'm a vegetarian."

"See – fruits and nuts," Bud laughed.

"Bud and I were just talking about going up to Alaska," my father said. "He has a little shack up in Fairbanks."

"Quite a road trip," I said.

"Would we drive up through Canada?" my father asked.

"How the hell else would we get up there?" Bud asked.

"Who will take care of the motel while you're gone, Bud?"

"That old battle-axe of a wife sure won't. I can't trust her not to take off shoppin'. She'd spend her whole life in Wal*Mart if she could. Which leaves Becky, I guess."

Becky was Bud's daughter – we were the exact same age and had attended the very same schools and the exact same classes.

"But what if she doesn't want to?" my father asked.

"Come on, Herb. She's wanted to be a chambermaid her whole damn life. If she does this for me, then she's got the job. She'll be a top banana, full-time."

I looked around at the dingy room and suddenly found myself defending the dreams of a girl I would no longer even recognize on the street, "She wanted to be an astronaut in grade school."

Bud frowned at me, "We're not that la-di-da, Tracy. We don't have them big ideas like you do."

James snickered and I felt a pinch of anger sprinkle through my body, and I didn't think I could ever tell him about my grandmother.

"Becky's not even here to defend herself," I said.

"She doesn't need defending," Bud said. "I can speak for her just fine."

"There's nothing wrong with having dreams," my father said.

"And nothin' wrong when you dream of being a maid," Bud said.

A vision of an alternative future flashed through my head – I was working here full-time as a chambermaid, dragging the giant pail of sudsy water that was chained to my leg. The image made me shudder and I scratched at something on my thigh; I was certain it was a hive, but my thumb and index finger revealed the body parts of a swollen dead mosquito.

I turned to James, "We'll have to be sure to follow up with Mitch – quickly. We can't just let it languish."

"Tell me about it," he said, and looked around the room as if it were a torture chamber.

"Listen, Bud," I said. "You're totally right – there's nothing wrong with being a maid, and there's also nothing wrong with writing scripts. Each world deserves respect."

"Fruits and nuts," he repeated.

"Forget it, Tracy," James whispered.

He mumbled something about species, and I realized that I was thoroughly annoyed with every person in the room – including myself.

"If I go up with you, how long am I gonna be gone?" my father asked.

"At least a month," Bud said. "And there's new seasons. Hell – the days up there are all jumbled up and backwards. I used to build cars at two in the morning in the summer."

"I'll bet the yard's covered in them," James whispered.

I frowned at him.

"What was that?" Bud asked.

"Nothing," James said.

"Pardon me for not havin' yer snotty tastes," Bud said. "I think this gentleman here thinks he's better than us. You and me, Herb –

we're just a couple of guys. That's what we are – just regular guys. Not opera lovers, or expensive people. Just meat-eating guys."

"Not everything's so simple," I said.

"Yes it is, little girl."

"My father loves vegetables. He loves them more than you could ever imagine. So I guess you don't really know him so well."

I looked over at my father; he gave me a thumb's up.

Bud burped and I scanned the floor, quickly counting ten beer cans. I wondered how many more were under the bed and out on the deck.

"Yeah, I'm not sure I can be away from my vegetables that long."

"Your wife's gonna rip 'em all down anyway," Bud said. "When she puts up that new shed."

"Actually!" I said. "Good news. Mom took that new shed back to the store."

I watched my father's droopy posture straighten, "What?"

"So you're now the proud owner of some new veggie seeds and a big credit – in case you need a hoe, or something."

"That's incredible."

My father sat on the edge of the bed, with his arms stretched out like airplane wings.

"Thought you needed some space from that old bat," Bud said. "You can plant a garden up there, for Cripe's sake. Edible flowers for all I care. I already said so."

"She's not an old bat," my father said. "Watch yourself there, Bud."

"Hell she ain't. And a nutter too. You told me she irons her pillowcases."

My father shrugged, "They smell better ironed."

I wondered if he'd ever seen her iron *towels*. I'd only seen it happen once, but I'd still seen it.

"Our housekeeper used to iron the pillowcases," James said. I could tell he regretted saying it, but it was too late.

"Housekeeper, heh?" Bud asked. "See, this pretty little guy doesn't just think he's better than us – he *knows* it."

"He does not," I said.

"Look," James said, "you created a great place here. You built it, you run it. Tracy tells me you can even fish here. And I think it's terrific that you're both going to Alaska."

"Don't *condense* me," Bud slurred.

I winced and looked to my father.

"I think you mean condescend," my father said. "Which means to patronize."

"Ah, fuck it," Bud said. "What difference does it make what word I use? It's just a word. The world was built with hands, not words. It was built by men, not Hollywood fruits."

James gave him a dismissive glance, and I wasn't sure I'd ever seen him look so smug.

"You haven't built a thing in your life," Bud said. "You got hands like a girl. And yet you'd turn up your nose at the men who built the very roads that your pansy ass trots along. You got some grand notions of yerself."

I looked around at these three men and couldn't believe that it only took a handful of minutes to unearth such deep-seated and mutual resentments.

"Dad, I'm sorry. I think James and I should leave."

"Yup. Good idea," Bud said.

James walked out to the parking lot, and my father walked me to the door.

"I'm sorry, Tracy. We've been drinking."

"It's okay."

"James seems like a nice boy."

"He's a man."

"Okay. I'm glad you brought him by."

I peered back into the room – Bud was baiting a hook with a lure made out of dead insects.

"You can come home now," I said. "It's really okay."

He squeezed me so tightly that I had to imagine rabid dogs gnawing through my gory remains to keep myself from crying.

"Dad?"

He burped and wiped his nose with the back of his hand, "But now I want to go to Alaska."

"For that last license plate?"

He nodded at me like I was the coolest person ever, and I left him to his friend and their tall tales and future plans.

chapter 48

HE WAS NOT going to catch me.

James chased me through the parking lot and down the hill to the creek, which I tried to cross but only ended up soaking my right foot.

"Tracy, wait!"

"I need some air," I yelled.

"I'm sorry."

"Just forget it."

"But the other guy started it."

"His name is Bud. And that's my father in there," I yelled over my shoulder. "The man who raised me. I've got his blood running through my veins."

"I know."

I started tossing stones into the creek and worked my way up to the twigs and larger branches that were scattered about. He joined me at the edge of the water, grabbed my arms and turned me to face him.

"Tracy, I'm sorry."

"You're a snob, James."

"I'm really not."

"You are."

"Then so are you, Tracy."

"I am not."

"You never grew up wanting to be a chambermaid."

"But why do we have to judge it?" I asked, angry spit flying into his sweet, handsome face.

"We don't."

"Why can't we just let people be – no matter who they are? Or what they want? Or what they have to do to survive?"

"You're right – I'm sorry. I guess I was just being defensive – trying to make myself feel better."

I sat in the creek and started crying.

"Tracy? You're going to get sick."

"I can't trust you now."

"Why?"

I wiped my nose on my arm, "Because some of us have to thrash around just to stay afloat."

"Tracy?"

"Forget it," I said, and threw a twig at him.

He lifted me out of the creek and into his arms where I cried into the exquisite contour of his neck.

"Tracy, talk to me."

"No."

"Please."

"I can't."

We both stared down at the creek and let our thoughts swim. The movement of the water was soothing; Nature wasn't concerned, just gently running her course.

"My grandmother was a prostitute."

I watched him closely but he didn't flinch.

"And I didn't want to tell you because I was afraid you were going to judge her. And if you judge her, you judge me. And if you judge Bud, you judge me."

He flicked his pocket change into the creek.

"Because that's the world I come from – the world of survivors."

"I'm not judging anyone, Tracy."

We watched the water for a few minutes longer until he grabbed my hands and managed me onto his back. I didn't once struggle as he carried me up the hill and into the front lobby of the motel.

An older woman, slathered in make-up – who I assumed was the old battle-axe – asked if she could help us.

"We need a room," James said.

"Newlyweds?" she asked.

"Yes," we said, in unison.

I peeked over my shoulder, hoping we could remain unde-tected by *the guys*.

"That'll be seventy-five dollars."

James handed her a crisp hundred and told her to keep it. I wanted to ask where he got the money but didn't want to ruin the mood. She smiled and handed us a key and two cold sodas.

"It's like going back in time here," he said.

"It's nice," I said.

"Yes, it is."

We snuck across the parking lot to our room, which was only two doors down from my father's. There was only one bed in this room, a queen that was covered in a heavy beige quilt to match the worn chocolate carpet.

James went outside to inspect the deck and the creek below. I was relieved that he was outside, though his chemical trail was still crackling through the room. The nerves in my stomach were starting to pile up on top of each other – like an exotic troupe of the heebie-jeebies.

I ran into the bathroom and stared at myself in the mirror – I was in desperate need of a complete overhaul. I turned on the shower, hoping to scrub away old grease and new pounds. The hot water brought immediate relief, like it could even wash away the jitters. I closed my eyes and tried to imagine all the ways my life might change once we took our relationship to the next level. Would we end up like so many couples before us, struggling to stay together while trying to remain free?

But something was different now. James and I shared the same dream. Perhaps the cosmos was benevolent and wanted to give us a signing bonus or head start.

"Tracy?"

I once again opened my eyes to the sound of his voice, knowing it was far too late to figure every last thing out. I'd just have to go with it.

"I'll be out in a second."

"There was a hummingbird out there."

I wrapped my head and body in huge faded towels and left the warm safety of the bathroom.

"You're too late," he said.

"It might be back."

"Maybe."

James tried his best not to register my naked body under the towel, but his face revealed too much. He hurried back to the deck, like it was his safe corner after an exhausting round circling an equally matched opponent.

I fell backwards on the bed and stared up at the water-stained ceiling.

"A fish!" he shouted.

He came running in, "A big green-brown fish just did a twist-flip-turn in mid-air."

I loved how he was like a child, enjoying all the amusements of the natural world.

"That's great, but the guys are gonna hear you."

James looked down at me like I was a tempting feast; I rolled over into a ball, certain I contained an excess of calories that would surely weigh him down.

"I'm hungry," he said.

"I know."

"Pardon?"

"Nothing."

"I'll go get us some food."

"Where?"

"I noticed a little Asian place on the walk over. Rice for you and fish for me?"

"That would be nice, or you could catch your own off the balcony."

I winked at him but he was out the door like a flash, and I thought it was rather charming to discover how nervous he was too. I crawled under the covers, careful not to disrupt the towels.

The sound of flowing water outside the room lulled me again, and I thought about how oddly everything had turned out. My grandmother had supported her family as a prostitute, my father was planning a road-trip to Alaska, and my mother's own constructs were being so pulverized that she might even end up as a new being – never another thought given to garden sheds nor a hand raised in the service of ironing a pillowcase.

And I'd soon be back in L.A., trying to catch that newly oiled brass ring – something more slippery than a motel fish. We'd all shift our literal geography again, but I knew it was my inner landscape that was changing the most. No one had to stay stuck forever, even if they'd spent a lifetime trying.

I fell asleep dreaming of James. We were lost somewhere in a wasteland, having just survived a terrible storm. The worst was over, but we were surrounded by a space that was vast beyond measure. Neither of us carried a compass and we were unsure what direction to travel.

"Should we split up?" I asked him.

"Why would we do that?"

"Because we could cover more ground, and maybe you'll find something before I do."

We both watched a tumbleweed blow across the vista.

"And how would I ever find you again?" he asked.

I thought about his question awhile and then shrugged, "You may not."

"We'll stick together then," he said, irritated.

It seemed as though we were on some kind of desert planet or perhaps we had just come through something like the Great Red Spot, the never-ending crazy storm that rages in the southern hemisphere of Jupiter. I shuddered to think that three Earths could fit within its boundaries. But even in my sleep, I knew I was exaggerating. We were probably just in Nevada.

"Okay," I said. "We'll stick together."

chapter 49

A COLORFUL FEAST had been laid out on paper plates.

And James was grinning at me like the Cheshire cat.

The drapes were closed, but two candles were burning. I wrapped the quilt over my towel and joined him at a small wooden table in the corner of the room.

"How long have I been sleeping?" I asked.

"Couple of hours, maybe."

"Where'd you find the candles?"

"Discount store next to the fish place."

He served me a huge helping of rice, broccoli, and fruit. Then he sat down across from me; I watched him shove chunks of curried salmon and halibut into his mouth.

"How do you like it?" he asked.

I wasn't sure since everything that I put in my mouth almost instantly dissolved with nerves, and like an idiot, I had to keep swallowing saliva.

"Yum."

He stopped eating and looked at me.

"Do you want to talk about your Grandma?"

"No, although somehow my mother seems better for it."

"What's wrong?"

I sucked in my cheeks and began to study my rice in earnest.

"Tracy?"

"I just think it's weird that my father's only a stone's throw away. Things are just weird."

"Do you think he'll move back in?"

"I don't know. Plus, I'm worried about my sister. She planned all this and ended up going home with her feelings shattered."

His nails looked manicured in the candlelight.

"Is there polish on your nails?" I asked.

"I went to the spa."

"Tan?"

He nodded.

"Any insights?"

"She poked me a lot."

My own chest was tightening and my stomach felt squishy, like I was on the verge of diarrhea. I had to wonder if she'd accused him of being in love.

"Does a facial suit me?" he asked.

"I can't tell – it's too dark. Turn on some lights."

"Believe it or not, the lighting was supposed to be romantic."

I looked back longingly at the tall lamp near the bed, and knew there was a big switch attached to the cord.

"Are you okay?" he asked. "You've barely touched your food. Aren't you hungry?"

"I prefer looking at it."

He watched me while I watched my plate. Though I felt like a jumbo supply of silly, it was just too hard to look him in the eye. While his beauty increased by the second, my own was in the midst of a swan dive.

I had turned into a donut. Foolishly, I had somehow supposed that I could turn it all around before this moment arrived – the glorious touchdown – but James had intercepted me.

And here we were – only a pocketful of inches from a big comfy mattress.

"Tracy?"

I gave him a brief glance and looked down at my food again. This was not the time or place to notice that his neck was just a little more tanned than when he'd left me to my nap. The candlelight was making objects appear a thousand times more attractive than was humanly possible.

"I'm getting sleepy," I said.

"You just took a nap."

"Right. And that reminds me – I had a dream."

"Yeah?"

"We were lost."

"No kidding."

I cut my pineapple cube into four smaller ones.

"And you suggested we split up?" he asked.

"How did you know?"

"I had the same dream."

"You did not."

"A variation."

I shook my head at him.

"It's a running theme, Tracy." He laughed and had no trouble chewing on another piece of fish, "So what happened?"

I sucked on a red pepper, "I'd rather not say."

"You gave me a chance?"

"Maybe."

"I know you did."

"Are you wearing contacts?" I asked. "Your eyes seem more blue than usual."

"I thought you couldn't see anything in here?"

"Must be my vivid imagination."

He pushed his plate away, like it had been nothing more than a precursor for the main dish.

"Alrighty then," I said. "Wow, I'm stuffed."

"You didn't eat anything."

"Minor detail."

"Are you nervous?" he asked.

"Pardon?"

"You're clutching your fork like it's a lifeline."

I dropped the fork and stared down at the soggy pineapple chunks on my plate – praying to every goddess ever conjured that I wouldn't get hives.

"Look at me, Tracy. It's okay."

I looked at him and suddenly wondered about so many things – like especially how he could understand my protagonist so clearly.

"What is it?" he asked.

"I was just thinking about the script. You knew exactly how he longed for immortality. That's why he was always moving outwards, trying so hard to exceed his own grasp."

"Because he never felt worthy just standing where he was."

"Right," I said.

"And so he goes too far – literally."

"The sad little space man."

I giggled but James had turned very serious.

"It's your story, Tracy. The space boy is you."

I lifted my eyes to the velvet Elvis Presley hanging crooked on the wall, letting my suspicions sink in, "I know."

"It's all you," he said.

"And it's you too," I said.

I remembered visualizing all the different versions of James in the park – the afternoon my father moved into the motel. Somehow, my subconscious had been trying to speak to me through him. And I now knew what he had wanted to tell me. Each and every James had a corresponding Tracy – no matter the age or the station, the source within was always the same. The same source that my space boy had forgotten about – forcing him to seek his worth in the far reaches of the heavens. Forcing me to seek my own even farther still.

"You really were in the park," I said.

"Pardon?"

"Part of you. Close enough. Your essence reached me before you did. But you were coming for me."

"I have always been coming for you."

We laughed a little, but I felt like I might fracture into pieces of stunned wonderment.

"We're just two small souls," he said. "And we jumped into the bubbling stew to save ourselves."

"From what?"

He shrugged, "I don't know – maybe the quiet peace that comes with the acceptance of mortality."

I stared at him like he was some sort of magical well, so much deeper than I thought.

"So I wonder what Mitch will think," I said.

"There's nothing left to prove."

"Exactly. So my motivation is pure."

And on that note, I was able to chew the first bite of the greatest meal I had ever known.

chapter 50

JAMES WAS WATCHING me suck on a water chestnut.

And I was straining to hear my father's voice.

"Tracy?"

"Yes."

"If I don't touch you soon, I'm gonna collapse. Right here on this ratty old carpet, and you'll have to call the paramedics – but by the time they arrive it may be too late."

But if you touch me, I might lose my mind. The part of my mind that is still my own.

"Oh."

"Is that all you can say – oh? What are you so afraid of?"

"Nothing. It's just that I'm hearing Lucy's cries in my head. She's going to want her dinner soon and I'm not there."

"You haven't been away long."

"But I have to feed her."

"She's fine, Tracy."

"She'll only eat her tuna if it's in a light syrup and a black bowl."

"After everything we've shared, you still want to close up on me?"

He got up from the table, turned on a bright light, and sat in front of the television. I went and stood beside him, not exactly sure what to do.

"But we didn't share it together – at the same time. You just sprang it all on me, and I need some time to catch up."

He turned up the volume, "Fine."

"What I'm trying to say is that I'm just terrified – that's all."

He turned off the television and stood up slowly, never taking his eyes off of me; I was only an inch or so shorter. We were millimeters from each other but he put his hands behind his back.

"Lucy," I whispered.

"No – *James.*"

"But – "

"Let go, Tracy."

I wanted to run for the bathroom but my knees felt like meringue.

He put his hands up over his head and brought them down to rest on my cheeks.

"James?"

"Thanks for giving me a chance."

He kissed me tenderly on the mouth. My body finally freed itself from my brain and my hands let the quilt and towel drop to the floor. We fell on the bed but not before I was able to flick a switch on the lamp cord and plunge us back into darkness.

His hands were all over my face and skull and then my arms and back and ass. His tongue was opening my mouth, searching for the truth beyond words. Before I could think another thought and get the situation back under control, I felt his mouth on my breast – circling my nipple without a care in the world. And I forgot entirely what it was I had wanted to protest.

And then we were back on the expanse. Still walking. There hadn't been a tree for miles, no sign of anything life-giving. My mouth was parched; the sun boiled my skin. I was slowly dying from dehydration. But then we heard something that sounded like water, and we started running as best we could in that direction.

My eyes stung with the sight – the yellow flowers and orange birds. The red berries and green melons. But it was the water that amazed us most – gushing forth down every possible face of rock – gushing forth to wash away the barren dry dust that had so long coated my throat in pain.

And then I was on top of him – and it was so hard and it hurt but then it melted into me – like something I'd needed for so long. All I was aware of was feeling full and then more full, like there wasn't a molecule of space left inside. And we were rocking and pushing and he was lifting himself up and pulling me down until we both exploded at the core, the sweet scent of milky water everywhere. We found each other's mouth and we gulped in life and we laughed and there were no more words.

Only silence.

James and I woke up stuck to each other. I removed my sticky limbs from his and turned over to look at the time. The motel clock read 12.15 a.m.

"Tracy?"

"I'm right here."

"Are you okay?"

"Yes. I haven't done that for a while."

"Is that why you're not sleeping?"

"No. I'm thinking about the script."

I turned back to him and placed my hand over his hairless chest.

"What about it?" he asked.

"I don't know. It makes me sad – how he can never come back."

"His choice."

"But he didn't have all the information."

"None of us do."

I gently ran my finger along the line of his jaw.

"Do you want to change it?" he asked.

I dug my fingers into his armpits in an attempt to tickle him, and then tried to pinch a stomach that was nothing but muscle.

"It's still your story, Tracy."

"It's ours now."

"What should we write about next?" he asked.

"So this partnership continues?"

"Yes, but this time we'll collaborate together in real time. Naked and happy."

"How about people who live together for years but don't really know each other at all. Something like Strangers Together."

"Sounds like a made-for-T.V."

"What's wrong with television?"

He drew me closer to him, and I could feel my extra softness against his hard body. I tried to pull away without him noticing.

"What?" he asked.

"Nothing."

"I want to see you, Tracy."

"I'm here."

"I want to make love to you and be able to see you at the same time – not in the pitch black."

"That's how I'm comfortable – you can feel me – why do you need to see me too?"

James pulled me closer to him, but I pulled away.

"Tracy?"

"Will you still love me if I'm just myself?"

"That's the only way I can."

He rolled on top of me, and looked me in the eye. And then he buried his face in my neck, eyelashes on my skin. And then gentle lips along my collarbone. And once again, I was too supple to argue; all my rough edges were blurry. So I got up, turned on the light, and shut my eyes against the extra weight and odd blemishes that he could now fully scrutinize.

"No hives," he said.

"Not funny."

"You are so beautiful."

I turned away from his gaze, "This makes me uncomfortable. But a little less so than it would have a week ago."

I opened one eye and could see that he was hard again.

"James."

"Come here."

I went to him and he helped me maneuver him inside.

"Just relax," he said. "It's okay. It's me. You have to be yourself – whoever she is or decides to be – or we won't have a chance."

"I know."

"And I'm not perfect, and I can't ever be. But I try, Tracy. And I can feel, and I feel you."

"I really want to let you in, James."

"I know you do."

He rocked me tenderly, and I held his cheek against my own. And soon he was inside as far as he could go.

chapter 51

JAMES AND I were playing games.

Of the healthy sort. I watched him prance around naked, stopping only to strike a Saturday Night Fever pose in the center of a room that was probably furnished the very same year the movie was released.

We were smiling at each other like goofballs, still lit from before by the considerable afterglow.

"Do you think Mitch is reading it yet?" I asked.

"Not yet. Give him a year."

"I don't have a year."

"You have many years."

"We could cut down on the effects, streamline everything."

"Do you think your father heard us?" he asked.

I looked at his naked body, a thin layer of sweat starting to take shape.

"I muffled myself – remember?"

James turned the room fan to the max. He was dancing again – whirling around like a dynamo, but I was staring up at the paint flecks that were now clinging desperately to the ceiling.

"You don't need your father's money."

He stopped dancing.

"It weakens you."

I couldn't believe I'd say such a thing after what we'd just done. But maybe it was because of what we'd just done.

"It's just that you look so strong and beautiful, James. And now that I know what you're capable of, it just seems like it's holding you back somehow."

"How?"

I sighed, "Because the wealth is like a sneaky thief. It will steal your motivation. And with a dream as big as ours, we need motivation more than we need anything else. We need our drive, and our perseverance, our insatiable hunger and unquenchable thirst. Without it, there is no fuel and we simply run out of gas. And the dream just sputters out and dies on the side of a lonely highway."

"God, Tracy."

"I'm sorry, James – but it's true. And you know it."

"Even knowing that we're already worthy, you have ambition so big?"

"Especially knowing it."

"I need to go for a walk."

"That's okay – I need to make a phone call."

He put his clothes back on and left the room. I grabbed my purse off the floor without leaving the bed, and rifled through crumpled notes until I found my cell phone. I wanted nothing more than to hear the voice of my baby sister.

"Hello?" she answered.

"Hello, Jenny – it's me. Where are you?"

"South Dakota. It's after one in the morning."

"I'm so sorry. You left without saying goodbye."

"You weren't around."

"You could have called."

"Is Dad back home?"

"No. He's going to Alaska."

"With Mom?"

"No – with Bud from the motel."

"That stupid fucking motel."

"I'm here too – at the motel. With my boyfriend."

"Your what?"

"He flew in from L.A."

"Don't play games with me."

"I'm not. His name is James."

"Why didn't you tell me?"

"Because I didn't think we were going to work out."

"You and him or you and me?"

"Jenny, you're my sister."

She started whimpering.

"Why are you crying?"

"Talk about something backfiring. I tried so hard, trying to honor their union. What a fucking joke."

"That's what I wanted to talk to you about," I said.

"What, Tracy? You want to tell me I'm a laughing-stock? Or that you win? That you're so much smarter than I am? What?"

"None of those things."

"Well a trip to Hollywood sure beats the fucking shed – if I'd known it would have led to my parents' demise, I would have just stayed home."

"Can I just say what I wanted to say?"

"Go ahead."

"I think that you've fixed something."

All I could hear was her aggravated breathing.

"Jenny?"

"Are you being sarcastic?"

"No."

"I don't get it then."

"Look – something was fundamentally broken. But it wasn't so much the marriage that was broken – more like our perceptions. There's stretching room now. You helped expand something."

"That wasn't my objective."

"Jenny, listen to me. By bringing us together at this exact time, by forcing us on each other – you made us deal with stuff. You initiated something new and different and good – whether you wanted to or not."

"Good?" she asked.

"Yes. You instigated a healing process."

"I did?"

"Even I feel better about everything. And it's all because of what you did for us. Your timing is impeccable. You're a healer, Jenny." There was a dead silence and I thought I'd lost the connection. But then, for the first time in as long as I could remember, my sister released a big, sweet, and sincerely happy laugh.

We said our goodbyes and I leapt out of bed and wrapped myself in a sheet. I walked out onto the deck and looked down at the creek. Moonlight had transformed the green water into a shimmering silver spectacle; I wondered if my father saw it too. He was probably passed out by now.

The door slammed and I walked back into the room. I sat on the bed beside him, "Are you mad at me?"

He turned on the television, "No."

I put my head on his shoulder and drew a heart on his back with my index finger.

"When I left the spa, Tan told me I had a golden spoon lodged in my throat. And until I removed it, I would have no true voice."

I giggled and rubbed his knee with my thumb.

"When are we going home, Tracy?"

"Soon."

"And you want to keep going with this thing?"

I wasn't exactly sure what thing he was referring to, but I knew the answer anyway.

"Yes, most definitely."

He looked at me with uncertain eyes, "And you think we'll make it?"

I nodded my head.

"Why do you think so?"

"Because there's really nothing left to do."

chapter 52

THE PLANE WAS chasing the sun when he'd said it.

"You're going to have to give the money back too."

It was the last thing I wanted to hear, but much like a season or a subway, I knew it was coming. Still, I was extremely proud of him.

"I know."

"If we're really serious about this, Tracy."

"I know."

"We're in this together. Students enrolled in the school of tough shit. Because your car wasn't worth twenty-five thousand."

"I know!"

"We'll get real jobs and it will force us to write our guts out – every spare second that we find. No squandering time on television or video games."

"Sex?" I asked.

"Very necessary to keep all the juices flowing."

"And then all the forces of the universe will join us in our efforts?"

"Yes."

"I also think that we should keep our separate places – at least for now."

"That may change," he said.

"It may."

We were thirty thousand feet above Colorado. My parents were in seats behind us, although Mary had insisted on buying their flights as a belated anniversary present. And given the choice between Alaskan freedom or familiar mayhem, my father chose the latter. But my parents were quick to point out that just because they were coming to Hollywood did not mean they were back together – although the fact that the old shed was still standing bode well for their continuation as a couple.

"What are you thinking?" I asked him.

"We'll keep writing because we love it, because we are worthy of it. We're already worthy, and that's why. We won't do it because we're empty, but because we're full. We'll write as an expression of love – something we want to share with the world."

"Right. And we'll need wine."

We landed at LAX and took a shuttle bus to James' one bedroom apartment in Woodland Hills. The four of us found seats in the center of his bachelor pad and stared at the old movie posters that were tacked to his walls.

"What's your all-time favorite film, James?" my father asked.

"Star Wars."

"You know, I haven't even seen that one yet." My father said this like it had just been released three weeks ago.

James looked at me as though a major crime had been committed.

"Why is it your favorite?" my mother asked.

"So many reasons. But I actually really like the effects. Everyone talks about how dated certain effects look these days – with all this new and perfect digital technology. But you know what, some of the new stuff looks pretty damn phony too – the computer graphics can really look goofy behind the live action stuff."

My mother nodded her head politely.

"I mean, I'll take old-fashioned models over any modern day action film where the invading armies are – very obviously – millions of little digital people."

"Interesting," she said.

"And what's your favorite film?" he asked her.

"Let me see – I'd have to say Giant. You're never going to see three better looking people on a screen. I mean, James and Elizabeth."

"And Rock," I said.

"Yes, of course. Rock. My eyes twitch just thinking about it."

As my mother and boyfriend chatted about movies, the invisible weight that had long ago crash-landed on my chest seemed to be dissolving.

"So what would everyone like to do tomorrow?" my father asked.

"James was thinking you might like to see the big car museum. And then we can all meet for a drink at Bar Marmont, and then maybe a quirky indie over at the Laemmle."

"You lost me at bar, Tracy."

"I'm suggesting a movie."

"That sounds alright," my mother said.

"And I was thinking I might take you for a spa treatment, Mom. We can get a facial and a massage – whatever you want."

"I've never been to an actual spa."

"Then it's high time. Plus, there's someone who works there that I'd like you to meet."

James announced that he was going to make pancakes for dinner. He insisted that no one was allowed to help him in the kitchen, which meant my mother was left to steal peeks as he cracked eggs and stirred batter.

"Your boyfriend's really cute."

"I know."

"And you were brought together by a car crash?"

"A mild one."

"There's a lesson in there, sweetie."

We watched James study his syrup supply.

"Sometimes crappy events can alter the entire course of a life," she said. "Like a bump in the road."

"Or a junk heap."

"Yes," she said. "Especially a junk heap."

I looked between my father and mother.

"What?" she whispered.

"What's happening with you and Dad?"

"I'm not sure yet."

"Any ideas?"

"We're just going to hang out and see how we feel."

"Hang out?"

"Yes, sweetheart – hang out."

"So you don't really have a plan for your life?"

Before she could defend herself, I was snickering, "I'm just teasing you."

We ended up insisting that my parents take the bed with the good sheets, while James and I struggled with his old lumpy college pullout – but even as I tossed and turned, I knew that I wouldn't have traded a second of it.

I listened to the rhythmic snoring of my father, hoping to subdue the excitement in my gut – but some feelings were just too rare to sleep through. I wondered if my parents were glad to be sleeping side by side – like finding a trusty old slipper that had long since disappeared behind the fridge.

In this little block of space on a non-descript street in the Valley, something beautiful had happened – a beneficial sort of give and take. And I knew it was possible to compromise in a way that didn't mean slipping into oblivion.

chapter 53

I STARED LONG and hard at my bank account balance.

I'd asked the teller to print it out for me one last time. Part of me was skeptical that I'd ever see a figure like that again – at least one belonging to me.

Damnit. I could've kicked myself for inspiring James into such drastic measures. I'd asked him to at least wait until we received word from Mitch, but he said that would be playing it way too safe.

"Anything else?"

I looked at her as though she were speaking Swahili.

"Oh yes, I'd like to take my balance and put it all in one big money order."

"The whole thing?"

"Everything less a thousand."

James and I agreed that finishing the script had earned us some grocery money.

"And who would you like to make it out to?"

"Paulette Wilson."

"Could you write that down for me?" she asked.

"Pardon?"

"The name."

I inhaled deeply, checking every corner of my interior for the hives.

"Certainly."

I left the bank, walked to the nearest coffee shop, and pulled the money order out of my purse. There was something else in there too. Mary had sent me a package, but I hadn't been ready to open it. It was wrapped in simple brown paper and sealed with a string. I slowly untied the book and stared at the cover. A woman was sitting in a chair. Her back was turned and she was looking out an open window, but I instantly knew that she *knew* things. Perhaps she knew that she'd been thwarted somehow. And perhaps she was going to do something about it.

Mary had sent me *A Room of One's Own* – the extended essay of Virginia Woolf. I opened up the front cover:

To my tenacious granddaughter,

"A woman must have money and a room of her own if she is to write fiction."

V. Woolf

(Use it if you need to; the universe loves to help those who try… and then try again).

At the back of the book was a blank check folded into a tiny square. I put it on the table next to the money order, and pondered the synchronicity of it all. It was as if some powerful force wanted me to keep writing without worrying about anything else in the process.

I stared out at the busy street and thought about Virginia Woolf. No matter what happened, I wouldn't fill my pockets with heavy rocks. I'd keep going and going until I either succeeded or my time simply ran out.

James and I had already started a series about a child who can see the repressed thoughts of other people. We'd started it the same day my mother had called to tell us once again how much she'd enjoyed Los Angeles – especially the spa.

I closed my eyes and remembered that day – Tan hadn't been around but that didn't stop my mother from reaching an important conclusion on her own.

"He *should* have a license plate upstairs."

We were lounging together after hot stone therapy treatments, and I had to turn and make sure it was she who had said it, and not some super-relaxed voice in my own head.

"At least one."

"I think he's earned it," I said.

"Me too."

"Which state?"

She carefully slurped up the remnants of her pineapple smoothie, "How about the state of recovery?"

"Dad should have taken you to one of these joints earlier."

She turned serious, almost sad.

"What is it, Mom?"

"Do you remember being a baby?"

"Not really."

"Then you'll never know how much I cared for you – changing your diapers, spoon feeding you mash – wiping up your milky puke."

I nibbled at a large piece of mango.

"You were so easily the most precious thing in existence."

She looked as though something of meaning had simply disappeared right before her eyes, and there was nothing she could ever do to get it back.

"But somewhere deep inside I do remember, Mom – it's probably what allowed me to come here in the first place. To have the audacity to think that anyone would give a shit about what I thought about anything."

"Really?"

"Deep inside me there is a tiny little girl who can still feel the warm fingers on her belly and the gentle whispers on the crown of her head."

I didn't mean to make my mother cry, but it happened anyway. And it was probably a good thing – a long overdue thank you that I'd needed to extend.

"I know which one I want to read," she said.

"Yes?"

"I want to read the one about that ambitious little boy. The one who makes it all the way to the Pinwheel Galaxy only to discover that he misses his family – but can never return to them again."

"Space Boy."

"Yes – the one you guys keep talking about."

"That's the one."

"It sounds sad, Tracy."

"It is."

"Why?"

I reached for my mother's moisturized hand and squeezed, grateful that we'd both returned, "A cautionary tale."

I handed her my bowl of mango slices and a small warm stone fell out of my ponytail. We started laughing – mild at first, but soon tears were running like rivulets. And it was hard to imagine that my life could get much better than this.

I closed my eyes and whispered a thank you to my grandmother – the one person in the universe who was able to whip us into something as light as a mousse.

chapter 54

It was a very bad sign.

Mitch was taking forever to come to the phone.

I was hunched over in the bathroom of a Starbucks across from the Creative Artist's Agency – on the slim chance that he'd want to see me immediately.

He'd emailed me two days ago. There were only four and a half words in the body of the email, but they held the possibility of a life I'd always dreamed of. Not to mention the happy face that would most surely usher in a new era for me.

FINISHED SCRIPT >>> LET'S TALK...☺

I'd emailed him back and he'd given me an exact time to call him. But that was four minutes ago and I was still on hold. I had to wonder what he was doing that could possibly be more important than this very phone call, because nothing more important had ever happened to me – in the history of my life.

Maybe he was chatting with Alan Ball or Woody Allen – but still. This was *our* time – our one tiny segment of allotted time in the multi-billion year existence of the universe. And I would guard it with my life.

I'd even banned James from this moment – telling him that I had to handle it alone. He understood and had stayed in his apartment practicing vegetarian recipes. But the truth was, I didn't want him to see my insanity. Especially since we'd both agreed that *Space Boy* had re-established our self-worth. But it was such self-worth that made me want to go for it harder than ever – almost like I'd be slapping God in the face if I didn't.

In any event, it was a good thing that he had no idea I was currently crouched in the corner of a bathroom, on the verge of dry-heaving my nerves and the tall green tea latte I'd just downed.

Oh God – the nerves. I'd always tried to keep my optimism in check, but any smidge of encouragement had always sent my hopes veering wildly out of control.

And this phone call was anything but a smidge. It was more like a healthy slice of salvation – a steady hand for a shaky target.

Perhaps I was assuming too much.

What if Mitch was mere moments from blowing away the rainbows, pulling me out of the clouds, and reuniting me with my clear-headedness? He'd politely suggest I attain my real estate license or enroll in an accounting course. And I'd have to thank him for his precious time while he'd had no problem taking mine.

Five agonizing minutes had passed, but what did he care? All he had waiting for him was a serious case of delusion.

Well I wouldn't let him do it. No way. There would be no u-turns on this track. It was fast-forward or bust.

I'd almost convinced myself to hang up when a man's voice rang out like a clarion call, "Hello – Mitch here."

"Hi." I, on the other hand, sounded like a pip-squeak.

"Ms. Johnston?"

"I'm here."

"I finished your script."

"Okay."

"Some interesting elements – I really liked your use of symbolism."

"Okay."

"The way you managed to get it across visually."

"Kay."

Story Girl

If I possessed any other words in my vocabulary, this would probably be the time to use them – before he thought me a total fraud.

"The main character was deeply imagined."

Deeply imagined? Shit. This could be it! Let all the choirs in heaven raise their voice in a single and triumphant exaltation. Let every angel in the kingdom soar through the cloudless sky.

"Okay."

"The scenes were tight."

And it just kept on coming like a turning tide.

"Great."

And?

And then came the pause – the iconic dividing line; that good old fork in the road – sharper than any knife – able to split a possible fate into two separate and very distinct futures.

"Unfortunately however, it isn't right for me."

But I didn't hear him clearly because someone was knocking at the door.

"Is *not* right?" I asked.

"Correct."

"Not right at this time?"

"Not right ever."

The angels were crashing hard. At least I was near a toilet.

"Okay."

"However – and this is what I wanted to talk to you about."

Now I was literally holding my breath.

"I'd be very much interested in your take on an idea that's been swimming around in my head."

"Okay."

"Yeah. What do you think you could do with something like this – and here's the premise... the epic frustrations of a modern day girl."

The bathroom seemed to be swirling, but I wasn't yet sure if my life was again going down the shitter.

"The frustrations of a modern day girl?" I asked.

Seriously?

"Yeah – you think you could toy around with that?"

This had to be a joke.

"You mean write a movie around it?"

"Of course, a script – you wanna play with the idea?"

"I do – yes. I absolutely do."

"You think you could flesh it out?"

"I know I could."

"Well, why don't you start on it, and then get back to me when you have a first draft."

"I can do that."

"How long do you need?"

"Not long."

"Good."

"Do you have any other details about this girl?" I asked.

"She's stressed, you know – but I figured you could come up with the particulars. Just make it tight. Throw in some humor – nowhere near as bleak as your last one."

"Okay."

"Call me when you have a decent draft."

"I will."

And with that, the call was over.

I opened the door to an angry woman who informed me that she shouldn't have to wait so long to take a simple miserable pee.

Part of me wanted to enlighten her about the awesome elixir known as patience. Instead, I walked out onto Wilshire Boulevard where the sun warmed my air-conditioned flesh. Creative Artists Agency took up a large section of the block, casting imposing A-list shadows.

Imposing and impenetrable. But I'd still caught a chance, and I was going to run it to the very end of the field. And I knew it was in me – I was the lead expert on the topic.

I made it to the bus stop ten seconds too late, but it was okay. In fact, it was more than okay. It was all material now — so bring on the aggravations.

Ninety minutes later I was home. Lucy greeted me with a quick brush against my shins — she already sensed I was revved for my mission. I'd have to quickly call James, shower, and heat up a frozen quiche. Then I'd have to disappear for a while — an extended visit back to the place I'd been struggling so hard to escape from. This time the irony was more delicious than a box of fresh pastries — but anyway — I would have no more time to ruminate on such things. There was simply too much work to be done.

And my epic frustrations were waiting.

About the Author

KATHERINE CARLSON GREW up in central British Columbia. She studied English and Sociology at the University of Victoria, and graduated with a Bachelor of Arts degree in 1997; that same year, she moved to Los Angeles to study film and theater. She joined the Screen Actors Guild in 2000. After many years in California, she moved to Vancouver, B.C. to study anatomy and write books.

Carlson is the author of *Arrows Across Eons: Becoming Tina Turner* – a spiritual tale chronicling how synchronicity worked magic in her life. She currently resides in Alberta, Canada – safely nestled between the mountains and the prairie.

CPSIA information can be obtained at www.ICGtesting.com
Printed in the USA
LVOW13s2125300913

354770LV00001B/64/P